EASY TRAVEL TO OTHER PLANETS

"AN ABSOLUTELY REMARKABLE BOOK...
almost absolutely original;
it takes materials we have with us every day
and puts them together to make a totally strange
but utterly recognizable world....
The last chapter is a lyric masterpiece."
Los Angeles Times Book Review

"Ted Mooney's prose is...mercurial and provocative—
a strange brew of interfaced idioms, dialog vérité, filmic
transitions, and straightforward narrative—as it would
have to be to generate the controlled hodgepodge of
gunplay, lovemaking, dolphin sagas, reverie, biotechnology,
and jive that make up the novel...remarkable."
Chicago Tribune

"BELIEVABLE AND DISTURBING...
compelling...extremely witty...
Mooney controls a large, richly imaginative canvas, making
both his realistic and futuristic images seem accurate,
powerful reflections of our own anxious times."
Women's Wear Daily

For Faye

It was more or less in the area where we were now sailing that Columbus encountered mermaids. "The three mermaids," he relates, "raised their bodies above the surface of the water and, although they were not as beautiful as they appear in pictures, their round faces were definitely human." The manatees have round heads and their breasts are at the front; since the females hold their young close with their paws as they suckle them, it is not surprising that they should have been taken for mermaids, especially at a period when people went as far as to describe (and even draw) the cotton plant as a sheep tree, that is a tree bearing not fruit but whole sheep hanging by their backs with wool ready to be shorn.

—LEVI-STRAUSS

I T took Melissa nearly the full three weeks to grow used to sleeping in the bed that hung suspended from the ceiling of the flooded house, and even then, even after she had surrounded the bed with shower curtains to protect herself from water splashed or slapped, she would find herself awake in the night's stillest hour, listening to the pump's dull pulse as it circulated fresh seawater through the rooms, listening beyond that to the sea's slow suck as it entered the cove on which the house was built, and from the center of her insomnia she would gaze up through the skylight above her at the meteor showers that streaked the Caribbean sky, and she would think: I am going to die from the strangeness of this. By morning I will be dead of the aloneness and the strangeness.

But when the dawn did come, and with its first light the sound of Peter's speech—clicks and whistles and high-pitched creaks like an unoiled door as he swam into the elevator's harness and pushed the start button with his beak, leaving the deep pool on the first floor to greet Melissa on the second and demand his breakfast —when she was again in the knee-deep water with the dolphin, stroking him and preparing for the day's first

1

lesson, all her despair slipped away from her like
clothes shed, and she was glad of everything.

And the dolphin: the dolphin was patient, mainly:
what else if not patient? His belly was scraped a bit
from the rough spots on the floor, his back peeled a
bit from the sunburned hours he and the woman had
spent together on the flooded observation deck. In shallow water, a dolphin thinks about the danger to his
skin, which is twenty times more sensitive than a man's
and which dolphins feel to be the organ of dreams,
though they do not sleep. Peter, under Melissa's daily
tutelage, had learned to thrust his head out of the water
and, with his blowhole, to approximate a few words of
English, for which he was rewarded with kisses that
created praise in his skin and a sad remembrance of the
sagas handed down from the distant times of his dry
ancestors. In shallow water, a dolphin will sometimes
fall to dwelling on the shortness of life and will seek to
make the best of it with amazing feats of attention.

Melissa awoke, on the last of the twenty-one mornings, in full moonlight. Without bothering to change her
leotard, she flung back one of the shower curtains and
stepped out of the bed into the warm and glittering
water. Her breasts were swollen, slightly but painfully,
with the approach of her period, and she explored them
absently with the fingers of one hand while she listened
for Peter. From the level below, faintly audible over the
noise of the pump, came the creaking of his nighttime
sonar as he moved about in the deep pool, unaware as
yet that she was awake. Melissa drew the shower curtain shut, then splashed slowly across the room to
where the plastic thermometer was tethered to the floor.
She examined it and, on a clipboard hung high on the
wall, noted a water temperature of 84°F.—normal for
St. Thomas in April.

At the freshwater sink, Melissa felt a swell of appre-
hension pass over her as she drew the mildewed wash-
cloth across her face, and she found herself thinking of

Jeffrey, who was awaiting her in New York, at the other end of her day. He would hate the cut of her hair at first, short against the constant wetness and the salt, but later, in rooms made warm with appetite, he would savor the suggestion of danger skirted and of distance successfully traveled. Melissa believed that only she knew how to return to him, though there had been, and would be, others. She released the drain, and the water flowed out of the sink onto the bit of ocean which covered the floors.

Below, Peter briefly sonared a lizard fish that was feeding on the algae at the pool's bottom. Then he swam into the elevator and, punching the button with his beak, allowed it to hoist him up to the second story. He was still fascinated by the fact that electric lights were not fish, a discovery he had made by splashing water on Melissa's desk lamp, and now he turned on his side to stare again at the floodlights as the elevator swung him out of its shaft and through the air over the flooded room. Once in the water, he looked for the woman. She had left her bed early. He made a noise like a human being with a cold and, when she did not appear, began slapping the water rhythmically with his flukes. Three slaps; Melissa appeared.

"Hello, Peter." She had been in the dry area in back and held a bowl of cereal.

"CCccccxxxxxx." He lifted his head out of the water and opened his beak to show he was hungry.

"Okay, okay, you greedy thing. Just a minute." She stepped down off the dry catwalk into the water and, reaching out her hand, offered a caress.

Peter swam rapidly toward her, then glided between her legs, forcing them apart with his body and striking her shins with the front edges of his bony flippers. Melissa tried to swat him, but he was already out of reach behind her.

"Goddamnit, dolphin! I've told you not to do that." Her shins were bruised purple from three weeks of this game. "One more time and I'll leave you alone the rest of the day."

Peter regarded her appraisingly. It is an attribute of the dolphin's eye that it is clear-sighted in both air and water.

Melissa fed Peter on the observation deck, taking freshly dead butterfish one by one from his plastic feed bucket and giving them each a short toss, not more than an inch, to indicate they were his. He caught them in jaws containing eighty-eight conical teeth of a sharpness and whiteness so imposing as to be hypnotic, and several times they had figured in Melissa's dreams: as mountains, as rows of prehistoric monuments, as a threat about to descend upon her leg. She looked out over the cove, listening to the faint reggae pulse coming from the radios of the fishing boats at anchor there. Dr. Ehrler had instructed her to make meals as dull as possible in order to avoid reward associations, so she never spoke to Peter during feeding. He nudged her leg and squawked, wanting another fish. She stared at the moon. On one of the fishing boats in the cove, a young down-islander discovered he had the wrong-size replacement batteries for his transistor and flung them angrily into the water; they sank forty feet and nearly hit a horseshoe crab. The moon traveled away, the sun rose.

"That's all there is," said Melissa, putting the empty feed bucket down in the water, letting it float aside like a toy. And she was halfway to sadness before she knew it.

Then Peter emitted a loud series of humanoid squawks, blats, and chuckles—the sound of English without the meaning—and when he knocked Melissa off her feet with a flip of his tail, soaking her, she, charmed, burst out laughing and said, "What do you know anyway, shithead? What do you think you know?"

Inside, beneath dangling microphones, Melissa and the dolphin labored fixedly at the lesson. Melissa said her name one hundred fifty times and Peter, absorbed in the strategies of human pronunciation, said it back. His vowels and *s*'s came easily in air now, and he had learned to shape an *m* sound by rolling over so his blowhole was just underwater; only the *l*'s were truly problematic. Melissa coached, gently touching his blowhole to indicate when he should listen to her. Both were drawn increasingly into the exchange, hearing the improvements, bearing down on them. She said his human name one hundred fifty times, and he said it back to her. They named his beach ball, his rubber rabbit, his brush. They counted to ten and back ten times.

In late morning, Melissa held up a diamond-shaped piece of plywood for him to identify. Peter rolled sideways to look at it, at her, then squirted the shape out of her hand with a blast of water and took off across the room at top speed, turning aside just before reaching the wall, so that close to a ton of water was thrown against it in a miniature tsunami. Without a pause, he swerved back toward her, trying, in the rub of water against his skin, to work up a vision of a place he knew in the deep ocean hundreds of thousands of body lengths away, a place free from the approach of shark yet decorously inhabited by all other manner of sea life: the rabbitfish, the butterfish, the spookfish; the croaker, the eelpout, the comb-toothed blenny; the starfish, sea horse, crab, and eel. He circled Melissa twice at high speed, then reared up on his flukes and stared at her. She had hair on her head and flexible lips.

"Peter, calm down," said Melissa, a little alarmed. "You're right: enough is enough." She picked the diamond out of the water and hung it on its wall hook.

Peter let himself back down into the water and swam to her. She leaned over, hugged him. "You did very well today, Peter, and on your last day, too." She could feel he was unusually tense. "Such a smart cookie," she crooned, kissing his back. He began to relax, then thought better of it and, slipping out of her arms, swam to a point a few meters away. With a heave of water, he reared up again, looking at her.

"Okay," she said to him. "If that's the way you want to be."

In the electronics room, she switched off the recorders and filed that morning's tapes next to the others. Out of the water, it seemed to her too easy to move now, as if the world below her knees had gone ridiculously insubstantial, and in response she had developed the tic of constantly wiggling her toes at the dryness. In certain parts of the island unfamiliar to Melissa, this tic, called obeah dance, is well-known and conclusive evidence of possession by jumbies, who may be banished only by the prompt and concentrated attentions of a red cloth dipped in goat's urine. Melissa sat on a high stool, lit a cigarette, and thought about her mother. There was a gecko perched atop the digital clock, drawn by the electric warmth even in the day's gathering heat, and it kept a lidless eye warily on her as she smoked. Each time it exhaled, Melissa could see its ribs, fine as thread. She stubbed out the cigarette and, reaching for the telephone, dialed her mother's number in Connecticut. The gecko fled; the phone rang only once.

"Hello?"

"Hi, Nona. It's me."

"You! But I thought you weren't back until tomorrow."

"I'm not back. I'm flying in tonight, but I wanted to talk to you now." She meant: I wanted to find out how bad it was before I got there.

"Well, it's good to hear you, Lissy. You don't even sound seriously waterlogged. I mean, I never thought I'd have a mermaid for a daughter, much less one who was an emissary of science, and you know what I—" She stopped.

"How is it, Nona? How are you feeling?"

A pause, blossoming into static, decaying back to silence.

"Pretty punk, Lissy," she said at last.

"Pain?"

"I have these pills."

"What happened at the hospital yesterday?"

"Bone scan okay, blood test okay, scarring of lungs from radiation treatment not too bad, and according to the X rays bronchial tumor shrunk by sixty-five percent. How does that sound?"

"It sounds wonderful."

"Doesn't it? But there's this other thing: I'm dying anyway."

"You are *not*."

"Don't treat me like a child. I know how I feel."

"But *I'm* the child around here," said Melissa, raising her voice. "*I'm* the fucking child around here." It seemed to Melissa that the tears came out of her skin, not her eyes. "I'm *your* child, Nona."

A pause.

"I love you, Lissy."

"Nona . . ." It seemed to be an appeal. They let it fade into the hum of the wire.

"Well, have you taught that fish to sing yet?"

"Not a fish, a mammal," she said, wiping her eyes. "He can talk."

Peter swam restlessly around the rooms of the house, onto the deck, back into the house. Use of the telephone disturbed him; the faint cast of its electromagnetic patterns on his skin reminded him at up to fifteen body lengths of what he did not wish to know and caused dreams to flicker at terrible speeds along the length of him like shadow dapple. He swam to where his soft-bristled brush was anchored to the floor and rubbed against it, closing his eyes. It had come to him that the woman was leaving today. In some of his dreams, he was able to move about in the dry world, swimming freely through air and bearing without damage the full crush of gravity. In some of his dreams, the woman had grown cold to him and, with a variety of devices that resembled electric eels, would torture him, or remove his teeth, or prod him into metal boxes. He ceased rubbing and lifted his blowhole above the surface to breathe. Dolphins regard decisions made at the moment of respiration as more serious than those made underwater. Peter savored this luster of seriousness, then, using both eye and sonar, set off in methodical search for his yellow, plastic, melon-sized ball.

He found it slowly orbiting the outflow fixture in one corner. With his beak, he nudged it back along the surface until it floated beside the woman's desk in the opposite corner, then he took up position behind it, eye fixed on the door, mouth slightly open, and waited.

Melissa did not see him immediately. She was tying a kerchief over her head as she came in and was ticking off a mental list of drugs, treatments, and attitudes that Nona might yet be convinced to try. After she had hung up the phone, she had had an alarming vision of herself flying alone through a viscous, black outer space. In the vision, she had flown at first in a sitting position, as if in an imaginary chair, then, as she accelerated, she had tipped gradually forward until she was soaring along belly down, legs out, like a rocket, utterly without fear.

The yellow ball flew at her. She caught it in a defensive gesture, not comprehending immediately how it had arrived there, in front of her face. Twenty feet away Peter made a noise like a cocktail party heard through wax paper.

"You damn fish-that-sings! You're impossible!" she shouted, and threw the ball back at him hard.

He caught it in his teeth, then released it onto the water and butted it into the air with his forehead. It fell one body length short of Melissa, and was briefly, as it sat upon the surface between them, the object of their separate contemplations. Melissa splashed slowly forward to get it.

"God, how used to each other we've gotten! It's getting so the shape of my own body surprises me when I look in a mirror after watching you all day."

Melissa tossed the ball into the air in front of her and punched it over to Peter with her fist. He had to leap to catch it, water falling away from him on either side in great swashes.

"Sorry," said Melissa. "My fault."

They played catch with a concentration that mounted gradually, centering now on the ball, now on each other. Neither of them made noises beyond the small aquatic commotions involved in the game's toss and catch, and those sounds blended with the pulse of the pump downstairs, with the chirrups of the banana quits under the eaves, with the buzz and click of invisible insects at the window louvers, until Melissa's sense of the house itself became acute, as if it were clothes she was wearing—indeed, more than that, and she saw that she had come to regard the house, with its brothy blood of seawater, as a living thing in which she and the dolphin had come miraculously to take up residence.

She was surprised when there was no more room between them for catch. Each of Peter's return tosses had fallen short, and, dreamy with the heat, she had each time waded slowly forward to fetch the ball. Peter, at her knees, opened jaws that another time had bitten a six-foot barracuda in two. Melissa dropped the ball into them. In Connecticut, Nona dropped a cup of coffee onto the kitchen floor and, lacking the patience to clean it up, kicked the cup fragments under the table and left the room.

And when Peter did not release the ball, continuing instead to mouth it gently with his eyes shut, Melissa hesitated, but seeing that his jaws could not easily close on her hand while the ball acted as a prop, she reached

into his mouth and massaged his gums gingerly until his
grip relaxed and the ball rolled onto her palm.

She lifted it above her head, and as the dolphin
turned on his side to peer at her with one bright, assess-
ing eye, she heard herself say strange words. She said:
"I've tried and tried and *tried*."

She dropped the ball into his open mouth, and Peter
this time let it roll farther back into his jaws, where it
was less certain a prop. Her hand drifted in among his
teeth like an unruly starfish, and she was reminded for
an instant of the story Nona told about sitting once on
Clark Gable's lap in the lobby of the Algonquin Hotel
and counting his teeth.

Peter drew away from her. Her arm, in his jaws
nearly to the elbow, came free. Without loosening his
grip on the ball, he let himself sink on his side to the
floor, and, underwater, took her ankle in his mouth.

She shuddered and, at the same time, so did he.
Their eyes met, and held.

Moments began to topple.

Melissa tried to touch her shoulder-length hair, but it
had been cut away.

She said: "I'm frightened, Peter."

Slowly, Peter began raking his teeth up and down her
leg, opening his jaws gradually wider under her whole
calf, knee, thigh moved through his mouth, and the
yellow ball slipped out and away.

She reached a hand down and touched his back, the
enormous muscle of it, the silken skin. In some of his
dreams, the moon was again honored among dolphins
and had come in full yellow light to settle slowly into
the sea and be rubbed against in praiseful places by
dolphins.

Melissa untied her kerchief and set it in the water
behind her. She maneuvered the leotard off one shoulder, then the other. Her nipples were taut, and the
sensation of Peter's teeth on her legs was like this taut-

ness spread to the rest of her body. She rubbed his skin.

She began repeating his name.

When the dolphin's cock appeared, emerging erect from the slit on his underside, Melissa stepped away from his jaws and pulled the leotard past long red scratches and off her legs. Peter saw the hair. She moved toward him uncertainly, drawing the fingers of one slow hand upward through her cunt. She is very wet, and as she repeats the gesture her knees begin to quiver. She is surprised suddenly by the need to say something and can think of nothing.

She says: "Love?" And her legs buckle under her.

For two seconds, she is fully underwater. During that moment, she has the impression that she and Peter are moving at a speed so extreme that movement itself has subsided. When she lifts her head, spewing saltwater and gasping for air, the sensation vanishes at the same speed. Peter, his eyes half-closed, is ramming himself against her, and it comes to her that he does not know how or where to enter her.

On her knees, she pushes with both hands just behind his flipper until he understands he is to roll over on his right side. As she takes his cock into her hands, Peter makes faint quacking sounds, and she herself begins to murmur. He is concentrating utterly on the effort of keeping his movements to human scale; she, the fragile one, is aware of his restraint. Both hear with new intensity their quiet splashing as the sound of air and water mixed. Straddling him, she is entered.

They were making love in the shallow water.

When Jeffrey returned to the apartment after his day of teaching fifth-graders what was to be expected from them in life, his telephone was ringing. It was Nicole. She was going to California for a day and wanted to know if she could catch a ride to the airport with him when he went to meet Melissa's plane. Nicole's father worked for TWA, so she could and did fly anywhere for free—as long as she didn't get married.

As they sped up the ramp to the Cross Bronx Expressway, Nicole said, "How's Lissy taking it about Nona?"

In the air there were jet planes, helicopters, invisible particles. Jeffrey looked at Nicole through dark glasses. "I think she's doing okay," he said.

At the airport an Irishman with a bottle of Jameson's in his back pocket had climbed out on one of the hundred flagpoles overlooking the main lobby and was trying to pull down the South African flag. Melissa's plane was not due for an hour and Nicole's not for two. They had drinks.

"I forgot to ask what's in California this time," said Jeffrey.

"You know those costumes I've been working on?" Nicole began. "They're due at a studio in L.A. tomorrow, and since it's cheaper for me to fly out with them than to mail them, I thought I'd take a little jaunt." She smiled at him.

"Nikki," he said, "I admire your sense of proportion."

"I know you do," she answered. "It's what you like best about me."

This seemed indeed to be true, so Jeffrey finished his gimlet and ordered another. At the first taste of it, it occurred to him that Nicole, who was not taking her eyes off him even when sipping at her Dubonnet, might again be pregnant. She had had five abortions and her gynecologist was in L.A.

A sadness passed over him as he looked at her. "You know," he said, noticing it for what was easily the twentieth time, "you become absolutely beautiful in airports; you have no idea how radiant."

She gave a short laugh, finished her drink in a double swallow, and put the glass down in front of her. "I was born and raised at a ticket counter, Jeffrey, born and raised."

They played electronic ping-pong. Every time they hit the video ball with one of the video paddles, the machine produced a beep of deeply satisfying, quarter-inviting tenor, and after three such beeps, a child sitting nearby but out of sight began to accompany it loudly. Jeffrey won, then won again, then ran out of quarters.

"There's some change in my bag," said Nicole, who had decided on another Dubonnet and was on her way to the bar.

Melissa, in a stainless-steel bathroom twenty thousand feet above Washington, D.C., looked at herself in the mirror, then took a yellow pill to wake herself up. I look like shit, she thought. She wondered why there were never any windows in airplane bathrooms.

Jeffrey's hand, in Nicole's canvas carryall, touched a thing that was startlingly unlike quarters. He lifted it partway out of the bag, holding it by the barrel. He let it drop back down into the suddenly enhanced depths of the canvas darkness and lit a cigarette. The child was now beeping unaccompanied; its parents were trying to hush it.

When Nicole had safely installed her new drink on the console of the machine in front of them, Jeffrey inquired, in the calmest tones left to him, why she was carrying a loaded Walther automatic in her purse.

A commotion of what seemed to him to be genuine surprise passed over her. She reached into the carryall and, hauling the gun out by its barrel, dangled it in the air between them like a dead rat. "Why, this little thing? Is that what you mean?"

The bar's patrons were mostly gathered in one corner beneath a surpassingly large color television set and did not appear to notice this grossness.

"Nicole, put the gun back in the bag." She did so, then shrugged and, with lapidary attention, examined the ice cubes in her drink.

"It's Diego's," she said. "I'd forgotten all about it. We've been fighting a lot and he started waving it around at me a bit too often, so I took it out of his drawer when he wasn't looking." She had found Diego in Barcelona a year ago with the aid of her TWA pass.

"He still beating you up?"

"Nothing really unfriendly."

In his distaste for this arrangement, Jeffrey ate a handful of very salty peanuts and fed the hungry machine a quarter. Nicole's shoulder, touching his as they played, seemed to request tolerance, and he summoned it up—though with misgivings, since to whom was it directed?

"You know," he said, "you still have to get it through baggage search."

Nicole, who had failed to consider this, gave him a fond, infected look and won the game. When they left the bar, the beeping child was in noisy tears from the cuffing its father had administered, and Diego's gun had been transferred from Nicole's canvas bag to Jeffrey's leather one, where it was to remain for safekeeping until her return from California.

At a newsstand, as they leafed through a copy of *Curious Creature Magazine,* Nicole asked him if he thought they would ever have an affair.

"I don't know," he said, truthfully but elliptically. Melissa's imminence was making him a little anxious.

"I don't know either," she agreed.

Melissa's plane arrived on time. He and Nicole waited for her by the security gate, watching metal detectors detect belt buckles and sets of keys on the persons of those who wished to fly somewhere. In the seven years Jeffrey and Melissa had known each other, they had parted so many times, rejoined each other after so many absences, that knowledge of her physical approach had begun to invoke in him a ritual succession of conflicting feelings which, by their very opposition, ramified with blinding speed toward the erotic. He removed his dark glasses, the first passengers appeared, Melissa was among them.

"Tell me I smell like fish," she said as they embraced, "and that's the last time you'll ever get close enough to know."

"You smell like fish," he said. "I missed you. Welcome home."

She laughed and, turning to Nicole, kissed her too. She had known her longer than she had known Jeffrey, and every time she saw her, Nicole was wearing a different essential oil.

"What is it this time?" asked Melissa.

"Verbena," replied Nikki, with harrowing sweetness.

Jeffrey's eyes met Melissa's and he saw that she had been lately crying. Travelers skated by on all sides, moving in and out of time zones with their colorful luggage. While Nicole explained about the studio in L.A., Jeffrey took the heavier of Melissa's suitcases from her, and the three of them set out for the TWA building.

"What's in this, anyway?" asked Jeffrey, hefting the silver-colored suitcase.

"Twenty-one days of dolphin talk on tape." She kissed him on the neck as they walked. A sea turtle caught sight of a plastic freezer bag floating on the surface of the deep waters just beyond the cove and, mistaking it for a jellyfish, attacked it. Attuned to its transparency and not its texture or taste, the turtle began to eat the bag. When it had swallowed half of it, it suffocated.

"Are you exhausted?" asked Jeffrey.

"No, actually. I'm okay."

They stepped aside to let a string of baggage carts pass by.

"Hey, where's Nicole?"

Melissa peered left and right at the people streaming

around them. "I don't know. She was right here a second ago. Maybe she's inside."

An electric eye winked open half a ton of sliding glass for them, and locating her gate number on a video monitor, they started down a long, carpeted corridor. When they were still fifty yards from the end, Jeffrey glimpsed Nicole far ahead, passing under the parabolic arch of the security gate. Her canvas bag was traveling through the metal detector on a conveyor belt, and she was smiling and nodding at the official who was running it.

"There she is." They shouted her name in unison.

Nicole, who was just being given back her bag, looked up but did not see them until Melissa began waving her free arm wildly about. Smiling broadly then, Nikki lifted her bag, blew them a kiss, and was gone.

In the parking lot, Melissa looked at Jeffrey across the top of the car, a BMW the color of baby aspirin, and said, "I want to get in back first."

USE OF THE RAY GUN

Melissa points her right forefinger at the BMW, whose color has always caused her acute distress. The sunlight seems so feeble up here, she thinks. She aims carefully and fires. Everything, including the BMW, turns blue.

"Hold me," she said to Jeffrey. He lifted her astride him; the seat springs groaned. When the steely thrum died away, he asked:

"How are you, Lissy? Are you okay?"

"Just a little shaky," she answered. "This helps. I've missed you very much."

He kissed her. He stroked her body, clothed in brilliant blue.

"Have you talked to her?" he asked after a time.

"Nona? Yes. Have you?"

"Several times. I went out there twice."

"How'd she seem?"

"The same but more so: hungry, speedy, troublesome, wonderful."

"Okay." She took a deep breath and ran a hand through his hair. "Let's not talk about it yet, okay? Just hold me a little longer. Hold me, then we can go home."

They sped into the difficult city.

At the restaurant, Jeffrey ordered the shredded beef with hot pepper sauce, and Melissa the "strange taste chicken." He asked her if Nicole was pregnant; Melissa, eyeing him, said yes, it was true, and that made six times in all. A melancholy silence ensued, during which Jeffrey decided to postpone telling Melissa about the pistol incident. Instead, he mentioned the name of a *Times* reporter who had called repeatedly while she was away. "He wants to do a story on Ehrler, but only if there are pictures of you and the dolphin."

"Pictures?" He caught the alarm in her voice; he saw the clipped gesture with which she reined herself in; and he at once recognized that keenness as partially chemical.

"You know: a few black-and-white vignettes of Beauty and the Beast. Here we see them sharing a bucket of butterfish after a long day of water polo. Here the prize pupil is reading Conrad aloud while his charming teacher looks on proudly. That sort of thing."

Melissa poured them tea. "John will be pleased to be written about."

"And you," said Jeffrey, "have no doubt been overcome with tropical modesty since last I saw you?"

She allowed her irritation to wash over and past her before she answered. "Perhaps it's a bit more complicated than that," she said.

Jeffrey looked at her, accepted the warning temporarily, talked to her of himself. He spoke of teaching, of seeing friends and films, of taking weekend trips to the country. Melissa believed he had also spent part of that time in bed with wide-mouthed women who cared for nothing but their dangerous appetites, which Jeffrey had contrived to sharpen. But maybe I'm being defensive, she thought.

Their waiter, impatient to return to the kitchen, where the cook's nephew was threatening the cook with a long knife, motored by, delivering fortune cookies to them on an aluminum platter as he passed—three fortune cookies like pale, invaginated blossoms.

"Do you have a cigarette?" she asked.

As he reached into the leather bag, his hand brushed against the gun inadvertently.

They smoked, paid, and left without touching the cookies.

USE OF THE THIRD RETURN POSTURE

Entering the apartment, they embrace. From where they are, in the foyer, she is able to see the enormous serigraph over the bed: a distant but unspeakably inviting view of puffy clouds seen from above, as though from an airplane. She wishes to go there, closes her eyes. He can smell maritime smells in her closely cropped hair. Why did she take the speed? he wonders. They kiss lengthily. Once the movement of their lovemaking has begun, they grow casual about it, as they have grown casual about physical distance, and they separate. Jeffrey goes into the kitchen and swallows twice from a bottle of gin. Melissa goes into the bedroom, shedding clothes. He thinks: we are getting very good at this, but life goes faster and faster. He puts the gin away and walks down the hall to the bedroom. Melissa is sitting naked on the blue rug. She has assumed the third return posture, also known as the memory-elimination posture. Selected sets of neurons begin tentatively to rearrange themselves. He squats before her and kisses her hairline, feeling refreshed, awaiting her refreshment. Her eyes perform little dances of fear and desire.

* * *

"It got so lonely," she said.

On the bed, she lay back, and he saw for the first time the long, red scratches on her legs, the oblong bruises. He touched them.

"It was harder than you thought it would be, wasn't it?"

She did not answer, but drew him slowly down to her until his face was three inches from hers. At the far end of the apartment the telephone had begun to ring and ring. "Fuck me," she said.

Their kisses, quickly breathless, seemed to Jeffrey centrifugal, their mouths impelled past each other by appetite at the very moment of tasting. He sought her elsewhere: in the profusion of salt-jacketed hair beneath her arm, in her swollen nipples, in the glistening of her cunt, quickly wet. She took the fingers of one of his hands one by one into her mouth. There was sea-water in her ear, and when she moved, she heard her motion amplified by the roll and pitch of that droplet. The speed of her arousal alarmed him slightly; he feared she might burst past herself, lose the moment. She took hold of his cock and guided him into her. The dolphin, in the deep pool, sped upward through water and burst, amid a storm of sea droplets, into air.

Sometimes she moaned, sometimes she raked his back, sometimes her mouth was clamped in concentration, and other times she gasped for air, but now, as she began to come, she laced her hands together behind his hips, holding him to her tightly, and what started as a word caught in her swollen throat became by increments a scream. He took a scant handful of her hair into his fist and ascended blindly with her, afraid of being left. When she felt him start to shudder, her scream streaked past the both of them and away by itself into the wide, wide dispersal of space.

For a long time they lay together, their legs tangled in the blue sheets and around each other. Jeffrey could feel Melissa's toes wriggling convulsively. He stroked her head.

"Jeffrey?" she said.

"What is it, Liss?"

"It's about the dolphin." She raised herself up to look at him, sight already supplanting touch as they subsided slowly back into the world. "He's been my lover."

Jeffrey's pupils opened wider to admit this news. "You know," he said, "I don't believe you're lying."

"Why should I lie to you?" She was trembling, but was able, with one deliberate shake, to still herself. "Why should I have to?"

He gently moved her off of him and got out of bed. In the living room he rolled a joint on top of the previous day's *New York Times*. The headline read: "Uranium Deposits Discovered in Antarctica, Called 'World's Largest.'" "Well," he called back over his shoulder, "who seduced whom then?"

SHE SHIFTS AMONG SHEETS, CAUSES EXTENSIVE DEPOSITS OF FUTURE-ORE TO LEAK FROM HER TO "CERTAIN DEATH"

With some difficulty, she stands up in the knee-deep water, naked and battered. Peter is swimming slow figure eights around the room, brushing against her as he passes. On the windowsill, a banana quit is perched, its tiny head cocked, its amazing eyesight trained upon her. It chirrups. She thinks: It was watching us the whole time. Absently touching her thigh, her fingers come away webbed with the dolphin's semen, opalescent in the sunstruck air. She is crying.

"He seduced me," she said. Jeffrey leaned against the doorjamb and breathed a cloud of smoke into the room. Through it, they regarded each other. The telephone rang. He strode down the hall and tossed it

through the window to dangle down the side of the
building until it was wanted again.

"You know," said Melissa, "that that was probably
Nona."

He sat down on the edge of the bed. "She'll call
back."

In spite of herself, a half-smile settled over her face.
She took the joint from him and drew on it, peering at
him sideways. "You're jealous?"

"Of course," he answered. In the walls and crannies
of the apartment, cockroaches went about their omni-
directional lives, silently waving their feelers. Do I want
to know about this? Jeffrey wondered. When he asked
her how it had happened, she told him.

Their love, the second time, was more deliberate,
each of them conscious of the other's patience. They
grew intensely aware of how damp the fronts of their
stomachs were, how wet the sound of their exchanged
movement. She had the further sensation that her cunt
was fully continuous with her skin, so that she was at
once enclosed and enclosing, and the impression allowed her to concentrate utterly on the man who was
making love to her. He recognized her attention and
returned it. She closed her eyes. Toward the end they
fell partially off the low bed and it half seemed to him
they were drifting down the hall as they fucked.

FIRST LUNAR UTTERANCE

The moon is distressed. It has come since 1969 to
understand that the animate/inanimate distinction
taken for granted by human beings has made its own
"aliveness" imperceptible to them. It had had hopes,
perhaps excessive ones. Instead, on its surface it now
has human footprints, not more than six inches deep
but certain to last over a million years, and these footsteps seem to the moon the emblem of a disturbing
future. Brooding on it, the moon reflects light down
onto the earth, into Jeffrey and Melissa's bedroom,

across the face of things. It continues to loop through space, moving around the earth, but away from it also —up till now at the rate of two centimeters a year, two meters a century. It has, all at once, a "sense of acceleration." It says: "Why am I not adored?"

When Jeffrey woke up in near-darkness, Melissa was shaking him by the shoulders violently and peering down at him.

"Wake up!" she was saying. "Wake up!"

He saw the wetness on her cheeks. "Okay, okay. I'm awake."

She sighed, sank back into his arms. "I'm sorry. I just got scared for a moment. You looked so . . ."

He stroked her head. She slept.

Nona watched the first sunlight hit the corner pane of her bedroom window. Then she let the three dogs in and made breakfast for herself. At the table, she spread open *The New York Times* and put her plate and a copy of *Elle* on top. She read from the newspaper about territorial disputes in Antarctica, then from *Elle* about how an Italian film star furnished her glassy tree house in Provence. One of the dogs, who had been swimming in the pond, stank happily at her feet.

She drank coffee, assessed the pain, decided to try to do without the Percodan, which made her sleepy. In the lower garden, she slowly and methodically turned over two rows of earth, fifteen yards long. Then she vomited. She was in the kitchen, washing her mouth out with soda water, when Jill arrived. Jill was her assistant in the real-estate business and lived with a boy who had once, in a fit of mutual convenience, been Nona's lover.

"Hi, Nona. How're you feeling?"

"Too early to tell yet, really."

Jill spooned honey into her green tea, thinking about the peculiar dream she had had. "In this dream," she said, "you were my sister. And you insisted that we stay

23

near a radio because there was going to be an invasion and you wanted news of it."

"Did we get the news?"

"I can't remember."

Jill had stopped smoking because of what it had done to Nona and because even other people's smoke sent Nona into horrible fits of coughing. Nona mentioned that Melissa was coming out to the house today.

"So she's had enough of the porpoises?" Though Melissa and Jill had gone to school together, they were not friends.

"Dolphin," corrected Nona. "In the singular. No, I think she's probably had anything but enough. We'll find out, though, I'm sure."

In the office, a sunny, oak-paneled room whose windows Nona had enlarged, Jill telephoned a prospective buyer. Nona examined the cash flow, then, referring to a set of Polaroids, sketched perspectives of the alterations she intended to make in one of their cottages: larger windows in the bedroom, a balcony in back, another fireplace. She thought about Jeffrey, wondering what had caused him to give up his career as an architect in order to teach small children in badly designed rooms. Then she received an invitation in the mail from the Connecticut division of NASCAR: her attendance was requested at a champagne brunch that was to precede the Fossil Fuel 250, scheduled for the end of the month at Windsor Locks.

"I didn't know you were still into stock-car racing," said Jill.

"I go when I can. Priorities have changed a little."

Jill put a pencil in the electric pencil sharpener, causing a tiny but measurable amount of energy to be consumed. Nona fell to coughing, throat tearing at the air, face gone red. When Jill rushed back with a glass of water, she drank it gratefully in small sips.

"Do I frighten you that much?" she asked, when the glass was empty.

"It's scary."

"Will Lissy be scared?"

"No. Angry maybe, but not scared. I've never seen her scared." It was not a compliment.

Nona smiled. "Maybe you're right."

In the bathroom, in the mirror, Melissa regarded her face, no longer puffy, her breasts, no longer swollen, and as she swung the medicine cabinet open to see if there were tampons, she felt a soft movement inside her. She stepped back. Between her feet on the tile floor: a star-splash of blood.

And so, when Jeffrey came into the bedroom to kiss her on his way to work, she was thinking about their decision not to have children.

"Is it awfully chilly of us?" she asked. "Life loves life and all that."

"It's a different world," he answered.

In the kitchen, she poured soda water into her orange juice and looked through a pile of his students' papers: their cramped handwriting; their strange, new thoughts. On one sheet, larger than the rest, was a crayon rendering of a little girl, tight of line and strident of color, but where the head should have been there was a television set, twice the size of the rest of her body. Melissa decided she knew nothing.

She stepped off the train feeling primed, flexible, fleet. She looked up and down the platform for Nona. And she had readied anecdotes, confessions, reassurances, so when Nona was not inside the station house she glided past the empty benches out to the sidewalk and took up a position whose confidence dwindled as the minutes passed. She smoked a cigarette. Nona arrived in her hatchback, the fat yellow Labrador riding behind her.

"Look at you, Lissy—brown as a coffee bean."

When they embraced, Melissa caught a dank scent on her mother's breath, something deep and ruined.

"Nona. I've missed you so."

They hurtled home in the little car, past the dairy farm, past the training center for the handicapped, past the county art depot.

"Jeffrey was very good to me while you were away," said Nona.

Melissa regarded her mother, wondering what might be seen there by an unfamiliar eye. "He likes you a lot, I think. How did you two amuse yourselves?"

"He came twice to dinner. I wanted to get some idea of what hc fclt for you, whether it was anything I recognized."

In the sky, bird events took place, high white cumulus movements. "Well?" asked Melissa after a moment. "Was it?"

"He loves you," Nona answered. "That much was clear to me."

And, after a silence, Melissa recalled aloud what Nona had temporarily forgotten—that as a child Melissa would sit beside her father while he drove and would weigh her sneakered foot surreptitiously upon the accelerator to hasten the progress of a cautious man. He, the day after she turned twenty-one, had without a word to anyone and with only a note to Nona, left them both for good.

"I thought maybe we'd have a drink and a bit of lunch, then take the canoe out to Patterson Swamp," said Nona, after another silence.

Melissa thought: *She's so thin.*

In the sun-room, Jill put a twist of lemon peel in each of the three glasses. "I thought you knew this story, Nona. Anyway, just as the elevator is closing, in breezes this young lawyer-type complete with half-inch-thick attaché case. He looks around at us and says: 'This must be my lucky day—starting out the morning in an elevator with seven beautiful girls.' Then Melissa looks him in the eye and, completely deadpan, says: 'We're not "girls," as you put it. We're vagino-Americans.' No one cracks a smile, the lawyer looks from one of us to another, begins to sweat, and up we go: one hundred twenty-eight floors of terror."

Nona was studying Melissa's haircut, her brilliant-blue clothing: *she looks different—sort of . . . jet-assisted.* They ate soup and salad and croque monsieurs.

"Aren't they supposed to be as smart as humans?" Jill asked. "Do they have emotions? Are there family attachments? What do you suppose they think of submarines? Are they afraid of the future?"

When Nona coughed, she covered her mouth with her napkin.

"I believe they have language," said Melissa. She washed the dishes, and when she went to fold the napkins, she found Nona's wadded in the trash.

The canoe glided upwater among oaks, elms, maples. And from the back Melissa seemed relaxed, attentive, young, so Nona spoke, as she ruddered, of a few of the things she did not know, such as whether to dredge the pond to make it swimmable again, what had driven the redwinged blackbirds away, what was meant by the term "information sickness," and whether it was true, what some people said, that the President had it.

"No one knows for certain," said Melissa. "But he's certainly in the right risk bracket."

The water surface was still and perfectly reflective; they seemed to be skimming along on a glassy membrane between the sky above and the sky below, trees and fronds and grasses growing both ways in the double sun.

"Nona, what do the doctors—"

"The doctors don't matter."

Melissa ceased paddling but did not turn around. She could see a catfish behind the sky off to starboard, chewing water.

"What does it feel like, then?" she asked, scooping her paddle forward again.

"It's terrifying. Not the pain, not the weakness, not

throwing up all the time from the radiation treatments. It's how I frighten people that frightens me. I've lost my greed, my violence."

Melissa turned around: Nona looked greedy, violent.

"I don't know what you're talking about," Melissa said.

"Exactly," Nona said.

They skirted the edges of a marshy islet where turtles, frogs, salamanders repeated feats of livelihood in excited camouflage. In the islet's single tree, Melissa and her friends had built a tree house; several silver boards of it still hung in the upper branches like Indian bones. And when Nona told Melissa she was thinking of stealing Richard from his wife for good this time despite the quarrels that had ended their affair two years previously, Melissa wondered what her mother had felt during the radiation treatments as doctor, nurse, technician had one by one retired behind shields of lead. In shallow water a dolphin thinks about the danger to his skin, which is twenty times more sensitive than a woman's.

"Does Richard know you're sick?" Melissa asked.

"I won't tell him right away."

"That seems a little cruel," said Melissa after a time. "Are you thinking of him or his wife?"

"I was thinking of you."

"So was I. Let's speak of something else."

The canoe grazed a partially submerged log on which a brilliant-green beer bottle had been placed; it toppled into the water like a frog. And Melissa continued to paddle, getting angrier and angrier and more helpless and more helpless.

"When I wanted to take a shower," she said, "I would have to stand knee-deep in seawater during it, dry myself, and then wade back to bed. When I got there, my legs from the knee down were wet with saltwater, and no matter how carefully I dried them, they'd still make the sheets clammy, and the salt would make the cuts on my legs sting, and I'd lie there awake for hours. Watching the moonlight on the water make moving shadows all over the walls and ceiling, listening to that fucking pump pound away, hearing the dolphin move about below like some intelligent creaking door from outer space. And after a few hours there'd be no doubt in my mind: I was the last human being on earth. I mean, I'd actually get used to the idea. And that feeling hasn't gone away; it's begun to change me in ways I don't even know about yet."

"But you have Jeffrey," Nona said. It was almost a whisper.

"I have Jeffrey and I have you and I have my friends, but—"

"Lissy, I'm terrified. Every day I am. And I don't want to die."

And the dolphin: the dolphin was patient, mainly: what else if not patient? He swam slowly around the perimeter of the deep pool where he was confined, avoiding boredom by reviewing in exquisite detail every moment of the near-month with Melissa. Since the evolutionary trauma that occurred when they moved from land to sea millions of years ago, dolphins have relied heavily on their memories, which are limitless—growing more elaborate and agile with each generation. Peter toyed with the images of Melissa, running them by his mind's eye in various orders. Repeatedly, he swam into the elevator's cradle, seeking to join the man who had fed him that morning, but when he punched the button with his beak, nothing happened. Nor could he feel the throb of the pump any longer against his tympanic skin. The sudden changes, the intensity of what had preceded them: Peter grew confused. Drawing breath, he dived to the bottom of the pool.

In deep water, dolphins pass into a meditative state caused by the weight of the water upon their skin. Peter ceased bit by bit to think of Melissa, dwelling instead on those subjects recommended by the sagas. He performed the exercise which is begun by thinking simultaneously of all 9,017 names for the taste of water. As he surfaced to breathe, he tasted traces of dolphin urine in the waves that swept over the inflow apron of the pool, and when he had counted seven different scents, he leapt several times from the water in an attempt to catch a glimpse of the animals in the cove beyond. He was unsuccessful. Beneath the surface, he began a series of exchange calls—long, high-pitched whistles which, cut off by concrete and air, went unheard by the others.

Above, the biotechnician who had replaced Melissa was draining the flooded house. Its floors needed cleaning and another coat of Thoroseal. As Melissa had suggested, he had hired three young men in Charlotte Amalie to help him, and they stood about in bathing suits, scrubbing the floors free of algae with push-brooms and listening to the transistor they had hung on the wall. "Etty in the room a cry," sang the radio, and tallest of the men sang along.

After gym, Jeffrey divided the subject of Antarctica sixteen ways among his students for the purpose of reports: geography, history, wildlife, natural resources, popular conceptions of, etc. Then he gave them some fraction problems and went to the teachers' room for coffee. All morning and afternoon he had seen swatches of brilliant blue out of the corner of his eye; a frock, the bobbing cap of a pen, the cover of a textbook blazing like clear points of fire until he looked directly at them. He was trying to understand: were he and Melissa moving closer together or farther apart? He called Clarice.

"Not far enough apart," said Clarice. "Besides, I told Neal I'd go with him to Philadelphia this weekend."

Jeffrey found he was relieved. "I think of you a lot," he said.

The children punched their calculators. They spoke

to one another across their short, radiant attention spans.

"Bunches of old persons with their balls hanging down to here and saggy tits."

"Bet that hurts."

"Already has some."

"Used to build buildings and he turned sideways on that."

"Started to change channels and I heard someone coming."

"Tried to get an ounce and she only got half."

"Too bad."

"Yeah, too bad."

"Never seen one in person; have you?"

"What'd you get for number seven?"

"Twice as much as we were before."

"Nobody mention it."

"You don't have to mention it."

"Some of these guys never did mention it."

"But he's a traveling head."

"Yeah, he's a swiveler."

"Older than us and he comes into the club sometimes."

"Got to turn sideways on that."

"Put your patch on, put your patch on."

"All the songs are fast and they play them all at the same time."

"Meet everybody all over again."

"With your radio on, and other radios on . . ."

"Wondering how do I work this?"

"Millions and millions and millions of years ago."

"She said it. Not me."

Jeffrey explained that he was not concerned about who said what, and that as long as they did the required work a certain degree of self-direction, not to be abused, might obtain. Then he collected the papers and had the children read aloud from their reading books one by one until the bell rang.

He lay down on his bed and took a nap. Nicole slowed the enormous red car she was driving and was passed on the left by an enormous green car out of whose window a blond child leaned to yell: "If you can't drive it, park it." That was what she was trying to do. She was on Wilshire Boulevard in Los Angeles.

Jeffrey answered the phone and sleepily accepted the charges.

Nicole said, "I need to talk to Lissy."

"She's at Nona's." Jeffrey dangled the clock before his face by its cord. "Is everything okay?"

There was a brief transcontinental silence.

"Everything's just fine," she said. "I've rented this gigantic red jackrabbit of a car and I've been driving it all morning—eating up the highway and seeing friends. All I need now is an ashtray full of cocaine and a—"

"Nicole. What's wrong?"

"Well, nothing's *wrong* exactly." She was watching a sports car drive up over the median strip that separated her parking lot from the next. "It's just that I've decided not to go through with this abortion after all. Five is enough, don't you think?"

Jeffrey hesitated. In this case he did not think five was enough; six was enough, followed by an intensive review of birth-control methods made available by modern science. He shut his eyes for a moment.

"Does Diego know?"

"That I'm pregnant, yes. That he's an incipient father, no."

"And if you get married, you lose your TWA pass. Am I right?"

The lines hummed. Almost no one knew how telephones worked.

"Well . . . I have nearly eight months."

Jeffrey tried to think up an entertaining lie then, to distract them both from the alarmingly rapid accumulation of sadness. Instead, he said: "Do you suppose I ought to keep the gun while you inform Diego of the content of his next twenty-one years?"

"Sweet of you," answered Nicole.

And when she asked how he and Melissa were doing, he said that to the best of his knowledge and belief they were an ongoing proposition, though a turn for the more peculiar had certainly taken place. The dolphin, he explained, had made a number of personal disclosures of a disturbing nature and had occupied Melissa to distraction for more than a month. She and the dolphin, he continued, were now exchanging cassettes by mail and all signs seemed to indicate that an understanding had been reached, the relationship amicably terminated. This, he concluded silently, was the entertaining lie he had sought unsuccessfully a moment ago.

"I love you, Jeffrey," she said.

"I love you, Nikki. You have to take care of yourself."

She agreed. "But could we keep what I told you just between us? I don't think I want Lissy to know after all."

Through the window, Jeffrey saw the moon: why did it look so small?

"Of course," he answered, pleased.

Then Jeffrey pressed the button and the elevator arrived. Ignacio was at the controls. He was reading the biography of Albizu Campos while the television, plugged into the lightbulb socket, narrated famous moments from the history of prizefighting. Between the ninth and tenth floors, Ignacio stopped the elevator and the two of them discussed a few aspects of the international struggle for liberation of the present from the oppressive apparatus of the tentacled past. They smoked cigars.

"No, amigo. We have learned from the case of Cuba one thing: first, the people's army. Entonces, we build the party around the army. No is good the other way."

"Iggy, I still cannot agree. What was good for Cuba

may not be correct for Puerto Rico. In history and revolution, every case is special."

"We will see," said Iggy, pouring them each a shot of
Bacardi. "And now: to our children's children!"

When Jeffrey got out at the first floor, the woman
who was waiting there would not enter the elevator
because of the smoke.

A CASE OF INFORMATION SICKNESS

On his way to Diego's, Jeffrey discovers a woman
harmed by information excess. All the symptoms are
present: bleeding from the nose and ears, vomiting,
deliriously disconnected speech, apparent disorienta-
tion, and the desire to touch everything. She has a rubber mat rolled up under her arm and is walking around
one of the soft, new park benches recently installed by
the city, palpating it hungrily. A small crowd has collected around her, listening to her complicated mono-
logue: Birds of Prey Cards, sunspot soufflé, Antarctic
unemployment. Jeffrey hesitates. I've never seen one
so far gone, he thinks. But, judging her young enough
to warrant hope, he gently takes the rubber mat from
the woman, unrolls it upon the pavement, and helps her
to assume the memory-elimination posture. After a
minute, the bleeding stops. "I was on my way to dance
class," she says to him, still running her ravening fingers over his leather coat sleeve, "when suddenly I was
dazzled. I couldn't tell where one thing left off and the
next began." She is rather pretty. Jeffrey explains that
he believes information sickness, like malaria, recurs
unpredictably. "Please let me through," comes a voice.
"I'm this lady's husband." The woman and her husband thank Jeffrey profusely and he leaves.

Jeffrey rang the bell, while inside the loft Diego
coaxed flamencoid eruptions from the stainless-steel
electric guitar he had recently designed. Jeffrey was
feeling good, enmeshed again in the civic fabric after

a day in which the world had seemed to be exploding away from him in all directions. The door was not locked.

"Hello?" he said.

Diego was looking out the window as he played, the amplifier turned up past the pain threshold. Jeffrey clapped him hello on the shoulder, and Diego, taken by surprise, spun around, his hands halfway to fists before he saw who it was. He relaxed, he switched off the amplifier.

"*¿Qué tal, Jefe?*"

And for a moment Jeffrey thought: she's already told him.

The year before, in California, this had happened: Jeffrey was driving home from the architecture office where he had already begun to distinguish himself, though only three years out of architecture school. It was a very prestigious firm that undertook only the largest corporate commissions, and Jeffrey worked exceptionally hard for them. So hard, in fact, that he had time for little else, and yet, as he started the drive back toward Oakland, he had doubts about the worth of what he was doing. The time for erecting monuments to modernism was past; architecture itself was beginning to seem anachronistic to him; the future seemed to demand a less monolithic vision. While he considered these reservations, waiting on the expressway's entrance ramp, his eye fell on the car's ashtray, which he had not emptied for months. A pyramid of butts made it impossible to close the ashtray, and the very fact of that negligence seemed at once to accuse him and architecture itself. He was still looking at that cenotaph when, from the left, a blue convertible swerved off the expressway, as if trying to exit onto the entrance ramp, and exactly as Jeffrey caught sight of it, slammed into the front of his car, throwing it sideways and lifting the contents of the ashtray into the small atmosphere of the compartment like a swarm of flies. Neither he nor the black woman who was driving the convertible was hurt, and as Jeffrey stepped out of the car, brushing the cigarette ashes out of his hair, out of his eyes, off his clothes, he found he had already decided to quit his job. It was shortly after that that Nicole had telephoned Lissy from Barcelona to say she had met a Cuban there whom she intended to import, that he believed in UFOs, and that his name was Diego.

"Heard anything from Nikki?" Jeffrey said at last, surveying the empty beer bottles and dirty dishes scattered about the space like cairns.

"No, man. You know what she's like."

Jeffrey relaxed.

Diego put the fish-skeleton-shaped guitar in its case. Then they went into the kitchen area and smoked a joint. Thinking of Diego's pistol, inhumanly patient as it was, and regarding Diego, tense and mercurial as he was, Jeffrey said: "How about a little billiards?"

At the Laws of Physics Pool Parlor, Eddie, sipping a Dr. Pepper, clocked them in at the choice corner table by the window. Diego won the lag, sank two balls on the break and four more in succession before missing a difficult combination. When he suggested upping the stakes from fifty cents a ball to a dollar, Jeffrey, looking up in surprise from the shot he was lining up, readily agreed.

They split two racks evenly, not speaking. They were watching each other in the table, as men do: intimate with the evidence or rules. Jeffrey had a run, then another. Diego thought: He's got something up his sleeve, but I'm faster than he is. Then he sank a reverse bank, opening up a sequence of easy shots for himself.

"How is it, having Melissa back?" he said.

"I'm not sure she is back," Jeffrey answered. At the adjacent table, a father who had already mastered the game was instructing his small son in the kiss, click, and roll of it. "And I'm not sure I know how it is."

Diego chalked his cue with excessive zeal. He left tiny spots of blue powder on the felt with every shot.

"Let's say you do know how it is. Let's say it's the best it's ever been. In bed, the earth moves. Out of bed, you are afraid of nothing."

Their eyes met. "Okay, Diego. Let's say that."

Melissa moved through the rooms of their apartment, turning on all the lights.

"Then, Jefe, you begin to notice a funny thing." Diego leaned fully out over the table and, lifting one leg for balance, scratched. He shrugged as he gave the cool, white cue ball to Jeffrey. "You begin to notice she never uses birth control anymore."

After the look, long and level, and the silence, long and fragile, Jeffrey placed the ball carefully behind the head string.

"You ask why. She says she's safe. You count the days, going back in your mind: you find she's not. You ask again why. She says she has used no protection for three months, and nothing's happened. She tells you she's not going to start worrying about it now. She says if you want to do something about it, that's up to you."

The women of the city were growing tired of waiting for their futures, although many were tired of other things instead. Jeffrey sank a rail shot, difficult to miss. He kept an eye on Diego, who was beginning to alarm him. "What did you do about it?" he said at last.

The table held diminished possibilities and the cue ball was frozen against the rail. Diego looked up. "I beat her," he said.

Melissa shivered. Then she realized that her socks and canvas shoes were still wet from the canoe, and sitting down on the bed, she took them off. It was Jeffrey she wanted now, as she watched her chilly toes wriggle in sly reminder of days and nights in seawater, and it was with Jeffrey that she was happiest. She rummaged through her drawer for socks. The dolphin grazed the surface, exhaling into the dark with a hiss.

Then through Jeffrey's drawer. Her fingers came up against something cold, metallic, dense.

Turning the gun over in her hands, she thought: What are we—all five years old? Despite herself, she began to cry. When her head hurt from weeping, she walked across the room to the closet's full-length mirror, pointed the pistol at her puffy, tear-blurred image and said:

"Stop it."

With the hand not holding the gun, she dried her eyes. It was actually rather interesting to be holding a gun. She fell again to inspecting it.

THE RAY GUN: AN EXPLODED VIEW

Some ray guns are constructed of steel, some of seed pods and titanium wire, still others of bone, clay, or Rhoplex. Melissa has turned away from the mirror as she studies the weapon that has wandered into her accelerating life. Removing the clip, she cannot avoid noticing that as an object it is beautiful. She sights along its blade and notch.

Some ray guns discharge with a bang, some with a hum, some with the sound of rock-'n'-roll music that owes nothing to the blues. Points of friction are eased with Teflon, but use of graphite or light fossil oil is not unknown. Other models have no moving parts at all. As with all weapons, the ray gun's function is to quicken the rearrangement of human affairs, understood to include objects. Feathers on the barrel enhance range, accuracy, performance . . .

Melissa wonders: Does Nona own one of these? It does not seem entirely out of character, though Melissa has never before considered the possibility. She is considering it still when the phone rings. The sound throws her into a small fit of panic. Before she realizes what she is doing, she has hidden the weapon—not in its former nest of underwear and socks but at the back of one of her filing cabinets, in her study. She is alarmed at what she has done, but by the time she picks up the phone, on the eighth ring, it no longer seems to be something to think about.

The ray gun, although an instrument of man and dependent upon him for locomotion, cannot be "owned" in the ordinary sense.

Racking the balls up, Jeffrey spoke to Diego. "We were in a hotel room—Dallas, Kansas City? I can't remember. The three of us on the bed talking and drinking. Lissy and I had been fighting, but we were trying to make the best of it since we hadn't seen Nicole in months and she'd just come in from L.A. Nikki was doing most of the talking, and she was feeding a stack of quarters one by one into the Magic Fingers. You know—a vibrator attached to the bed? The ice rattling in our drinks as if we were on a train."

Diego grimaced. "Nikki the traveler." He was up fourteen balls on Jeffrey and would have to pocket only one on this rack to win. Jeffrey, whose turn it was, would have to clear the table. He broke; sank two.

"Then Lissy said something to me, I don't even remember what. But it was something only Lissy would know—a tiny betrayal, but complete. As soon as she'd spoken, she jumped up and ran for the door. Halfway down the corridor, I caught her."

Sighting along the tops of the balls, stalking them, Jeffrey sank four more in a sequence of shots that left the table open to him.

"And I began to strangle her. It was automatic, amazing, awful. It was not a game, not pretend. I remember how surprised we both were—me through my rage, she through her triumph—that it had come to that, that it was finally out of control . . .

"I don't know how far it would have gone. All at once I became aware of Nikki standing beside us in tears—the only time I've ever seen her cry. She must have seen me hesitate, because at that moment she grabbed Lissy and me by our sleeves, pushed her face up between us, and screamed, 'I've just had a fucking abortion and I want you two to listen to *me!* '"

Diego, who had been watching Jeffrey's progress at the table looked sharply up at him. In his mind's eye, he saw the hotel bed—full of quarters, shimmying by itself in the empty room.

When Jeffrey returned to the apartment, all the lights were on. He walked down the hall, past the kitchen, living room, dining room, study. The heavy double doors to the bedroom were ajar.

He said, "Melissa?" and pushed the doors open.

Her clothes were scattered about the room; her suit-case, open on the bed, was half unpacked. A chair had been turned to face the door, and a belt was slung over it. On the buckle, a note was spindled:

J: Forgive me, love, but the Aquarium's dolphins are being flown in tonight from their winter quarters in St. Aug, and Pamela called to ask me to help. (They'll be traveling in those fiberglass cases you and I and John designed last fall, so keep yr fingers crossed.) Don't know when I'll be done, but hope not later than 3. Ehrler to arrive from Europe early tomorrow p.m.—with funds, I trust.

     Must talk to you about Nona. She wants you to call her. Also: call Kirk at home.

     Jeffrey, I can't tell what's happening to us. What it means when I loosen my legs to you; when I come, when you do . . . It's different than it was. Are we all right? Am I?

I love you,
M.

In the kitchen, Jeffrey poured himself a drink and telephoned his twin brother Kirk in Houston. No one answered. Jeffrey studied an ashtray containing five of

Melissa's cigarettes, each less than half smoked. Then he took the D train to the Aquarium. "I'm part of the dolphin reception team," he explained to the guard, who answered that the truck had just arrived from the airport and everyone was down by the sea pool in back.

Passing through the empty, carpeted halls, silent galleries lit by tanks where sea life hovered, swarmed, and dipped on every side, Jeffrey thought: Skin. He stopped before a wall-length tank containing three beluga whales, twenty-five feet long; their smooth, white, amazingly sensitive skins gleamed as they pressed against the glass and turned their intelligent heads sideways to inspect him. Behind him, electric eels crackled and popped. He decided everything was possible.

Pushing open the back door, he saw a truck, floodlights, a knot of excited people. He decided everything was possible. The sea pool had been drained to knee level and four men in wet suits splashed about talking among themselves. A woman with braids rigged a small hand crane. After a moment's hesitation, Jeffrey approached Melissa, who was sitting on the end of the open truck bed, swinging her interesting legs and pointing and giving directions to people. Her gestures faltered; she jumped down.

"Jeffrey! What are you doing here?" Her eyes were anxious, guarded, pleased.

"I got bored," he answered, kissing her. She looked at him. Of the group, only she had preferred swimsuit to wet suit. And when he inquired how the transport cases had worked out she invited him up onto the truck bed where six fully grown dolphins lay calmly in their form-fitting, water-filled boxes of fiberglass. Holes at the top allowed room for dorsal fins and breath; soaked bed sheets kept their backs moist.

"We're waiting for the forklift so we can unload them," Melissa explained.

Jeffrey squatted down before one of the boxes, semitranslucent under the floodlights. She's in a state, he thought. From within the box came a series of three short whistles, to which Jeffrey responded in kind. The dolphin answered with four whistles, giving the last one a rising inflection that made it sound interrogative. Jeffrey whistled four times and stood up.

"They seem happy enough in them, don't they?" he said. The forklift, a hundred yards away, approached on steel treads. Melissa jumped to the ground. "Feel like helping?" she asked.

Jeffrey stood among the caskets, listening to the dolphins breathe—short, rushing hisses that came unpredictably from one quarter, then another. Melissa flagged the lift forward. Maybe it's good he's come, she thought. With the help of a man whose foot had a tugboat tattooed across it, Jeffrey pushed two of the cases onto the steel forks. The lift withdrew, and the four remaining dolphins began a rapid interchange of clicks and creaks, easily audible through the polythene-padded fiberglass. Jeffrey spoke to the man beside him. "Do you think they understand what's happening to them?" The man looked up in surprise. "Of course."

Volunteers with cameras recorded the operation, staff members pulled the cases one by one from the lift and aligned them carefully poolside—smooth they said, safe they said, the fiberglass design a vast improvement. Jeffrey leaped from the truck as it began to move; the lift departed in the opposite direction.

"I don't know, Pamela," Melissa said to the woman with braids. "I think it might be easier if we take the tops off the cases and drain them first."

"They'll float if you do that," Jeffrey observed, and when Pamela agreed that dumping the dolphins out that way might harm them, Melissa grew impatient.

"Okay, I'm overruled. Let's go."

Attaching a rope sling to either end of one of the cases, and the slings to the hook of the hand crane, they began carefully to raise it—Pamela at the winch, Melissa and Jeffrey steadying the load. When the case was chest-high, Pamela paused while the man with the tattoo reached into the hole and removed the soaked sheet (*hovering in the sudden air, and something was happening! and there were humans on all sides! and cold light!*) for fear of suffocation.

"Okay," he said to Pamela, holding the sheet up.

"Okay," Melissa said to the men waiting in the pool.

Pamela cranked the case slowly higher, beyond Melissa's reach, beyond Jeffrey's. When the case was ten feet above the pavement, spinning lazily, Melissa nodded and Pamela began to swivel the crane so its load moved out over the shallow water.

But she turned too fast and water gushed from the air hole in a gout which unbalanced the case, quickly upending it.

"Lower it, lower it!" Melissa shouted as Pamela struggled with the winch and the men in the water tried to be in the right place at the wrong time. The case danced drunkenly to the right of them and to the left of them, and Jeffrey put a restraining hand on Melissa's shoulder. Pamela released the ratchet, cable whirred, the case fell into the men's arms.

When Melissa unfastened the lid, the dolphin peered up at her with a bright, inquiring eye. She stroked its back. "All right," she said softly. "All right." The animal, released into the pool, was skittish but unhurt.

Pamela fetched a plastic siphon from the shed and, removing the lid of the second case, drained it. The dolphin plainly suffered at the loss of buoyancy; its breathing grew labored and short. Jeffrey asked if it would be all right like that; Melissa, fastening the ropes, said it would.

"Do you mind managing the crane this time?" Pamela asked her, tossing her braids back over her shoulders with either hand. "I'm afraid I don't have the hang of it yet."

Melissa walked over to the crane, took hold of the winch (*moonlight condensing across a great distance*

*into words and ranks of data upon the dolphin's hot,
tympanic skin)*; and began to turn.

TALES OF PRAISE AND GLORY

As the dolphin is lifted slowly into air, Jeffrey becomes
aware of the ocean, five hundred yards to the south. He
can smell it and hear it. Afterward we'll go look at it,
he thinks. Pamela, at the other end of the transport
case, is still angry with herself for having mishandled
the crane, and she compensates by staring intently at
the dolphin. Its breathing sounds like a bad cough.

Melissa decides to crank the case as high as the cable
will allow, elminating the pendulum movement which
caused so much difficulty before. Deciding this, however, she is not quite able to ignore another, less practical reason for raising the dolphin to the crane's full
height: she simply wants to see what it looks like up
there. As she anticipates the moment, she suffers in
brief reprise the previous day's vision of herself soaring
through space—solitary, rocketlike, unspeakably swift.
She continues to crank, the case rises out of Pamela's
and Jeffrey's steadying hands, it begins languidly to
turn.

Behavior of the first dolphin: It is swimming around
the pool's perimeter at top speed, sonaring frantically.

Behavior of the men in the pool: They are distracted
by the movement of the first dolphin.

Behavior of the rest of the staff, spectators, volunteers:

They watch as the case reaches the summit of the
crane and remains suspended there in the glare of the
floodlights. No one speaks. Melissa is about to swivel
the crane out over the pool when, with a tremendous
exertion of its complex musculature, the dolphin leaps
from the case, rising fully six feet upward into the air
before falling headfirst in a graceful arc toward the
pavement below. Some of the onlookers instinctively
cover their eyes; others, their ears; most do neither. The

dolphin strikes the concrete with the muted smash of wet laundry and is immediately still. Pamela, her hands over her face, is covered with blood. Jeffrey, beside her, is covered with blood. Melissa is running toward the dead animal, crying. The others converge.

WHEN Nona stopped the hatchback in front of Jill's house the following day, she remembered, because Jill was always talking about her own dreams, that she had dreamed the night before about Antarctica, In the dream, it had been a hospitable land, rich with birdlife, abandoned temples, and a warm blue snow which her companion had called "singing ice." Sliding into the seat beside her, Jill kissed Nona on the cheek, while Mason, her lover, got in back.

Nona smiled into the rear-view mirror. "Hi, Mason."

"Hello, Nona." The two of them were mildly but enduringly amused over their single sexual episode, which Jill did not know about.

"Let's go," said Jill, rolling her window partway down. "This is my first time and I don't want to miss anything." Then they drove to Windsor Locks, to the stock-car races. Nona parked behind the speedway in a field already full of casually parked automobiles in pastel colors—late-model Chevys, Dodges, Fords, very much like the ones their owners had come to watch. The air smelled strongly of exhaust fumes and burnt rubber. Nona, getting out of the car, had a coughing fit. It was Saturday.

46

"I told Richard we'd meet him over by the beginning of the front straight," Nona said to Jill as the three of them walked across the field. "We'll have to save him a seat."

They waited while Mason ran back to the car to get his sunglasses. "Are you nervous?" Jill asked. A blue haze hung over the speedway's concrete bowl.

"It's been over two years," said Nona.

They took seats near the top of the stand so they could hear each other speak. The qualifying runs had already started, each car in turn running three solo laps, and in the sunny spring air Nona confessed she was a fool for the smell of burning gumballs.

"Gumballs?" said Mason. It was strange to hear her talk like that. He was glad to see her enthusiastic and he knew there was more going on here than just the race. But it was strange to hear her talk like that.

"Gumballs are the special tires they use in the qualifiers," Nona said, brushing the hair out of her eyes. "Too soft to race with, wouldn't last ten laps, but see how they hold the turns?" And as she scanned the aisles for Richard, as she remembered what it had been like between them, she began to feel she had set herself up for a calamity.

Jill put her hand on Mason's thigh. Everyone she looked at in the crowded grandstand had a transistor radio pressed against his ear; some had televisions. "As the Chinese say," Mason observed, " 'We must cripple ourselves to use the crutch which gets us to the stars.' " In the time it took him to pop the top on a can of beer, a Plymouth Superbird raised a ring of smoke around the two-and-five-eighths-mile circuit.

Nona leaned forward to ask the man in front of her for the time, but when he pressed the button on his digital watch, nothing happened. He shrugged. Nona drank two beers, and so did Mason. Then a Mercury Cyclone went up against the wall in the number-three turn, spun out, rolled, and burst into flame. Jill did not let go of Nona's arm until the driver crawled out the window, unharmed, insolvent, angry. Tearing his helmet off in rage, he flung it up into the crowd by its chin strap.

"It was a bad idea to call him," Nona said. "I can't imagine what I—" But she said no more. Jill's fragile gold earring jiggled in the sunlight. Richard, his corduroy jacket slung over his shoulder, waved and climbed the steps two at a time.

"I hope you weren't pulling for the Mercury," he said, a little breathless.

It had never been their habit to kiss in public.

Nona said, "They resurfaced the track a couple of weeks ago. It's like ice." She faltered. "You know Jill. And this is Mason, who does carpentry for me. Richard's a former client." The maintenance crew threw two fifty-pound sacks of Sta-Dri on the track where the Mercury had been.

Richard thought: I forgot to take off my ring.

Information in waves like birds startled into migration filled the transistor radios, televisions, imagination of the crowd as the one o'clock news broadcast itself. Richard talked to Nona about his new job. He was assistant commissioner of mass transportation for the State of New Jersey.

"Does it give you pleasure?" she asked.

He leaned forward, clasping his hands. "I want to move twice as many people daily at peak usage. Before I leave the job, I mean. That would give me pleasure."

Nona laughed, bit her knuckle, looked at him sideways. "And how many people do you move now?"

A roar went up as the last of the qualifiers came in, a Ford Talladega at 152.228 mph. Mason studied the infield, ablaze with brand-new cars so fast they could tear the tires off their casings. These belonged to spectators who had arrived early enough to park there and who were now sitting among their cars in aluminum lawn furniture or lying face up on their cars in the tireless sun or stooping beside portable barbecue pits. Mason put his feet up on the empty seat in front of him. "It's good to be us," he said.

The sight of Mason's feet—antique wing tips incongruous at the cuffs of his carpenter's jeans—reminded Richard of his own sons, so ready to insult the customary. It was cause for wonder that Nona should know such people, should always have chosen them as friends and sometimes, as he suspected, lovers. He once had told her it was because of the way her husband had left her, and she, shrugging on her bra, had not disagreed. He had thought at great length about her husband.

"Richard, I've just had a marvelous idea," said Nona. Over the loudspeaker came announcements for the pre-race chapel service and drivers' meeting.

"What'd you say?" said Richard, putting his hand on her knee. "I couldn't hear because of the—"

"What you ought to do," she said, leaning against him as she spoke into his ear, "is invest in a fine . . . racing . . . machine."

She looked at him intently.

"I knew it," he said. "You want me to become a race-car driver. What would the Mass Transit Authority say?"

"No, no, no. I just want you to help that guy buy a new car—the one who wrecked his Mercury in the qualifiers." She consulted her program. "Lud Roberts. He's an independent, which means the factory doesn't pay his bills, but look at his list of wins: he's a good driver."

"Nona, what do I want with a $26,000 car that might only last one afternoon?" He seemed genuinely puzzled.

"I don't know," she said, shifting her body abruptly away from his. "Perhaps you'll think of something."

Thirty stock-car engines started up on signal with a sound that began on dark country roads where men competed with the rumble of their hearts, histories, internal organs. The pace car glided onto the track. What am I so angry for? wondered Nona. And heading up the orderly field of cars, it led them twice around the track to gather speed. At the fourth turn, it peeled off, the green flag went down, and, as the crowd rose screaming to its feet in joy at this chorus of internal combustion, all thirty cars accelerated down the front stretch into the first turn.

Nona took two Percodan with a swallow of beer.

"You haven't changed a bit," Richard said.

Nona said, "As a matter of fact, I rather have."

She changed the subject then, attempting to squelch the glimmer of comprehension she imagined she saw in his widened eyes. Her hands were trembling. It was still Saturday.

"How's your wife?" she asked. Richard noted the conciliatory tone.

"My wife," he said, "has developed an interest in Oriental rugs. She buys them and sells them. We get along."

"Is she still happy with the house?"

"She considers you a very good designer," answered Richard. "And despite what you thought, she never really suspected anything."

"And you never told her?"

"I would have if you'd asked."

Jill felt a little sick. It's not like horse racing, she thought. At least you can hear each other speak at a damn horse race. The cars spread out around the oval, the slower ones dropping down to the low side of the banked track, while the faster ones attempted to "root each other out of the groove," as the expression goes. Mason explained the Doppler effect to Jill. "Like when a car speeds past you with its horn blowing," he said. The crowd roared a prolonged roar then, fringed here and there with applause, although nothing noteworthy seemed to have transpired on the track. "What happened?" Jill asked, but Nona didn't know, so Jill asked the man in front of her. He was wearing a straw hat with miniature beer cans on it and a sign that read: "Girls Wanted: No Experience Necessary." He removed the transistor radio from his ear and she repeated the question.

"Oh," he said. "Guy on the radio says before they go talkin' 'bout gas rationin' and takin' the gas straight out of our cars, we oughta find out why they fixin' to pass up all that land at the South Pole. Ain't nothin' *but* wells an' mines an' shit down there . . . Hey, you need a beer, baby?"

"No thank you."

"What'd he say happened?" asked Nona.

On the 110th lap, the lead car, a Thunderbird, broke an axle in the number-one turn, sailed across the track, and flipped end over end into traffic. The driver's arm could be seen flapping at the window in a peculiar way. "They control both the brake and gas pedals with the heel and toe of the same foot," Nona explained to Richard, and he wondered if she herself knew why she had called him. "By the end of the race, their heels are blistered from the heat of the gas pedal," she said.

It was she who had ended their affair two years previously, it was she who had been the more fearful of its deepening seriousness, and now, from the perspective of the one approached, Richard saw how much she might require of him.

"I see no reason why we can't at least talk to this Roberts guy," he said. "Find out how much he needs, what kind of angles he's got."

Nona, caught off guard, stared at him. She cast wildly about in her mind and in the chronicle of fragile, man-made objects with their hazards and imperfections and she said, "Are you sure you—"

"No promises," he answered. "But I am willing to look into it."

The drivers' heels were blistering in the furious

machinery, although some were not. Nona in her confusion leaned abruptly forward and with that gesture
found herself propelled into the larger movement of
gathering her bag, her sweater, her binoculars, and
standing up.

"Well then, if we're going to find him, we ought to
get down to the front now so we can beat the crowd."

That's what's different, thought Richard. She's quit
smoking.

"Meet you at the car in an hour," Nona said to
Jill.

"Is everything okay?" Jill whispered.

Nona smiled and shrugged. "I don't know." Mason
waved to her as she started down the steps after Richard.

A Pontiac slammed the inside front panel of a Ford
with its rear end as it passed, while white smoke spewing from under the hood of a Plymouth blew back
against the windshield of a Buick. A Dodge that
couldn't get past a Chevy kept banging into its rear end,
trying to bend its fender down to cut the tires, and a
Chrysler tried to force an Olds off the track "into the
country."

But why was it *singing* ice in that dream? Nona wondered as they descended. I'll have to ask Jeffrey.

"Ten dollars says the Chevy's got it," yelled Richard,
over his shoulder.

"You're on," she shouted. "It's the Dodge for certain."

In the front row, the crowd was pressed against the
fence, shouting. Nona climbed on a seat so she could
see over their heads. Richard, in front of her, said
something, and when she leaned down to hear him, she
saw a *Times* on the seat next to her, folded open to a
half-page story headed with a photograph of Melissa
sitting at a desk handing a fish to the dolphin in the
water at her feet. Putting one hand on Richard's shoulder and the other to her mouth, Nona began to cough.

* * *

Jeffrey woke up. Melissa was in the bathroom, brushing her teeth.

When she came out, he said, "I've just had the strangest dream. While you were in the bathroom. There was an Indian sitting in the middle of my parents' back yard in Dallas, and my mother told me he would kill us if I disturbed him. When I went out to talk to him, he explained to me in very flowery English that just as I needed a chair to sit in, he needed this bit of territory to himself. Then he handed me a pipe, saying, 'It's tobacco,' and I took it inside. In the dream, none of us had ever heard of tobacco before."

He rarely spoke to her of his dreams, and as she sat naked beside him on the bed, as she tried once more to shut out the events of the night before, something like distress passed over her.

"Lover, you're a solitary one."

"Not so very," he answered. "Not more than you."

She looked at the short white string hanging between her thighs. Then up at him. "And exactly how solitary *is* that?"

Sometimes, as now, he had the sensation when he kissed her that her body had grown suddenly borderless in the transition from sight to touch, and that she herself had willed this transformation. When he was much younger, this moment was what he had most sought in women. His hand strayed across her breast, hip, thigh —a single movement. Encountering the string, he drew the tampon from her and let it drop to the floor. She stretched out beside him on the bed's edge, fragrant and continuous. He spoke her name.

As she felt his cock grow in her hand, gently forcing apart her fingers, she thought: Someday we will be dead but not now. She opened her legs to him.

He opened his eyes. Or: they had not been closed.

They made love patiently, moving slowly across the bed with the momentum of their own exchange. He

grew conscious of thrusting slightly from the side so as
to exaggerate the sound of himself in her cunt, of her
enclosure and release of him. Toward the end, when
they were in danger of slipping off the foot of the bed,
Melissa rolled them back from the edge and, finding
herself on top, rose fully up on him. Looking down, she
saw their bellies smeared to their navels with her blood,
and as her eyes met his, the long syllable caught in her
throat loosed itself and she, anticipating him, began to
come.

TIME MEASURED BY THE CLAPPING
OF HANDS

Rounding the nunatak (NUNATAK *n. 1. mountain peak
visible above the ice cap*), the traveler comes upon a
large rookery of Adélie penguins. It is a spectacular
sight. The stalwart Adélie, though only 19 inches high
and weighing some 12 pounds, returns year after year
to the same nesting ground, and during this season
there are perhaps 200,000 in residence. Waddling energetically to and fro, their flippers stretched out wide for
balance, these penguins painstakingly go about collect-
ing the pebbles and small stones that serve as their
nesting material. While they will venture 100 yards or
more from the rookery in order to pick over a promising patch of warm blue ice, they are just as likely, given
the opportunity, to steal suitable stones from the nests
of neighbors, who frequently remain utterly oblivious to
this thievery. All the while there is a tremendous din as
the penguins bicker and squawk and cry.

Throughout this period, the birds avoid the water,
and as a result are soon quite filthy in appearance. In
addition, the whole area surrounding the rookery is
stained a vivid green by their guano. Strangely exempt
from their attentions, however, is the large temple of
pink granite which, long abandoned, marks the south-
ern boundary of the rookery. It is here that Shackleton
first observed the "ghostly handclapping" phenomenon.

On three successive "nights" in 1908, as the polar sun wheeled low about the horizon, he reported that a sound of rhythmic handclapping, involving what sounded like as many as a hundred participants, emanated from the temple, though no life whatever was to be seen within. The rhythms, which he attempted to set down on paper, were highly complex and caused the rookery to fall silent for the space of some minutes.

They lay silently together, his hand between her legs, a finger between the lips of her cunt. The warm liquid surrounding his finger was simply one way of locating the larger sensation that surrounded them both. She spoke to him.

"Jeffrey, what happened last night?"

Light streamed in at the edges of the bamboo window shade. "What are you asking?" said Jeffrey.

"If it was my fault."

"It wasn't."

"I can't accept that."

"No, what you can't accept is that you weren't really involved at all. The dolphin committed suicide."

The words had come unbidden, he had not even known that he believed what they seemed to say of their own accord, and both he and Melissa were momentarily silenced by them. His clothes, stiff with dolphin's blood, lay rolled up in a ball on the kitchen floor. The telephone receiver dangled soundlessly by its cord.

"And if it did?" she said. "If it did, whose fault then?"

Large jets crisscrossed the sky, their passengers subdued by seat belts and color films of handsome actors and actresses in stress situations. "I'll have the health-food platter and a glass of white wine," Nicole told the stewardess.

"I should never have cranked the case so high," Melissa said to Jeffrey. He stroked her hair, waiting for her to explain, but she said no more.

In the shower, where there was really not enough room for the two of them, they bumped into each other a lot and talked about their neighbor, the high-density-foam salesman. He was a friendly fellow who had recently taken to running his radio, television, and record player simultaneously at top volume. Jeffrey noticed Melissa's toes. "Why do you wiggle them like that?" he asked.

"I don't know," she answered, and they began to laugh.

Melissa turned on the kitchen radio, then turned it off. Jeffrey cracked eggs into a Pyrex bowl. "Did Nona say why she wanted me to call her?"

"If she knew, she didn't tell me." Searching the refrigerator for butter, Melissa couldn't quite keep from adding: "But I think she's rather taken with you."

"Don't be trivial, Lissy. I'm not Mason."

"Sorry." She kissed him as she delivered the butter. "But don't underestimate her. She's not Clarice."

Jeffrey overlooked this uncharitable reference to Clarice, about whom Melissa knew nothing for certain. The door to the apartment opened and closed. Melissa returned with the newspaper.

"And what about my brother?" he asked. "Was he calling from Houston?"

She leafed through the newspaper to see if life was an event much like it. "Yes," she said, "but he's planning to——" And confronted suddenly amid the print's rank-and-file by herself and Peter in halftone, she uttered a small cry and sank into a chair.

WOMAN AND DOLPHIN SET UP
HOUSEKEEPING IN ATTEMPT TO BRIDGE
LANGUAGE GAP; PROJECT TERMED
''GROUNDBREAKING'' BY SCIENTIST,
FURTHER RESEARCH EXPECTED

Jeffrey, one hand caressing the curve of her neck, is reading over Melissa's shoulder. Melissa, as she reads, is swearing under her breath at Ehrler. It is clear to both of them that Ehrler has sent the photograph, taken during a preliminary test of the flooded house, from Europe, and that the article, largely an interview with him, is both premature and self-serving. As he reads, Jeffrey understands that he is at that instant crossing some point of no return in his involvement with— Melissa? himself? the information structure?

Q.: Do you believe that, at some point in the future, full two-way communication between man and dolphin will be possible?

A.: I'm convinced that it is possible now. The real question is twofold: whether, on the one hand, we as human beings choose to pursue that goal, and, on the other, whether the dolphins choose to be receptive.

Q.: Are you hopeful?

A.: [*silence*] Perhaps if you rephrased the question . . .

Q.: When I was quite young, I don't know, maybe three or so, I would play in the living room while my mother wrote long letters to her father, who lived in another part of the country. She always typed these letters, and watching her, I noticed that her thumb would hit the bar at the bottom of the keyboard more often than her fingers hit any other single key. So I asked what letter it was, and she said, "It's a space," and I said, "A space letter?" and she, thinking this was baby talk, said, "Yes." "Can I see?" I asked, but when she put me up on her lap and struck the bar, I of course saw nothing because I was looking for a letter—a sign from outer space. She asked me if I saw, and embarrassed that I hadn't, I said yes, and went back to my toys, thinking how complicated outer space must be.

A.: Are you hopeful?

Q.: Someday we will be dead but not now.

A.: Did he tell you he had been speaking to the *Times* when you talked to him on the phone yesterday?

* * *

"Of course not," Melissa said, throwing the paper down. "He knew perfectly fucking well what I thought about publicity at this stage."

They ate toast and scrambled eggs with mushrooms. Melissa poured more coffee. "Now we'll have everyone on our hands from the ASPCA to Walt Disney."

Jeffrey helped himself to one of her cigarettes. When he had lit it, he said, "Maybe so. But you'd better put the phone back on the hook anyway."

She stared at him over the edge of the coffee mug, holding it steady against her lips. He rarely smoked now; for the first time she recognized the cigarette in his hand as an alert. Hanging up the phone, she thought: We're in this for the duration.

They dressed. Friends began to phone with their congratulations and questions, and Diego brought roses —six yellow and one red. "Nicole," he said, explaining the red one. He and Melissa laughed. Jeffrey agreed to lend him the car to pick her up later that afternoon.

When Ehrler called, Melissa was quite prepared. She brought the phone into the kitchen, where Jeffrey was correcting papers. The radio was on; she didn't turn it off.

Ehrler said, "We got the money, Melissa."

"Oh? From whom?"

He caught her tone. "Listen, I'm sorry about the article, Melissa. I didn't forget our agreement. But I think it's made the difference between being able to go ahead and not. I've just heard."

"How much?"

"Fifty thousand."

Melissa sat down. What was good about Ehrler was first he was eclectic as a scientist and second he was charming and intrepid as a capturer of funds. "Oh," she said.

"And I was hoping we could get together to talk things over." He hesitated. "How's your mother, Melissa?"

"Improving. Better than she thinks."

"I'm glad. And you?"

"I'm all right, John."

"Well then, what would you say to meeting here at the hotel around three?"

"Actually," she said, catching Jeffrey's eye, "I think it would be better if you came here."

When she hung up, Melissa went over to Jeffrey and, straddling him, sat down on his lap. She rested her head against his shoulder a long time.

Dolphins are students of the sonic, the tidal, and the gravitational. Through ear and skin, the dolphin receives forty million bits of such information per second and organizes them spontaneously into a changing musical replica of the world. Some of this music is useful; some is not.

Since the man had fed him in the early morning, Peter had not been aware of anyone in the house, but now, as he swam up from the bottom of the deep pool, his sonar picked out a seaweed-shaped head leaning over the railing above. Peter pushed his own head through the surface and peered up.

"Eh-eh, nuh! Why you don' seh somethin?"

There was hair on the man's face and smoke came out of his mouth. Peter rose up on his flukes to get a better look.

"Ai, ai, ai! Easy dong, mon." Laughing, the man held out something that smoked. "Y'would like to use a taste?"

Peter let himself back down into the water and swam to the bottom and back in rapid ampersands. In the tickle of his skin he dreamed Melissa riding a fish. There was blood on her belly and in the hair. When Peter burst through the surface, the man, singing, had moved out of sight.

A gecko skittered across the floor. Knolly could still smell the Thoroseal he and the other two boys had laid down the day before, but now it did not give him a headache. The long walk back from town, the dolphin, the package he was carrying wrapped in old sugar sacks —he felt excited. He flicked the last of the spliff, still smoking, through an open window. "Etty in the room a cry," he sang.

But in the electronics room he felt suddenly depressed. There were many more switches, lights, jacks, and tape decks than he had remembered. They seemed calmly to overlook him, demean his excitement; other hands were familiar with them. Reaching out defensively, he switched on one of several televisions, and when, instead of a Puerto Rican film, the dolphin appeared on the screen, swimming patiently around the deep pool, Knolly felt a little better. He threw switch after switch until a row of tiny red lights stretched across one wall and the hum filled the room. A millipede walked along the top of the only tape deck equipped with tape. Knolly said, "Hmm," and, picking up the bundle he had brought, untied the sugar sacking.

The sound of human music, of song or instrument, will transfix and exhaust a dolphin by its load of alien information. Knolly strummed a few chords on the battered Fender, using a folded matchbook for pick. Peter arced from the water, squawking in alarm, then dove for the bottom. Knolly laughed. In the two years he had owned the guitar, Knolly had never before heard it amplified. He pulled a second spliff from behind his ear and, lighting it, took up a slow-handed reggae skank, his eyes half on the video monitor, half on himself.

If a rude music finds you, it will tell you stories, or invade your skin, or make you forget things you have always remembered. Peter, floating on his side in hopes of catching another glimpse of the smoke-breathing man, blinked. In the music, humans were staying alive in complicated ways, in dry places, with their uncountable constructions. Peter's cock emerged from the slit beneath his belly for a moment, then withdrew. If she came back, perhaps the tide would again flood the rooms above.

Knolly pressed the red button on the tape recorder, but nothing happened. After checking the window to be sure no one was coming, he pressed the other buttons until the reels began to turn at what seemed the proper speed. He laughed and laughed, but his playing was serious, and as he played he walked slowly across the house, cord trailing behind, to where he had seen a microphone hanging from the ceiling. He hissed up at it, it was dead, he sang anyway:

> *I and I a keep de pressure up,*
> *And I an I, I naw break down;*
> *Let I'es is I'es in I'es is black,*
> *In I'es is red in I'es is dread;*
> *And I an I, I naw break down.*

He felt comforted by the tough sound of the words: their toughness became his own. As he tried to remember others, he walked over to the railing and, still playing, looked down into the dolphin's clear, intelligent eye.

"Hey, d'ya hear what the man seh?" Knolly shouted. He had been lucky to see the white man getting on the sea plane in the harbor that morning; he knew it didn't get back from San Juan until late afternoon. With his foot, Knolly flipped the yellow plastic ball over the railing to the water below. Peter punched it back up with his beak, and for a moment it hung suspended before Knolly's eyes, revolving slowly in sunlit space.

Ehrler pressed the door buzzer. He was wearing a suit of putty-colored linen and carrying a bottle of California champagne.

"Congratulations," said Jeffrey, referring to the money but looking at the suit.

"Thank you." Ehrler had a time-lag smile he used

to protect himself from those with unearned influence over his projects. "Is the lady of the house—"

"In here, John," called Melissa from the living room. She did not get up. Jeffrey followed him in with three wineglasses.

As she leaned forward to be kissed, Melissa noticed his skin: it was unusually dry and, under his eyes, slightly flaked. Her toes wiggled.

"You look wonderful, Melissa." He regarded her fondly, one hand in the pocket of his dolphin-colored suit. "Are you drying out?"

"A bit," she said, her fond gaze contesting with his while she tried to decide how much to tell him. There was a pop as Jeffrey persuaded the cork from the bottle. Handing champagne to the two of them, he said, "Melissa's invited me to sit in on your discussion. I hope you don't mind."

Ehrler turned sharply to Melissa and she nodded. "For my sake," she said. Ehrler began to formulate words of protest then, in his mind. It was not the first time he had formulated words of protest, concerning Jeffrey. But thinking of his own proposal, promising as it was, and Melissa, complicated as she was, he said only, "It's all right with me, but I can't guarantee we'll be all that entertaining."

They lifted their glasses then to interspecific communication and to the rich Californian in Montreux who had provided the fifty thousand. Melissa asked Ehrler if he had heard what had happened at the Aquarium the night before. He had not. She told him.

"And you think it was intentional self-destruction?" Ehrler, on the couch, held his glass before him at eye level, and gazed at the wine's horizon within.

"I'm convinced of it," Melissa answered. She glanced at Jeffrey.

"Did you do an autopsy? Any diseases? infections?"

"Yes, I did; and no, there weren't."

Jeffrey, looking at Ehrler, remembered a part of his

dream that had until that moment eluded him: in the dream, his twin brother Kirk had watched him from the window while he, Jeffrey, talked to the Indian. When Jeffrey returned with the tobacco, Kirk was crippled. He was on crutches. There was a wheelchair.

"I hope you're wrong about it being suicide," said Ehrler, putting the glass down on the table. Melissa watched the champagne slosh back and forth there. "It would complicate the ethics of the thing enormously."

For a moment they silently contemplated the ethical questions raised by the unhappiness of captive animals. Ehrler stood up to examine the painting on the near wall, a six-foot-square gestural diagram of a horse by Susan Rothenberg. "A friend of Jeffrey's," Melissa said absently. "It's by far the nicest thing we—" Jeffrey poured more champagne, and Ehrler, turning around, began to ask her questions.

How extensive was Peter's English "vocabulary"? What was the frequency ratio of humanoid vocalizations to delphinic? Did the night tapes suggest that Peter vocalized to himself when Melissa was not there, and if so, what percentage of these sounds were humanoid? How was his health? How was his appetite? With what other human beings had he had contact during the three weeks? Did he show any particular interest in the telephone? the television? the radio? Was there any suggestion that wild dolphins entering the cove were aware of him, or he of them? Did he appear depressed by the lack of contact with other dolphins? To what extent could Melissa impute to Peter a variable emotional state? Did it resemble the human model? Examples? To what extent did she feel the dolphin to be aware of her own emotional state? Examples? How had their relationship changed during the three weeks, and to what extent did she feel a specific "personal" attachment had developed between them?

Melissa poured herself another pale glass of tanglefoot and sipped it—the pale of the tanglefoot against

the brilliant blue of her chemise. She looked at Ehrler.
Jeffrey thought: A bit smug is what she looks just now.
Melissa said, "Peter and I were lovers."

Ehrler blinked. He looked to Jeffrey. "She'd already
told me," Jeffrey said. Melissa shivered—a palpable
but single shiver—and continued to regard Ehrler.

"How long?" he asked, and she said, "It happened
the day I left," and he said, "Your idea?" and she said,
"Peter's." Ehrler began to chew his lower lip then, for
the news of their intimacy, in combination with Jeffrey's presence, had made him feel momentarily old and
circumvented. He asked for details, she gave them.

"So Peter actually used his ball to put your fears at
rest. About his teeth, I mean."

"Yes," she answered. "He knew that would be an
obstacle."

Jeffrey answered the phone. One of his students was
in tears over her Antarctica report, although the report
was not the true issue. Puberty was the true issue.
"Doon, I'll have to call you back," Jeffrey said, looking
at the crescents he had drawn on the message pad.

"But why the last day, Melissa?"

"I know what you're thinking: that I projected the
whole thing on him because I was leaving. But it happened just as I described it. And I believe Peter knew it
was my last day."

Ehrler's lips were drawn back in a slight rictus—a
smile either forced or suppressed. "How?" he asked.

"I don't know." She regarded his slightly tinted
glasses, his neat gray sideburns. What is there to like,
anyway? she thought. Those awful glasses, that smirk.

Ehrler thought about her cutting her hair on the observation deck of the flooded house. She had thrown a
handful of hair over the railing and then, with the same
hand, waved to him as he pulled out of the driveway,
leaving her and the dolphin in solitude.

"It must have been hard for you out there," he said.

She hesitated. "Yes, it was hard. Evenings." She spoke calmly, almost absently, but in her eyes he saw distress, and he reproached himself with it. He looked at his hands to see what age they were. Then again, perhaps all hands were old, rightly regarded.

"Maybe we were wrong to go ahead with it, under the circumstances."

She said, "That depends on what you think of the results. I mean, I seem to have read somewhere about a 'ground-breaking project.' Well, now that you know just how much ground was broken, I'd like to hear your opinion."

Ehrler settled back in the couch. After a while he said: "I guess I need to know in what way you're emotionally involved with Peter before I answer."

Jeffrey sat down in the chair beside Melissa and put his feet on the table, near the flowers.

"I don't use the word 'lover' lightly," Melissa said.

Ehrler stood up and walked out of the room. Jeffrey and Melissa looked after him silently. Ehrler returned, putting his glasses back on. "I'm sorry about the interview; from now on, we won't release anything we haven't both approved. It will take Martin about a month to install the new computer down there, not counting day trips to San Juan for equipment. How do you feel about going back down after that? Another chronic contact situation, this time with on-line computerized frequency analysis. But it would have to be for at least three months."

The giant jet touched down, its tires sending little puffs of smoke into the congenially polluted air. Jeffrey drained his glass. "I don't know, John," Melissa said. "I need time to think. I would never forgive myself if my mother—"

When Ignacio opened the elevator door for Ehrler, fifteen minutes later, Jeffrey walked back to where Melissa was still sitting. She looked blankly at him. He took the empty glass from her hand. A moment later she smiled and, leaning forward, pulled her chemise off over her head.

SENTIMENTAL EDUCATION

He traveled.

He knew the melancholy of steamboats, the cold awakenings in the tent, the stupefaction of landscapes and ruins, the bitterness of interrupted friendships.

He returned.

He went into society, and he had still other loves.

Later the phone rings. It is Kirk. He is coming to New Jersey for a month of parachute lessons before being flown on camera assignment to Antarctica.

NICOLE turned to face the alarm clock's cantaloupe glow. Then she shook Diego awake. "Hey, *chingón!* Go down and answer the phone; it's your mama." He looked sleepily at Nicole and at the lemon-colored underpants she had insisted on wearing to bed the night before. "Nikki, you make us a great big breakfast. Okay?" Watching him climb naked down the ladder of the sleeping deck, she wondered what new weapons he had acquired in her absence.

The refrigerator contained a six-pack of beer, a brown bag of coffee, and a pot of black-bean stew. Diego's mother, who lived in Brooklyn, called every Sunday after church to pass along whatever new advice she had received from Diego's father, who was dead. Nicole put the stew on the hot plate. I feel sick, she thought. She turned on the radio, which was connected to one of Diego's amplifiers and permanently tuned to a country-music station. The permanent tuning she had accomplished by pulling off the proper knob with a pair of pliers.

"He said they make you work over there just like

here?" Diego repeated into the phone. "So what good is it to die?"

Nicole walked around the loft in search of the coffee-pot. She regarded the various costumes and dresses hanging on the Sheetrock walls. Some of them she had made this year and some a long time ago. But which were which? She found the coffeepot on the floor, next to Diego's collection of UFO books. It would be at least a month before she started to show, she decided, feeling her belly. On the radio a man was singing about truck driving, and on the telephone Diego had switched to Spanish.

Stirring the beans, Nicole thought about certain things that had happened to her as a child in Kansas City but would not happen to a child of hers. For one thing, her mother used to wake her up in the mornings by intercom, and for another thing, her father used to drive her around on Sundays to look at grain elevators. Diego kissed her on the neck.

"What is this?" he said, looking into the pot.

"All we had," she answered sweetly.

Diego put his hands on her breasts. The nipples seemed larger than ever. If we did get married, he thought, at least then she would lose that fucking TWA pass. When he asked her how she felt, she smiled at him and shrugged. I feel like throwing up, she thought.

"There is sugar?" Diego asked as he poured himself coffee. Nicole read the newspaper interview with Ehrler and looked at the photograph of Melissa. "She looks so—"

"That was before she cut her hair," Diego said. "Now it is very short."

"I know. I saw her at the airport."

Diego shook his head. "She is changing. She looks beautiful like that but she is changing. Jefe too. Like I go over there yesterday with flowers because she has her picture in the paper, okay? I have to leave after twenty minutes because I feel like I am talking to soldiers or something. *Guerrilleros*."

"Soldiers? What do you mean by that?"

He swallowed a mouthful of beans and looked at her. "I don't know. Nothing. It was just something I said." Diego's father had owned a nightclub in Havana until the revolution, when he had come to Brooklyn to have a heart attack in a parking lot.

Nicole sewed together a dress she had cut out of carmine cloth. She was thinking of former times, before the arrival on the scene of Jeffrey, Diego, and the dolphin project with all its unhealthy mental excitement, those departed summers when her parents would send her East to stay at Lissy's, the two of them consuming quantities of stolen tanglefoot in the coolth of the evening, speaking girlish trash and smoking cigarettes in the woods. If only they were still—if only Lissy hadn't —Nikki stood up, put on the carmine dress, and sat back down. It might, on the other hand, be less than a month.

"So I want to try to finish this song before the show tonight," Diego was saying. He drove a cab six days a week to support his musical ambitions.

"Where are you playing, again?" she asked. "We ought to invite Lissy and Jeffrey."

Diego, aware suddenly that she had not been listening, gazed at her and at the soft, injured part of the future where ranks of children are gathering to replace us. "It is painful?" he said.

"A little." She did not look at him.

"I was talking to Jefe a couple of days ago, and he told me about how you and him and Melissa got drunk the night after your first abortion. In a hotel."

A smile flickered over her face at the speed of regret. "He told you about that?"

"*Sí*. The whole story. He said you were a little hysterical."

"I was. I'd never had an abortion before, and I'd never seen someone being strangled. Also I was drunk."

The measured calm of her response startled him. It suggested a side of Nicole he didn't know, a side that had assessed her own capabilities and was able to act confidently upon them. The dress she had just made irritated him; clumsily, he became aware of his love for her. "It is different this time?" he asked.

"Very different," she answered.

He breathed his relief. In her tone and in the downward cast of her eyes he believed he discerned a note of capitulation. She admitted their large, handsomely furred cat to her lap, testing the softness of her cheek against the softness of its fur, and Diego, inexplicably, was moved.

"I do not say that we will never have children. Who can know a thing like that? But we must be intelligent. In Cuba, in Barcelona, in Brooklyn, I have seen many men ruin themselves with children they did not think about having. There are those who might say my father was one like that: to support us, he became a slave to his work, and once he left Cuba it killed him." Diego paused, glinting strings of incidents running to and fro in the history of regret, and watched Nicole come round the table to sit beside him. "With women it is different," he said, touching her hair. The cat scampered away across the length of the loft, terrified of open space. I can't tell him now, Nikki thought, and as she watched the moment slip by, her guardedness turned gradually to love, her love to lust. He seemed beautiful to her, foolishly brave. They kissed, and she swung one leg over the bench, straddling it to move closer to him. When he broke the kiss she was wet, breathless.

"Nikki," he whispered. "It is all right for us to make love?"

She shook her head, and as she leaned over the carmine folds of her dress to take him into her mouth, she imagined she felt a movement inside her: distant, tiny, precise. She closed her eyes.

In the rear-view mirror, Melissa surveyed the city—its dim cantilevers full of citizens, subjective reactions, synergy. She turned on the radio. At first she hadn't liked the new trend in popular music—away from melody and lyric, toward complex rhythmical figures—but now, when they played "Incorrect Thought" or "Amazonian Ghetto" she just . . . she felt sort of . . . A red light flickered on the dashboard to warn her she was running on empty.

In the women's room of the fuel station, Melissa ringed her eyes carefully with kohl which Nikki had once brought from Teheran. She tried to gauge the effect it might have on the various men she knew. It makes me look like a damn raccoon, she decided, and tried to wash it off. Outside, she phoned Jeffrey.

"You could take the train," she said. "I'd wait for you at the station and then we could drive out to the house together."

"You know I can't, Lissy. I've got to wait for Kirk."

After a moment she said: "I'm frightened, Jeffrey."

He said: "I know."

When she pulled up beneath the sheltering oak, she was relieved to see no other cars parked there but the hatchback. Nona's trio of dogs came running around the corner of the house, barking and carrying on as per the domestication agreement of some eight millennia's standing.

"Hello?" called Melissa, as she let herself in the front door.

There were lilacs here and there about the house, purple and white, in vases and bottles. There was the tick of the mantel clock, which Melissa would cease to hear by the time she left. There was the broken-backed copy of *Incidents of Travel in Yucatan*, propped open on a chair and untouched in two years.

"Hello?" she repeated.

The dogs circulated happily through the rooms of the house, wagging their tails and retrieving dull bones. Melissa followed them to the sun porch in back and stopped before the plate-glass window. In the far garden, Nona bent over green shoots, her face and shoulders shadowed by an enormous coolie hat. And you can never return home without thinking of what you will not do there, or have not done there previously, or have failed elsewhere to undo. Melissa picked up the plastic drug container and read the label. Then she opened the door and followed the dogs into the hot sun.

"You didn't bring Jeffrey," said Nona. To kiss her daughter, she had to push the coolie hat to the back of her head and hold it there with one hand.

"No, his brother is coming up from Texas, and Jeffrey felt he should be there. But he sends his love. He said he'd call." Melissa took a step backward, narrowly avoiding one of the tomato seedlings Nona had been transplanting. She stumbled, Nona reached out to her, hat falling to the turned soil, and they collided suddenly in brief, anguished embrace.

More seedlings were placed in the ground. Nona installed cutworm collars, Melissa mulched. "It gave me quite a turn to see you and your singing fish in the paper yesterday," Nona said, wielding her trowel perhaps a shade too busily.

"Me too. I wasn't consulted."

"All that about complete two-way communication . . . I guess I didn't really know how ambitious a project it was."

Melissa brushed a ladybug out of her hair, and it flew away home. "Yes," she said, "if it were any more ambitious it would border on the criminal. Probably it already does. But why did it upset you?"

"I don't know," answered Nona. "It can take a long time to begin to see, but then you just see and see and go on seeing. It's a vice, really. Or one of the symptoms of age."

Melissa wiped the sweat from her brow. The fat yellow Lab, a bone clamped in his jaws like a cigar, was sitting on the stone wall by the compost heap, watching over it with evident pleasure. "I think maybe I won't ask what it was you did see," Melissa said.

Nona hesitated. "Nothing very exciting, I'm afraid. Just that I'm old." And though in a way she had answered Melissa's question, in a way she had not.

She went back to the house and returned with another flat of tomato seedlings. Am I imagining it, or does she look a little better? wondered Melissa. They discussed the dolphin's teeth. Melissa rolled up her jeans to show Nona the scratches and bruises her young legs had received in the service of science.

"And you weren't terrified?"

"Not really. A little." She restored her clothes, slightly embarrassed. "I guess I mean the whole thing is so important to me that fear sort of gets lost in the shuffle."

Nona nodded, thinking about the shuffle. She said: "Tell me what that feels like."

Three small aircraft wrote the name of a suntan lotion on the sky. Melissa squatted down and hugged her knees. "Maybe a little like the way you want to feel about Richard."

By planting tomatoes near asparagus, the gardener may, without dangerous chemicals, ward off the asparagus beetle. "Since I don't really know what I do feel about Richard," said Nona, "or what I want to either, you're not being very helpful."

"I'm sorry." Melissa took a double handful of mulch from the red wheelbarrow parked nearby. "How was it, though? Seeing him."

Nona dug a shallow hole. "He wasn't really sure he was interested in a $26,000 car that might only last one afternoon."

"What? So you—"

"No, I didn't tell him. I took him to the stock-car

races. And in a moment of weakness, I convinced him to back a car for the big race coming up next Saturday. The Fossil Fuel 250."

"Your weakness or his?"

"Both. I've got a quarter share and he's got the rest. So we'll see each other about that, and then, who knows?" She lowered a seedling into the hole, that it might flourish there and ward off asparagus beetles. And she tried to think of a way to explain herself to this smooth-skinned daughter kneeling beside her in the dirt with her space-age felicities and dangerous habits. But the silence grew. Explaining anything was more than she could manage. And so they planted, like giddy homesteaders.

A LOW HORIZON

Nona coughs: an invasive sound. Melissa has already realized she will hear that sound the rest of her life. In reaction she imagines herself a child. She is trying to sleep. Her head is between two pillows. She hears the sound.

Walking behind Nona to move the wheelbarrow down to where they are planting, Melissa notices that Nona is not sweating although she herself is drenched. Why is that? she wonders. She reaches out as if to touch her mother's back and at that moment feels a pang of longing so intense she fears her knees will buckle. It is the first time she has missed the dolphin as a lover misses a lover. She points her index finger at the sky and fires. Everything turns blue.

The best way to prepare for the future is to keep an eye on the sky. That's where everything else is not. Meanwhile, information pours invisibly across its friendly expanse, and it is up to us to absorb as much of it as our systems can tolerate.

Look! Across the shallow waters from here to the horizon: the dolphins have thrust their curious gray heads into the air! They weave from side to side, peering patiently upward—first from one eye, then from the other. Spacemen are expected.

Nona and Melissa returned the tools to the shed, talking of Nicole. "She's sweet but that TWA pass has ruined her," said Nona. "She's utterly unlike anybody else," said Melissa. In the distance, the dogs barked furiously at a raccoon they had treed.

Nona put a twist of lemon in each drink while Melissa, in the bathroom, rummaged through her bag irritably. Did forgetting to bring Tampax while visiting her mother correspond to forgetting birth control while entertaining a lover? My mother is fifty-nine, thought Melissa. She stared at the bathroom cabinet for several seconds before opening it. On the top shelf: a box of tampons—half full, filmed with dust.

"And if nothing else," said Nona to Melissa as they sat drinking their drinks on the sun porch, "it's a wonderful way of finding out who your friends are. Imagine her suggesting a trip might 'take my mind off it.' I don't want my mind taken off it. Children have their minds taken off things."

I am twenty-nine years old, thought Melissa. She put lemon twists in their new drinks and brought them back out to the porch. "I've never told anyone this," she said, "but I might not be able to have children."

They exchanged a shy look. Nona felt a faint whinge within, as of something not quite remembered or forgotten, a lapse of some sort. "Darling. You never—I didn't know you wanted children."

"I don't think I do," answered Melissa. "But still, one likes to think it's a choice."

"Of course," said Nona. She remembered lying beside her husband after love, her legs folded in the air above her because she had been told it made things easier for the teeming sperm. "Is it something that could be—"

" 'Corrected?' Yes . . . maybe . . . they don't know.

But it could certainly have been prevented." Melissa drank her drink in half. "I was so stupid. I had an infection—this was before Jeffrey—and I refused to go to the doctor. Absolutely refused. I was fighting with my lover and I think I got a little mixed up about who I was punishing." Irony gathered in the corners of her mouth. "I had Nikki prescribe homeopathetic herbal teas. Or whatever they are." Staring into her glass, Melissa felt suddenly quite drunk.

"And there was scarring? Is that what—"

"Yes. The doctor said there was a chance I was sterile, but there was an operation I could have . . ." Melissa traced triangles in the frost on her glass. "Of course I could actually be as fertile as the Nile for all I know: I'm very careful about birth control."

Nona thought: Don't blame everything on your father, even though he deserves the worst you can give him.

Nona said: "Things have changed so much."

"When you were my age," said Melissa, smiling, "you had me."

In the kitchen, after lunch, Nona noticed the rings around Melissa's eyes, and Melissa, giggling, explained what kohl was and how she had tried to wash it off. After some consultation, they went into the bathroom together and put kohl carefully around each other's eyes, talking and talking.

Kirk stepped into the elevator with his canvas duffel bag, his white cowboy hat, and his Gila-monster-skin boots.

"How did you get down here so fast?" said Ignacio. "I just take you up, no?"

"No, I believe that'd be my brother Jeff." He smiled and held out his hand. "I'm Kirk."

Jeffrey and Kirk slapped each other hello on the back. The sight of twins greeting each other can be disturbing if you have been brought up in a culture that values the unique object. But Jeffrey and Kirk themselves were delighted at the reunion: they had not seen each other in over a year.

"Damn, Kirk, when are you going to stop playing cowboy?" Jeffrey put his brother's bag on the fold-out bed in Melissa's study and turned to look at him.

"Don't guess there's any real danger of that," said Kirk.

They drank black coffee in the kitchen and explained themselves to each other. Kirk, a freelance photojournalist, was on double assignment. "First I learn skydiving from this outfit in New Jersey—that's a portfolio of photographs and a thousand words of text—then I hop an army plane to Antarctica and *buzz* right into the big time: I stay as long as I want, *Newsweek* foots the bill and pays me royally for first crack at whatever I shoot."

"Including the representatives of Third or Fourth World peoples trying to get their share of the world's natural resources?" Jeffrey lapsed into wryness more often when Kirk was around. Wryness was a kind of invisible cowboy gear.

"Whatever," said Kirk, putting his feet up on a chair and grinning.

Antarctica was capturing the popular imagination. Private adventurers were adventuring there. It was becoming an international hot spot.

"But you'd never know it from what you see on TV," said Kirk. "My guess is the networks are in it up to their armpits, like everybody else."

"It would make sense," Jeffrey agreed, pouring more coffee.

"Sure. The last set of relatively quiet airwaves on earth: it's got to be worth a fortune. But what about you? You still glad you got out of the building racket?"

Jeffrey explained himself then, aware that his defection from the drafting table helped release Kirk from the familial role of bum, a reprieve in which Jeffrey was delighted to be of assistance. He left out only those parts which had to do with Melissa. Kirk and Melissa did not get along. They misunderstood each other. They disliked each other. They were on different wavelengths.

"You know, I never did understand the schoolteacher part, though," said Kirk. "I wouldn't have picked you for it, I mean."

"I like to see what the children are up to. You might say I think of them as a kind of early warning system for what's next in the world. Here we are getting older, and there they are getting different."

"Different as hell. You're not wrong there." Kirk regarded the dead Gila-monster skin on his feet with an air of melancholy and wonderment. "But let me be the first to tell you what's coming next in the world. Antarctica's coming next in the world. Next and maybe last."

Jeffrey and Kirk went to the expedition-equipment store. Jeffrey looked at the foil packets containing freeze-dried moo-shu pork while Kirk tried on the complete survival system, which was on sale.

"And you say these here are another fifty bucks?" said Kirk, putting on huge, gauntleted fur-back mittens or "bear-paws." The smiling salespersons gathered. He was still wearing his cowboy hat, though otherwise attired for Antarctic contingencies.

"A man got to have his equipment," Jeffrey said. Kirk paid in cash from an envelope he'd been carrying inside his shirt. Then they strolled about the midtown area, surveying its architectural marvels. Architectural marvels are deserted on Sunday, mostly, because the economy which they monumentalize has traditionally kept a low profile on that day.

"Mies van der Rohe," said Jeffrey as they passed the Seagram Building, which in the early days of modernism many people likened to an upended cigarette carton of golden glass. "He ordered those bronze verticals—

thirty-eight stories tall—bathed regularly in a special oil so the folk could more fully appreciate the rich beauty of the metal. Notice what that assumes about the continuity of values. Notice what that assumes about the folk."

Kirk's eyes cut to the side for just a moment. One thing about Jeff was that he was ambitious and another thing about Jeff was that he had both ears to the ground. "Arrogant motherfucker, huh?"

"Not that there aren't other things going on now. You've got the vernacularists, the post-modernists, the supermannerists. This ism and that ism. But it's all nostalgia: memories of architecture past. What we want are buildings like the people were becoming. We need an architecture that—"

They gazed up at the curtain wall of sleek bronze glass which capitalism had placed there.

"Guess sometimes you miss it a little, don't you, Jeff?"

"Nothing I can't handle."

In the bookstore, Jeffrey browsed through the art and architecture section while his brother asked for the diaries of Admiral Byrd. He opened Friendlander's *Landscape, Portrait, Still-Life* and read a passage at random: "A low horizon is always and everywhere a sign of an advanced contemplation of nature." He yawned. *Melissa notices that Nona is not sweating although she herself is drenched. Why is that?*

"Did they have it?" asked Jeffrey, when Kirk reappeared. They did. Jeffrey wondered suddenly how Melissa was doing.

They made their way further downtown, toward an undiscovered lunch spot Jeffrey knew. As a child, Kirk had been a sleepwalker of extraordinary skill and address, climbing stairs, turning corners, and opening doors without a slip; he still occasionally spoke in his sleep. Jeffrey did neither.

"The folks send their love and advice," said Kirk.

"Now don't tell me Dad expects *you*, the all-time, flat-out black sheep of the family, to talk me back into architecting?"

Kirk grinned in various directions. Their father, a CPA, was a fine fellow with displaced hopes.

At the restaurant, amazingly attractive waitresses rushed by in their wrapped skirts, the intermittence of thigh giving the room a slightly erotic cast. It was no longer undiscovered, as a lunch spot.

"You know it did hit Dad pretty hard when you quit. Not Ma so much, but him."

"I know."

"Not that he said much about it, of course. But you could see that all he felt like doin' was goin' on out to the patio and barbecuin' himself up a flank steak or whatever was around to barbecue. You know how he gets."

"Morose."

"Well, thoughtful. Course, I expect he'll be okay."

"Sure he will. You're just worried that since Dad asked you to explain me to him, you lose your black-sheep options."

Kirk grinned. "Well? Do I?"

"I doubt it. You're a natural."

The bluefish salad was satisfactory and the *moules marinières* were satisfactory, too. Kirk glanced at the strange new art hung here and there on the walls of the restaurant, while Jeffrey recalled something interesting he had read in *Xerox* magazine—that seventy-two billion new pieces of information were created yearly. What was good about Kirk was that he was smart in what he didn't now. Artists and dancers at the adjacent table discussed other people's movie material. Kirk ordered strawberries.

'Jeff, do you by any chance know a very blond woman, pretty, with a wide mouth?"

"Whatever are you talking about?"

"Thought so, by the way she jumped when she saw

me. She and a tall fella with spectacles just walked in. They were headed back here but then she made him take a table way up front."

Jeffrey resisted the temptation to turn around, although it was not every day he had a chance to see Clarice with her husband, the landscape architect. Kirk twisted lemon peel over his coffee and Jeffrey did too. If you are having an affair with a married person, a certain interest, inverse to the passion itself, accrues to the cuckolded spouse. "Melissa and I are doing very well," said Jeffrey, in answer to Kirk's question. Then he told him about Nona.

"You close to her?" asked Kirk.

"In a funny way. Yes."

The blond woman had situated herself so she could see their table but her companion could not. Repinning her hair, she glanced at Kirk. "Now, Jeff, you tell me if you'd rather I find someplace else to stay. I mean, seein' as you got trouble an' all, I—"

"No, no. I'm proud to have you. I just wanted you to know what's going on."

Kirk watched Jeffrey fiddle with his silverware as the waitress added up the check. There were ceiling fans on the ceiling.

Why can't he leave me alone sometimes? thought Clarice as she pretended to listen to her husband.

DISINFORMATION

Jeffrey and Kirk leave the restaurant. Kirk is thinking that perhaps Jeffrey's real reason for quitting architecture was to obtain more time for hugging other people's wives. Jeffrey is thinking about Clarice's two children. He and Kirk cross the sun-shot street, and Clarice's husband gets up to go to the bathroom.

I have to admit it's sort of frightening, thinks Clarice as she watches them through the window. Exact duplicates!

They are standing in front of a glass-faced building,

consulting one another as to their plans. There is dazzle on the glass behind them, and their double image is doubled again by its reflection. Then the glass door swings open, catching both the light and the reflection: six gesticulating clones.

When you love someone, thinks Clarice, turning the ring on her finger around and around, what is it that you love? Upon returning from the bathroom, her husband tells her an amusing anecdote that isn't true.

Ehrler stood in the doorway of his hotel bathroom, studying the spotless tile, the brilliant white light. Then he flew to the Virgin Islands, to the flooded house. On the doorstep was a letter from the local government saying that he, Ehrler, had not hired an adequate number of local people and would be subject to a special tax if he did not do so by the end of the month. Cactus, thornbush, and catch-and-keep pressed close against the pink concrete walls. Martin pressed a glass of iced tea in Ehrler's hand. Martin was a very hotshot biotechnician, but he didn't have Melissa's imagination.

"Peter went into sulking behavior when I drained the house, but he snapped right back this morning when I reflooded," said Martin. Ehrler put the tea down without tasting it. He changed into his bathing suit. He sat down on the edge of the catwalk and dangled his feet in the warm water. When he called Peter's name, the elevator started up from the deep pool downstairs.

Dolphins are lovers of attention and exchange, and no dolphin ever willingly isolates himself. There are personal likes and dislikes, but as these are the effect of electromagnetic patterns cast on the dolphin's skin by the nervous system of the other party, they are considered immutable and of no consequence in simple social behavior. Once in the water, Peter swam immediately to Ehrler and began a thorough study of his feet and ankles, bumping them gently with his beak. Ehrler spoke words of greeting. A horsefly bit Ehrler on the shoulder, raising a welt. I've let this whole project become too dependent on her, he thought, lowering himself into the bit of ocean that had been gathered there, in the house. Peter broke into a high-pitched humanoid wailing and dashed off to find his brush.

On the observation deck, Ehrler sat down in the water and stroked the skin between the dolphin's flippers, speaking loudly and frequently about whatever came to mind. Peter rocked back and forth on Ehrler's legs. In the rub of his skin he dreamed the woman had acquired protective coloring around her eyes, like a fish. Ehrler gently touched the dolphin's blowhole to get his attention. "Say your name for me now. Say 'Peter.' "

Peter broke away and, rising up on his flukes, turned a clear eye upon Ehrler. Then he swam full tilt toward the seaward wall of the deck, turning aside at the last possible moment so that three-quarters of a ton of water was sent gushing back over the railing to its source. A sea gull plucked a lizard fish from the torrent and flew off with it.

"C'mon, Peter. You can do better than that." Ehrler stood up. The dolphin swam figure eights around him, drawing the length of his body roughly across Ehrler's shin with each pass. There was dazzle on the shifting water, and the air pressed very close. When had that bird stopped singing—just now or a while ago? Ehrler went into the house and came back out again. He tossed the rubber rabbit, the floating ring, and the striped dishrag to the other end of the flooded deck, saying, "Bring me the ring, Peter." Peter returned with the ring on his beak and a look in his eye. But maybe I'm imagining the look, thought Ehrler.

Then he held up fingers and Peter counted them and he held up shapes and Peter named them. He held up some colors and a few more fingers. Peter brought the dishrag back on his flipper. Ehrler was sweating and shouting at Peter. "*I said to say your name,*" he shouted. "*Do what I say,*" he shouted. The dolphin began swimming slowly around the deck, as if Ehrler were not there, and Martin, who had leaned out the window to see what was wrong, went back to work on the computer.

God, I'm becoming ridiculous, thought Ehrler. Rubbing his eyes, he remembered the test question he had given Melissa before hiring her in San Diego: "Obtain a dead organism, and from what you can *see* in it derive arguments to show that it is an information-processing entity." The moon, white and gibbous, hung high over the ridge, while the dolphin swam patiently through the shallow water. Ehrler felt the need to get away.

In the electronics room, he showed Martin the government letter. "I think what we ought to do," Ehrler said, "is take on a groundskeeper." Martin agreed and said he would hire back one of the boys from Charlotte Amalie. Then he made a schematic drawing of the new on-line computer system he had designed for Ehrler. The objective was to turn the computer into a self-correcting translator through which dolphin and human might eventually speak. "To the extent that it could reprogram itself continuously, it could almost be considered alive," said Martin, in a rare flight of fancy. "Solid-state life, if you will." Martin's teeth were smiling. Ehrler picked up something that had caught his attention under one of the tape decks. Then he went for a walk.

It must be Melissa's, he thought, as he examined the brown cone-shaped cigarette. A mongoose darted across the path, and a cloud of mompies orbited Ehrler's head without biting. Of course, it was always possible there was a side to Martin he didn't know. Ehrler arrived at the end of the path, where the ruins of a Dutch plantation house, two hundred years old, were subsiding beneath bird droppings and jungle. He sat down. He thought about his children, who lived with his ex-wife in San Diego: What were they doing at this exact moment? When would be the best time to talk to them on the telephone? The spliff appeared to have been rolled from a brown paper bag, and after a moment's hesitation Ehrler lit it.

Ground orchid and wedelia grew where the house had been; the broken slab on which he sat had been its threshold. He had come here three years ago with his wife, just after purchasing the land for the flooded laboratory, just before the end of their marriage. He had used a cutlash to hack their way in, and she had spread a plaid blanket amid the orchids. A tiny green fly buzzing around their heads had made her hair even redder, the jungle even quieter. In the midst of their lovemaking, he had looked up to discover a very large dog sitting not a yard away, watching them. What was particularly unsettling was that, despite the heat, the dog did not pant. "What should we do?" Rebecca had asked, and he had answered, "What do you think?" and she had said, "Something will come to me." When they had finished, the dog was gone. Ehrler dreamed about it for weeks.

There was an ant nest of dried mud on the tree trunk next to him, and Ehrler watched the insects streaming in and out of it until the spliff burned his fingers. His hands were aging, all right. But they had heard about pleasure. They had heard about ambition. Bending over, he picked up a fragment of cast iron—part of the door latch to the ruined building. Then he walked back to the flooded house and sat down in the water, on the observation deck. The dolphin neither ignored him nor paid him undue attention, swimming ceaselessly to and fro, his sonar creaking. All right, thought Ehrler, I've just got to convince Melissa to say yes. He watched the dolphin for a very long time, thinking sometimes about the dog, sometimes about what had happened at the Aquarium in New York. *If anybody, any one man or woman, cares more than I do—* When the grass wore off, he felt lonely and went inside to call his children.

* * *

Jeffrey put the key in the apartment door, which he had double-locked. It opened with a single turn. "Melissa must be back," he said to Kirk, who began reviewing in his mind a little of the history of her bitchery and abomination, silently citing her penury in the matter of promising investments, her disapproval of a bit of friendly fornication he had conducted on a previous visit, her excessive control over Jeffrey's thoughts and inclinations, and numerous other offenses too pickyminded to recall.

"Does she know I'm staying here?" he asked.

Jeffrey restored the beeping telephone receiver to its cradle. The lights in the apartment were not on. The keys to the car were not in evidence. "Lissy, are you here?" he called, wondering suddenly if his eight-inch Gerber stainless-steel carving knife were near enough to hand. A man emerged from the bedroom.

"Buenas tardes, Jefe," the man said, yawning and stretching.

And when Jeffrey had introduced him to Kirk with an irritated look, Diego explained that napping at his own place had been impossible because the people in the loft above were sanding their floors, so Nikki had lent him her key, saying it would be okay. Diego always slept before a nightclub date, gathering new attitudes.

"But, man, you wouldn't believe your phone. Five people in an hour they want to know about that dolphin. You think they even know Melissa? No, man, they read about her in the paper."

Jeffrey looked at the phone. Not forgetting her stamina, compulsive and beautiful as it was, nor her desire to make herself understood, complicated and crucial as it was, Jeffrey wondered: Should I rip it out of the wall?

He handed Kirk the newspaper with Melissa's picture in it and turned to Diego. "How's Nikki?"

"She is good, very good. Now that it is over, we understand each other again." He smiled. "Sometimes it is necessary to talk, because a woman does not always consider what is the way the world is. We men must be more realistic, even in love."

"So the abortion went smoothly?"

Diego bowed his head. *"Sí."*

Jeffrey marveled briefly at the way a single well-placed lie such as Nikki's could cause multiple fractures in the bones of everyone who happened to be standing around it, or passing by it, or drawn naturally to it by the strings of some familiar emotion. He noticed Diego had shaved his mustache off. Then he went into the kitchen to see how much gin there was. There was half a bottle.

"Okay, Jefe. I got to go. But I will see you at the club later, no?"

"For certain."

At the door, Diego paused, his newly naked lip sly and slightly larcenous. *"Gracias, Jefe."*

Their eyes met. *"De nada, Diego."*

When he was gone, Kirk looked up from the paper. "Now what reason's he got to call you 'boss' all the time?"

"He's never told me and I've never asked," said Jeffrey, shrugging a little refrigerated gin into their glasses. Kirk finished reading the interview with Ehrler and put it on the kitchen table. He had trouble, however, keeping his eyes off the photograph of Melissa and the dolphin. "One thing I will say for that girl," he said. "She has a whim of iron." Jeffrey spoke a few sentences to the effect that this was true and that she had many other wonderful qualities as well. When he heard the night latch rattle, he tilted his glass a final time and replaced it on the table.

"You're looking lovely," he said to Melissa, as she came skating in, her dark, wary eyes sending messages in multiples of enough to both him and Kirk—and indeed the kohl seemed to suit her. They kissed. Melissa complimented Kirk upon his increasing resemblance to

Wyatt Earp, and Kirk, raising his glass to her, thanked her.

"But Earp always wore a *black* hat," he said.

"But I wasn't thinking about the hat," she said.

Jeffrey unstuck a third glass from the shelf and asked how Nona was.

"I don't know, she seemed better to me. Not coughing quite so much. But she's having a bronchoscopy next week, so we'll know more then." Melissa filled a vase with water and in it began arranging the lilacs she had brought.

"I guess you get along with your ma pretty well, don't you?" said Kirk.

She looked up, startled. "Why, yes. Yes, I do." He was so at ease it made her uncomfortable.

"I'll get it," said Jeffrey, and when he picked up the receiver, on the third ring, a female voice asked if Melissa lived there. He said, "Yes," and the woman said, "She's the one who had her picture in the paper yesterday with a dolphin?" and he said, "Yes. Who's calling, please?" and the woman, after a moment's hesitation, hung up.

"What was that?" asked Melissa, who had turned on the tiny kitchen TV and was holding on to the channel selector with one hand.

"Wrong number."

They watched the last reel of a silent movie, the 1927 version of *Loves of Carmen*, starring Dolores del Rio. Although there was a flamenco score accompanying it, Melissa kept the volume turned off so she could ask Kirk questions about Antarctica. I know he calls me "Honey" like that to annoy me, she thought as he answered them, but still— Toward the end of the movie they fell to making up dialogue for the characters, but the finale, in which Carmen is stabbed to death by José, was too bloody and peculiar for jokes—or, in fact, for words at all.

Jeffrey and Melissa took a shower together while

Kirk watched the news. Their bodies glistened, and in the way the water fell away from them in skeins, Jeffrey caught a glimpse of something squandered so recklessly and instinctively that the day had already half come when they might recall it only by its expenditure. The soap slipped from his hand as he soaped Melissa's back, but he caught it with his other hand. She turned around.

"What are you thinking?"

"I'm thinking that I miss you." He began to wash her breasts and stomach.

"But *why* do you?"

He laughed. "Life doesn't go on forever. Or weekends either. Maybe we're too ambitious."

The sound of his laughter, whose slight constraint would have been inaudible to anyone else, made her instantly alert, and that alertness took the form of a thought. "Well, that's a switch," she said. The thought was that she really hadn't wanted to believe he was having an affair, and now she did.

"More like a moment of weakness." He handed the soap to her and turned around. "But it would be nice if we had some time together. Are you going to accept Ehrler's proposal?"

She regarded his back and, in so doing, allowed it to remind her of the moment earlier in the day when she had reached out toward her mother from behind and had suddenly been overwhelmed with longing for the dolphin.

"I don't know," she said. She began slowly to wash him.

"Well, whatever you decide, we really ought to take a long weekend—just us. By the ocean, in the hills—I don't care. I mean, do you know how long it's been since we've had nothing to do but enjoy a long, cuntyfingered breakfast and worry about the weather?"

She laughed and kissed his soapy shoulder. "Long."

"Right. Too long. And sometimes we need that, even we do."

Stepping back so he might rinse, Melissa felt herself grow momentarily awkward, like a child running or an adult overcome with grief. When she was still, the impression faded without vanishing. She said: "Yes, even we do. I've never denied it."

Jeffrey stepped fully beneath the streaming water so that it encased him like a skin. "Well, then?"

She wondered if his other lover saw in him what the water streaming over him illustrated: that his solidity made no claims to being invariable in its outlines, or even, from moment to moment, distinct. But Melissa found she had only limited interest in the point of view of his other lover; that that point of view almost certainly belonged to someone she knew radically curtailed her curiosity. Reaching out, she placed a hand on Jeffrey's chest so that it was included beneath the water's flashing membrane. "Yes," she said. "I mean yes I want to go away. Not now but soon." She moved very close to him.

As they dried themselves, Melissa put one arm around his waist and, turning him so they faced the same way, said, "Look." In the tippable mirror: the reflected image of their naked bodies. Jeffrey, who was often asked why he was laughing, laughed now.

HARDWARE

They are dressing. As Melissa turns away from the closet, absently pressing to her body the skirt she has just selected, she sees Jeffrey throw a pair of socks into the laundry bag. What is it about socks I'm supposed to remember? she wonders. He opens the drawer to select a new pair, and as his movements grow suddenly agitated she remembers and turns quickly away.

Lissy?

What is it, darling?

You haven't been in my drawer for any reason, have you?

Of course not. Is something missing?

He shuts it. No, no. I just . . . I thought I left some money there, but I must be mistaken.

Jeffrey recalls the look of Diego's unmustached lip. He remembers his parting words. In a moment he will become convinced that Diego, while alone in the apartment, found and repossessed the gun with which he has threatened Nicole.

The figures of the digital clock rearrange themselves with a flicker. They are pumpkin-colored.

Melissa slips quickly into her underwear, blouse, skirt. It is unimaginable to her that the gun remain where it is—in the back of the file cabinet in her study —because it is unimaginable to her that Kirk, who will be sleeping in that room, would not find it there. She does not ask herself why that would be worse than Jeffrey finding it. He, seeing the tremor in her hand as she lifts an earring, decides not to tell her what has happened. He will speak about it to Nikki. Melissa kisses him and, saying she's going to fetch the kohl, leaves the room.

But why does he have a gun in the first place? she wonders yet again. Guns get fired.

Kirk lowers the needle onto the first cut of *Fracas,* whose opening bars confirm for Melissa his presence in the living room. She hurries into the study. Lifting the aluminum suitcase onto the foldout bed, she unlocks it. The rows of dolphin tapes, numbered and dated, have the momentary effect of calming her, and a taste, like the anticipation of citrus, rises to the back of her throat. She opens the filing cabinet.

In her hand, the gun subtly transforms everything else in the room. She confirms this by simply holding it an instant longer than necessary and looking at it. Then she places it carefully in the aluminum suitcase. She closes the suitcase, she locks it, and it is not until she turns around with it in her hand that she sees Kirk standing in the doorway. After a moment's hesitation, she smiles at him and squeezes by.

THREE CONVERSATIONS
IN THE NIGHTCLUB

Nikki, why did you disappear like that at the airport? Jeffrey and I were worried about you.

Oh, did I disappear? I'm sorry.

You're doing it again now. Please don't.

Why, mercy! It must be the loss of blood. They give you those little diapers to wear afterward, and I declare! I must go through five or six of them a day!

Nikki, you're being unfair. I'd just stepped off the plane, I hardly knew where I was. *Of course* I wanted to talk to you. You never gave me a chance.

I was upset.

Are you really bleeding that much?

No. In fact . . .

In fact what?

In fact, I'm not bleeding at all.

Nicole, you're impossible! Listen, the reason I didn't answer your letter was that I got it the day before I was coming back to the States and I knew I'd see you. Okay?

Okay. What's this you're drinking?

Rum.

Ugh. Here: take it back. By the way, I saw your picture in yesterday's paper. You really looked terrific. Like Amelia Earhart or something.

Amelia Earhart!

What's so funny?

Nothing. You just have a knack for compliments.

There've been those who say so. How does your friend over there feel about all this?

Jeffrey? He's been very good about it; I'm not sure I would have been able to get through it without him. And besides, Jeffrey has his own little intrigues to keep him occupied.

Such as?

Such as I don't know. That's why they're intrigues. Waiter, I'll have another rum when you get a chance.

I'll have a Perrier-and-lime.

You *have* stopped drinking.

I thought it would be a good idea. Were you really worried about me?

Nicole was right, Diego. Your band's getting too good for a little club like this.

Ah, Jefe, you exaggerate. But the second set will be better.

Y'all get too much better up there you gonna hurt yourselves. And we can't have that.

You are right, Kirk. We can't have that. *Salud*.

Salud.

Where are the ladies?

In the bathroom.

Jefe tells me you will be staying with him and Melissa for a while in their little Sierra Maestra. Watch out they don't turn you into a *guerrillero* like them.

Guerrillero, huh? Jeff, you been moonlighting?

It's news to me.

Still, you will see that I am not wrong, Kirk. You look closely at that one and you will see a desperate man with too many ideas. Alone, maybe he would not be dangerous. Who knows? But that Melissa! A soldier, a warrior, *una amazona*. You cannot be too careful.

She does keep her finger on the trigger, doesn't she? Tell me more. I'm getting interested.

Diego gets very romantic when he's had too much sleep.

And Jefe in his own way is romantic always . . . Ah, Nicole, Melissa: sit down. We were just talking about you.

What rock-'n'-roll star, Nikki? I don't see a rock-'n'-roll star. Do you see a rock-'n'-roll star?

A double this time. Keep my toes from wiggling me awake in the middle of the night.

It *is* the middle of the night.

So it is. You know, you could move this hand up a bit for company. Mm. There. What's Diego *doing*, anyway?

He broke a string on that last song.

Oh. I guess I missed it.

It was about buildings and food.

How Diego. By the way, what were you and Nicole talking about at the beginning of the set? Before I fell asleep.

Nothing particularly riveting. I don't remember. Why?

I don't know. You both looked so . . . serious.

Did we? Well, I guess I was trying to instruct her about birth control before Diego did.

Oh, that. It's not one of her keener interests, is it?

Not the control part, no.

Jeffrey . . . Don't have an affair with her, okay? I mean, even if you already are.

Even if I already am? What kind of talk is that?

I don't know. I love you. And I'm frightened.

Of what, darling?

Every time I close my eyes I see that scene at the Aquarium all over again.

Lissy.
Even when I blink.

Jeffrey removed the video camera from the case and checked the connecting cables. The children went on writing: if they were to travel to Antarctica next week, what would they bring, what would they feel, what would they hope to find there? The slight hum of the camera soothed Jeffrey and reminded him of other slight hums he had known. His hangover had vanished. Of course, she doesn't really think I'm having an affair with Nicole, he thought, that was just a guess. He trained the camera on Doon, who was shortening her pencil beneath the time line's pink Jurassic Age.

Melissa answered the telephone and explained that she did not want or need an agent. Then she pressed the first tape cassette into place and waited, nervously fingering the controls. The really crucial difference, she thought, the thing to keep in mind, is we have hands and they don't. From the speakers, Peter made a sound like the strum of a banjo. Melissa transcribed two and a half lesson tapes, trying to imagine what a language of pure relationship might be like. If you are handless, you do not fill the world with expressive objects but instead turn your attention to the shifting ribbons of connection which produce music, emotions, mathematical formulas. Melissa watched the cream cloud her coffee. Maybe it *is* Clarice, she thought; he never mentions her anymore. At the beginning of each tape her own voice said, "Good morning, Peter." She lay down on the sofa and pulled the plum-colored blanket over her feet. When she felt she was ready, she put on the first of the night tapes.

The sound of the dolphin creaking, whistling, wailing to itself as it swam tirelessly about the deep pool while she turned in fitful sleep on the floor above, saddened and exhilarated her now by its burden of beauty, longing, distance. Melissa punched the rewind button, wondering what was possible. She thought the answer might lie in the four chambers of her willful heart, in its robust contractions, but she couldn't be sure. The sound-level indicator skittered and jumped. Melissa's toes stirred beneath the blanket. Closing her eyes, she listened twice to the next two night tapes, growing dreamier and dreamier and more patient and more patient.

"I brought cheese," said Nicole as Melissa held the door open for her. "Okay?" They hugged.

And as the children organized themselves into three separate "expeditions," Jeffrey wondered how they felt sitting in their tiny chairs, waiting to be catapulted through the hole at the end of the mechanical age into their strange new lives. He moved among them with the video camera, zooming slowly in and out, sly with emotion.

"What are those?" asked Melissa, helping herself to some more Caprice des Dieux. She had had her doubts, but now she was glad she'd asked Nicole over to sit on the same side of the kitchen table with her for lunch and soda water.

"They're from the beach house last summer."

"The beach house? Don't tell me you've actually begun to *develop* all those pictures you take."

"Intimations of mortality," answered Nikki, with a fey look.

They inspected the photographs then, relics of the previous August when the two of them and Jeffrey had rented an ocean-front house on Long Island, Diego entering the picture plàne on weekends, from the corners, mostly. Much happiness could be read there: in the two-valued blue of sea and sky, in the caracole of their own frequently naked bodies, in the moist spots the brightly colored towels had made on the wooden sun deck.

Melissa reflected sadly on what it was the camera had captured: "Everyone looks so innocent in retrospect." Nikki said: "My breasts were a different shape."

The buzzer buzzed. A woman from down the hall

wanted Melissa to sign a petition to evict tenants displaying symptoms of information sickness. "That's against the law," said Melissa, shutting the door. Her favorite photograph, the one she looked at longer than the others, showed Jeffrey leaping into the air. He looked surprised there and very happy, crouching weightlessly against the sky.

"This year we really ought to get bicycles," said Nicole. "Remember how much we wanted them last time? And a wok—we've got to have a wok."

Melissa put down her steaming mug, the better to consider Nicole's tone of voice, whose exaggerated enthusiasm suggested she took less for granted than her words implied. Do dolphins have tones of voice? she wondered, looking at Nikki's hennaed hair. Then she said, "I'm not sure I'm going to be here in August."

"Oh. Where would you be?"

"With the dolphin. There's another project in the works."

"How long?"

"Three months if I decide to do it."

"Okay," said Nicole, giving her wintergreen tea an exciting look. "I'll bring the wok, and we'll buy our bicycles when we get there. I've never really been to the Virgin Islands before." Then she emptied her mug, went into the bathroom, and threw up.

"Should I read it?" asked the child.

"Whatever you want," said Jeffrey from behind the camera.

"Okay. Antarctica. The air would be very clear. We would all live in round houses and communicate by TV. There would be no more books or cars and everyone would know everyone else. It would be so quiet that we could read each other's minds, and talking would be like singing. Singing would be like I don't know what. Sometimes there would be big snowstorms, and your friends would come over and stay with you. No one would need to sleep anymore. There would be frozen dinosaurs. Sometimes in winter you would think the sun was coming back early but it would be a flying saucer. You would be able to see millions of stars and there would be no more tall buildings. Also I forgot to put in that I would study the customs of penguins."

Jeffrey decided he worried too much about the darker aspects of Melissa . . . who was holding Nicole's hair up out of the way while Nikki washed her face.

"It must be the aspirin I've been taking," said Nicole.

"Don't take them, then," said Melissa, giving her a kiss on the back of the neck. "Don't."

They sat on the sofa and listened to loudness from the street below. Melissa lit a cigarette. "I don't know what I'm going to do, it depends on all kinds of things. Jeffrey and I have got to have some time together before we get too perfectly casual for our own good. And there's Nona. I could never leave if I really thought—" Light fell through one edge of the ashtray. Nikki smelled of cloves.

"When do you have to decide?"

"Soon."

"Well, if I came with you I could take care of all the household chores—buy the groceries, wash the clothes, gossip at the water catchments."

Melissa put out her cigarette. "Nikki, you just can't."

Then a pigeon landed on the window ledge and Nicole thought: Of course, there's still my red, white, and gold TWA pass to consider. In six months I'll marry Diego and it will be gone forever. Nicole thought: Believing in destiny removes you, in a funny way, from those who don't.

"On the third day," read another child, while another child traced the route on a map held up for the camera by another child, "we come to the uranium place. You can tell where it is because there are millions of footprints all around and the snow glows."

"The snow what?" said Jeffrey, zooming in on the speaker's face.

The child looked nervously to the left and right, then grinned. "Glows," said the child, and Jeffrey thought: Freeze frame.

The scent of cloves lingered after Nikki's departure, and Melissa walked back and forth, thinking about their college days, when the two of them had set out together to educate themselves in the pleasures of city life. After all, it was possible to be too close to someone. Wasn't it? Melissa looked at the tape cassette in her hand.

The more she listened, the less she thought teaching the dolphin English was enough. If delphinic speech were in fact tonal, the information load of each utterance would go up by a factor of ten, and a half-hour vocalization would contain up to a hundred times as many information bits as the *Odyssey* or the Icelandic Eddas. Melissa remembered a few things that flew through the air: TWA jets, Peter's yellow ball, Amelia Earhart, the dolphin at the Aquarium. She pushed the volume on the tape deck higher. Opening her notebook, she used a fiber-tip pen to outline a black box in the center of one page; then, with a series of rapid strokes, she filled it in.

BLACK BOX *n. 1. a conventional and usually temporary agreement among scientists to stop trying to explain things at a certain point.*

She stares at the figure she has drawn. Some women would have considered it a sign that their attention was wandering unproductively; most men would have come to that conclusion without even consciously entertaining it. As she listens, Melissa pretends that the box contains everything necessary to make the dolphin's night utterances intelligible to her. Bit by bit, her mind takes on the qualities of the figure she is gazing at. When the tape ends, she blinks, and like water seeping back to its accustomed place, an image appears: it is her father, in rumpled khaki pants and a plum-colored sweater, standing as he did years ago beside the family pond in Connecticut.

"A glass of white wine," said Clarice. Everything she was wearing was more or less beige. If we rented a little studio somewhere, she thought, at least it wouldn't be so nerve-racking. From where she was sitting, she could see the entrance to the hotel Jeffrey had named over the phone. At least we could eliminate some of this creeping around.

Jeffrey kissed her on the mouth, whose ample cut gave Clarice a starved and beautiful look.

"But how do I know you're not your brother?" she asked.

"You don't," he said, sitting down on the bar stool beside her. He too ordered a white wine, and they drank slowly, their upper arms pressed together in an exciting way. Jeffrey thought perhaps she looked a shade unhappy, but maybe he was just feeling guilty.

"How was Philadelphia?" he asked.

"Boring. I missed my children. I missed you."

Once again, she _felt_ surprise at having become Jeffrey's lover, and it was to this surprise she returned each time they met. Had her presence beside him in the middle of the afternoon seemed too plausible, she would have been obliged, as someone who disliked predictable arrangements, to put a stop to their affair. Had it seemed too obviously incongruous, she would have suspected she was merely out to prove something. As it was, their intimacy aroused within her an acute curiosity from which she believed all else would follow. She smiled at him.

"It's very good to see you again," he said. "And you're looking suspiciously beautiful for one so bored." By way of answer, she clinked her glass against his—a pleasant sound. They drank.

"I'm sorry I was so flip on the phone Friday," she said. "It was a bad day."

"Never mind."

As they got up to leave, the bartender switched on the television, a six-foot screen suspended from the ceiling. Four orange helicopters were flying in a line toward a snowy peak.

"How long do we have?" asked Jeffrey. The sound of the hotel-room door closing behind them seemed suddenly to sum up the unreasonable demands they made on life, demands which could be neither met nor counted, there were too many of them. Clarice sat down on the edge of the bed and looked at Jeffrey, his question already irrelevant. For a moment, she did not know how to begin undressing—not because she was reluctant but because it seemed to her that by entering this room together and closing the door they had already left behind everything that opposed their love-making. Jeffrey stood beside the chest of drawers, naked. She unpinned her hair.

There was a wedge of sunlight at one corner of the bed, not quite touching them, as Jeffrey, cradling her hips, put his lips and tongue gently to her cunt. The taste he had come to recognize as her own made it impossible to recall other tastes—that of the wine, for example—at the same time that it seemed to allude to them. A tremor passed slowly from one of her thighs to the other and back again like a tide. She placed a hand on his head's hair, drawing him closer.

"Don't stop, darling," she may have said or whispered. "Don't ever stop."

When he entered her, the sun had reached her shoulder. He kissed the spot and left a strand of silver glistening there.

Afterward they lay together with their foreheads touching and the sounds of major traffic arteries drifting in through the small open window. Jeffrey's hand continued to admire one of her breasts. What was good about Clarice was first the greenness of her eyes and second the knack they had for seeing what they looked at. For a moment Jeffrey wondered what it would be like to have breakfast with her every morning—four little glasses of juice and the radio off. She propped herself up on one elbow.

"Jeffrey?"

"What is it, sweet?"

"It's harder than I thought it would be to go back to hotels."

He regarded the room they had rented, a fatigued-looking area it was true. After a while he said, "But do we have any choice, now that she's back?"

"Well," she said, running a hand through her hair's blond fluency, "what if we rented an apartment? Apartments are more discreet than hotels."

"And more expensive than hotels," he said.

"And more serious than hotels," she said.

They kissed each other in a companionable way, trying, at the speed of self-interest, to imagine the outcome of their dangerously successful affair. A year was a long time to continue loving someone you saw only infrequently, but there it was. Clarice's use of the word "serious," freighted though it had been with friendly irony, began to alarm Jeffrey.

"Oh, come on," she said, "If we couldn't tease each other sometimes, where would we be now?"

He smiled. "In the throes of faithfulness."

"Exactly. I don't mean to press you, darling. It's just that I got a little spoiled while she was away."

"So did I," he said. "And I do hate hotels. But I'm not sure renting an apartment is the answer either."

"Maybe not." Looking past his shoulder, Clarice could see their bodies partially reflected in the dressing table's mirror—part of her body and part of his. "I don't suppose she's planning another trip right away, though?"

He hesitated. "It's not impossible."

Their eyes met for an instant, and Clarice began to laugh. "The throes of faithfulness, is it?" She drew two fingers slowly up between her legs and touched them to his lips. "Poor Jeffrey."

Their love, the second time, was at once less patient and more sharply grateful. Both half imagined the hotel room door had swung open as they fucked and that there were people approaching; toward the last there was the sound of many hurried footsteps in the hall. He pressed as far up into her as her hips would allow, and she, clasping him tightly to her, began to moan.

But it is love's impediments that improve the world into which we must eventually subside . . .

They showered, they dressed. Clarice was sitting at the dressing table, brushing her hair.

"I wanted to ask your advice about something," he said, massaging her shoulders with his intelligent hands. And though it was the gun he meant to speak of—how it had glided in and out of his life with the unnatural stealth of illicit things—he ended by telling her the whole story of Nicole's pregnancy and pretended abortion, of Diego's stressful temperament, and of his own misgivings at all this dismal behavior.

"And you say Nicole and Melissa are best friends?"
"Yes."

"It sounds as if the plan was for you to tell Melissa anyway, then, don't you think?"

"At first I did. Nikki can be very manipulative when

it comes to getting Melissa's attention. But lately I've begun to see it differently—this as well as a lot of other things. Lately I've begun to think she told me out of some kind of self-protective impulse, so I would keep an eye on Diego and step in if things got too rough."

"Oh, come on. You don't actually think he'd shoot her because she's pregnant?"

Jeffrey walked over to the bed and sat down. "No," he said, picking up the tiny gold watch Clarice had left there on the table. "I guess I don't think that. But I'd hate to be wrong."

Kirk peered over the edge of the platform and jumped.

"That's it," said the instructor. "Feet together and roll." Picking himself up out of the sawdust, Kirk caught a glimpse of the next student's face atop the training tower. He reached for his camera.

"Now what in hell you suppose made us think jumpin' out of airplanes was gonna be fun?" Kirk said when they were back in line. A red Cessna buzzed overhead with somebody's haunch hanging out the side door. Kirk took a partially crushed Snickers bar from his pocket and ate it thoughtfully, keeping his eye on the plane.

"In a high-speed malfunction," instructed the instructor, "you'll have twelve seconds to deploy your emergency chute or in seventeen seconds you're dog food." The class became interested. White jump suits, heavy boots, old crash helmets, chest radios, and liability releases were distributed. The first student stepped forward to be strapped into his carefully packed parafoil.

Snapping a few pictures while he waited, Kirk overheard two of the younger students talking about the new emotion some people were feeling. "I know this girl," said one, "who thinks it actually began years ago with the whole ESP thing." Kirk himself had not ex-

EASY TRAVEL TO OTHER PLANETS   105

perienced the new emotion, but he wanted very much to believe in its existence, in its newness. Certainly the old standbys were getting a little shopworn these days, what with the proliferation of confessional therapies, advertising agencies, TV personalities. But could a whole new emotion really be preparing to move out into world life?

"It's like . . . I don't know, it's like being in a big crowd of people without the people. And you're all traveling somewhere at this incredible speed. But without the speed."

Kirk nodded. An elderly Cessna moved slowly out of the hangar, and a pretty girl walked by, a "Skydiver" patch sewn to the crotch of her jeans. Everyone regarded the gorgeous day and tried not to appear nervous. They also tried not to think about "going in"— "frapping," as it is sometimes called, or "bouncing."

Conversation stopped as a jump-suited figure crawled out onto the wing of the red plane, three thousand feet overhead. "If that fat mother fraps, half of New Jersey'll be seasick from the aftershock," observed one of the regulars, pulling on a Dr. Pepper. Kirk remembered standing on a roof in Dallas with Jeffrey, the two of them looking down past their Keds. Which of them had been the first to jump? Which? The fat mother hopped and popped, a perfect jump. Kirk reloaded his camera.

In the plane, nobody spoke. They had been told by the jumpmaster that if anyone's pack popped inside, the draft would suck the bandanna-sized pilot chute out the open door, tearing its wearer and everyone else through the fuselage of the plane. Kirk looked dubiously down at the radio through which he was supposed to receive directional signals from the ground. Then he looked dubiously at the ground. Of course, if he told Jeffrey about the gun right away, he would lose the chance to find out more on his own.

At twenty-five hundred feet the first student was motioned forward by the jumpmaster; a moment later, he stepped out, an expression of idiot panic on his face, and was gone. The plane seemed ominously emptier.

"Okay, you next." Kirk sidled up to the door, and his static line, which would open the chute, was attached to a hook. The jumpmaster made Kirk focus his eyes on his own to see what was left of Kirk's wits. Then he signaled the pilot to cut the prop. Kirk climbed out on the wing in the 90-knot breeze and, at the jumpmaster's nod, dropped off backward into the sky.

YOUNG, FAST, & SCIENTIFIC

1. Bright chunks of earth, sky, and departing airplane tumble by on all sides of him.
2. Arching his back, Kirk attempts to count, but the notion of consecutiveness has abandoned him.
3. Jeffrey was born first; *then* he, Kirk, was born.
4. He had been told to keep his eyes on the horizon rather than look down, but when he determines which way is down, he will look that way.
5. Fa fa fa fa fa / Fa fa fa fa fa
6. He passes a bird. Or: a bird passes him. Or:
7. Einstein's theory suggests that increasing intensity of gravity has the effect of slowing the passage of time, although this is not something we can observe in our own universe very easily.
8. Fa fa fa fa fa
9. *The wind in his helmet is very loud.*
10. He feels a tug and looks up: the main chute opens flawlessly and he is dangling from his crotch by a harness in the sky. There is, he discovers, a camera in his hand. He begins to photograph what he sees—the Pine Barrens below, the other parachutes opening above— but it is the unexpected silence he wants most to preserve. It is broken only by the occasional squawk of his chest radio directing him to the drop zone, reminding him that the air is full of airwaves. When he is three telephone poles from the ground, he uses the toggles to

steer his back in the same direction as the wind sock below, so his forward speed will neutralize the slight wind. He lands, rolls, leaps up to chase the ballooning chute.

What is wonderful is not to die.

After a late lunch in Trenton, Richard drove Nona into the city. Two hundred thousand other cars were going the same way, and as everybody rolled slowly forward, graying up the air, Richard said, "You realize owning that fine racing machine makes us partly responsible for all this."

"So it does: 'Win on Sunday, sell on Monday,' as they say in Detroit." Nona was concentrating on not coughing. "Does it make you feel guilty?"

"No," he said, smiling. "It doesn't." She put her head in his lap.

The point of their meeting, the reason they had lunched in the soft orange glow of the Holiday Inn was that their driver had bought the car he'd had in mind, a Chevy Monte Carlo, and he had wanted to tell them about it. The car was as brave as 625 horses. Although Nona knew she was right not to tell Richard about her illness, Melissa had also been right in saying the cruelty of that silence would fall as much on her, Nona, as on him. Today, for instance: when there was no one to talk to about tomorrow. She pushed the dashboard's cigarette lighter idly to.

Richard said: "You quit smoking."

She looked quickly up at him. The rimless sunglasses he wore while driving made him look slightly clownish, but his mouth gave a different impression. "Yes," she said at last. "Six months ago."

"Good for you. What made you do it?"

She was trembling slightly. "Oh, I don't know. The rage to live."

Richard regarded Nona's large gray eyes. He wondered if they saw how much his own marriage was a compromise with terror. Then he shifted lanes. "My wife's trying to quit and my youngest son's trying to start. That says it all, I guess."

The lighter popped out, startling them both. Nona inspected the fading glow of its coil, and Richard stroked her head gently. "How *are* your sons these days?" she asked.

He scanned the vast movement ahead, behind. "I don't know. They're strange."

In another part of the traffic, a driver leaned on his horn.

Nona stepped into the elevator. Between the eighth and ninth floors she admired Ignacio's turtle, who lived in a liquor box and ate iceberg lettuce. "He is very old," said Iggy. "Old," Nona agreed.

Kirk opened the door to Melissa and Jeffrey's apartment, and Nona embraced him, overlooking his two-toned shirt, intaglioed belt, porcupine-skin boots. "I believe you got me confused with my brother Jeff." Kirk said, letting a hand linger at her waist to emphasize the friendliness of the confusion. Blushing, Nona introduced herself, and Kirk led her to the kitchen, where he poured them each a glass of water, or rather vodka.

"I tried to phone ahead to tell them I was coming," said Nona, "but I couldn't get through."

"It's that damn dolphin." Kirk sat down beside her on the sofa. The aluminum suitcase was seated in the chair across from them, but Kirk had been unable to open it; it was locked. "Ever since that article in the paper, the phone just won't quit. If she's fond of her sanity, she's either gonna have to change her number or get herself an answering service."

They contemplated the telephone.

"Lissy says you're from Texas?"

"Houston. I'm up here for a month to learn how to fall out of airplanes, then *Newsweek*'s flying me to Antarctica. I'm what they seem to call a photojournalist."

Nona considered the thousands of feet through which one fell wondering if one's parasol were going to open to open to open. She put her glass down—dizzy, nauseous. "Why are you grinning like that?" she said to Kirk.

"I just this moment figured out how scared I was this afternoon."

"Of what?" she said.

"Heights," he said.

She looked closely at him. From the cowboy face, the cowboy-colored brow, Kirk's eyes were kind, calculating, unafraid. "You're a lot like your brother, aren't you?"

He unwrapped a Snickers bar and bit into it, washing it down with a slug of vodka. "We do take after each other some."

Nona's laugh became a cough and the cough became prolonged. When she finally caught her breath, she apologized. "But I'm not afraid of heights," she said, draining her glass.

They talked about stock-car racing. Kirk grew more intrigued. He discarded the possibility that the gun was actually Nona's and that Melissa was simply trying to prevent her from pointing the wrong end of it at herself. "I guess," said Nona, "that I just have a natural love for fine machinery."

Kirk nodded. The liquor was beginning to give everything a faint innuendo. Nona was in pain.

"It's almost poignant: all that sophistication and money just to send people zooming around in circles so fast they nearly die every time they blink. Amazing, really." When she inhaled sharply, her chest made a peculiar sound. "Not many people would understand that."

Kirk said: "You're a closet skydiver."

"No," she answered. "I just talk big."

Their eyes met. "From what I hear, it's not just talk."

And she wondered how she would feel when they

scanned the scene in her segmental bronchi, the bronchoscope's fine, stainless-steel machinery snaking down her throat: disgusted? frightened? resigned? And when they told her she had six, twelve, or another number of months to live, would she feel the same way she felt now, going into the other room to put vodka back in their glasses and think about a few things she didn't know, such as the origins of altruism, the proof of the vodka she usually drank, what her husband saw when he looked in the mirror? She handed Kirk his glass.

"Was it Jeffrey who told you, or Liss?"

"Jeff."

Nona nodded to herself. "Anyway, it's true: I have lung cancer, it's inoperable, and I frighten everybody but small children and animals. In fact, your brother is one of the very few exceptions. In fact, right now, he's the only exception."

His head inclined slightly to one side, Kirk said, "Jeff never did scare easy." Which seemed with the liquor's help to mean that neither did he, so Nona told him about the bronchoscopy she was to undergo the following day, a test meant to make clear in a way that X rays never could the past, present, and future of her invaded lungs.

"And Lissy still thinks it's scheduled for Friday," she said. "I've decided it's easier on me that way: fewer looks of contained terror."

"So there don't anybody know about tomorrow?"

"You do," she said after a moment.

Melissa and Jeffrey came in, their arms full of groceries.

"Oh," said Melissa, who knew intimacy when she saw it. "Hello."

Jeffrey put his bags down on the counter and kissed Nona hospitably. "How are you feeling?" he asked, although the answer was there in the soft, spoiled scent of her breath.

Nona smiled.

"We been havin' True Adventure time here, and I'm afraid your mama's got me beat," said Kirk, to whom a suspicious glance meant nothing.

They unpacked the groceries. Melissa could hear the new music, with its exciting sound, playing softly on a radio in the apartment next door. She turned on their own radio: the same music, strong and message-laden.

Jeffrey poured another round of drinks and listened to Nona's dream about Antarctica. " '*Singing* ice'?" said Melissa. "Why 'singing'?" They all looked at Nona's throat. "I don't know," she said. Jeffrey sat on the counter and dangled his legs.

"You say that in the dream Antarctica was a hospitable place—birds and everything?"

"Yes."

"And there was someone with you?"

"Yes."

Unsnapping the cuffs of his shirt, Kirk intervened. "Why, any damn fool can see you just got a craving to travel," he said, looking up sideways at her.

Nona laughed. "You're right, you know." She raised her glass to him. "Now, how is it I didn't see that?"

Melissa went to answer the phone and Jeffrey began sautéing chunks of meat for the beef daube. I'm just feeling guilty I didn't call her before this, he thought. Through the window, the sun could be seen setting over the divorced and the dead.

"John!" said Melissa into the phone. "What're you doing down there? How's Peter?"

Nona was once again noticing how Melissa had arranged the kitchen to resemble her own as closely as possible; she had even painted the little wall hooks red, an idea Nona had borrowed from Jill. "So what do you think of all this dolphin business?" she asked Kirk, who replied that he had nothing against it as long as it didn't become the sort of preoccupation that gave folks beady little eyes; he didn't much care for beady little eyes. Nona's hand chopped the air impatiently. "No, I mean seriously. Do you believe they're as intelligent as we are?"

Jeffrey, who was holding the refrigerator door open in search of carrots, held it open some more, and before Kirk could answer, he turned around and said, "But what do you think, Nona?"

She was surprised. She saw the veins in his temples, the set of his jaw, and for the first time it occurred to her how hard it might indeed be for him. Swallowing the last of her drink, she said: "I don't believe in the dolphin."

Kirk chewed ice. Jeffrey said: "What do you believe in?"

Nona put down her glass and shrugged. "I believe in my daughter."

There was a white towel around Ehrler's neck, and Peter kept an eye on it as he swam back and forth, six body lengths away, patiently back and forth, uncertain what the function of a white towel might be. Ehrler leaned back in his chair, letting his free hand dangle in the water. "No, I've been here since yesterday," he said into the phone. "I thought I'd better get a firsthand look."

Melissa lit a cigarette. "Well? Is everything okay? No problems getting him to eat or anything like that?"

"No," said Ehrler, "nothing like that."

The sound of water being slapped around made Melissa's knees shake; she sank into a chair. "I miss him. Can he hear me?"

Peter swam, his skin glutted with dreams and their transit.

"It's hard to say. He's interested, but he's keeping his distance. You know how he is about the phone."

"Yes." From the kitchen, the sound of laughter reached her, but she put it impatiently out of her mind. There would be plenty of time later for—for what?

"The first thing I wanted to ask you," said Ehrler, "is

whether you ever noticed any correlation between Peter's behavior and the movements of the moon—its phases, its rising and setting, whatever."

She had misheard the question. He had misphrased the question. It was not a question. "No," she said at last, exhaling a cloud of mentholated smoke. "I don't think so. Why?"

"Well, yesterday I hired this guy from town as groundskeeper—there's that new law about trying to find local help, remember?—and we got to talking." Ehrler looked out the window to where the last sunlight struck red from the shedding bark of the gumbo-limbo tree. "Now, Knolly's lived here all his life and he says the one thing everyone knows about dolphins is that, as he put it, 'the moon looks after her own.'"

"What do you suppose that means?" said Melissa.

"From what I can make out, there's some sort of folk tradition about the moon having taught the dolphins speech. I may not have that quite right, but anyway, it's meant to explain why dolphins are so much more vocal and active when the moon's in certain phases. Something I'd never noticed."

"Nor I," she said, her mind racing.

In some of the dolphin's dreams, water fell out of the woman's eyes and made the shallows deep, safe, alive with butterfish. Peter swam faster. In some of his dreams, she praised the wet life with many motions of her hands and arms.

"But I *have* been listening to the night tapes," Melissa said, "and what I can do is plot them against the moon for those dates and see what turns up." A herd of cockroaches stampeded past her foot. What was happening? Why wasn't she down there? Who was Knolly? "Not that I expect much," she added, without quite meaning to.

"I'm not sure I do either," Ehrler answered. "But it's worth looking into."

"Sure. And what was the other reason?"

"Other reason?"

"That you called."

Ehrler swiveled back around to regard the dolphin slim-slamming about in the water, its attitudes unknown to him, or only partially known to him, or lodged firmly in that part of time that used to be called the future. "The other reason I called," he said, "is to ask if there's anything I can say or do to convince you to agree to the three-month project. We can't really continue this line of research without you. You do know that?"

Melissa felt like coughing. "Yes, I know that."

"Of course there are other possibilities, other projects. But in more ways than I care to think about, this is probably it. When I came down here it was partially to see whether I could take your place if you decided not to go through with it. I'm satisfied now that I can't."

"What happened?"

"Nothing. Or at least not enough." Pushing his glasses up onto his forehead, Ehrler watched a hair drift past his nose to the rippling water below. And while it was true he lost only four or six hairs a day, who knew but what the rate of loss might not triple tomorrow? He closed his eyes and wondered what was manipulative. "If you need to come down here to decide," he said at last, "we can afford that now."

There was a silence. Melissa drew deeply on her cigarette and put it out. "How long are you going to be there, John?"

"A while."

Her voice was very calm and it said, "My mother's having a bronchoscopy this Friday. I'll have a better idea then about what to do. I'll call you when we get the results and we'll talk again."

"Yes," said Ehrler. "That would be the best thing."

"Thank you, John."

"Good luck."

Just before she hung up, a sound like baby laughter

came clearly over the phone. "Peter?" she said, pressing the receiver to her ear. There was a click, a sudden rush of acoustic space, a dial tone.

SECOND LUNAR UTTERANCE

She is lying in the center of an enormous bed, crying. The bed is so large that she cannot see any of its edges. At one of them, her father is standing.

Where is her crib? Where is her room? Where is her mother? She continues to cry. Her father continues to stand.

Her night-light has been brought in and placed in its customary place, high up on the wall just beneath the ceiling. It is in the shape of a smiling crescent moon with a cow jumping over it; lit up, it looks like the real moon. Her father sits down on one of the edges of the bed and says something with his mouth.

He hands her one of her blocks. He says something with his mouth.

She wants to be fed spoonfuls of strained apricots, but no matter how she propels this desire up from her stomach to her head and out of her mouth, the sound she makes is not the right one. Holding the block (which she will later learn to be in the shape of the letter *L*) by its short arm, she points it at her father. He raises his hands up over his head and pretends to be frightened. She laughs. He is wearing a zippered suit of brilliant blue and he says things with his mouth.

Later, in the dark, when she is alone, she gazes at the softly lit moon as if it were the real one.

"Who was that?" asked Jeffrey, pouring a gout of burgundy into the daube. Nona held a handkerchief to her mouth, and when she removed it, folded it quickly away. Melissa sat down beside her and, under the table, took her hand. "Nobody," she said.

Everybody else's glass was empty, and the radio signal was completely free of drift.

Kirk said, "So y'all plannin' a big cookout or some such for the day of the race?"

"Race?" said Melissa. Then she remembered. Kirk kept his thumbs hooked into his jean pockets and missed nothing.

"See, Jeffrey, I told you: she's getting all funny about it again," said Nona, running her free hand through her hair.

He smiled. He shook the rice level in the measuring cup and continued to smile. "Well, it's a handicap, you know—a mother who likes fast cars."

"Oh, screw you both," said Melissa. The sharpness with which she spoke seemed to surprise her; in a different voice she added: "And I think a cookout is a great idea; let's plan on it."

The cork had been pushed into the burgundy bottle, and by the light of the open refrigerator Nona saw it floating—sodden and solitary. Then the rice was done and she remembered she wasn't supposed to eat for twelve hours before the bronchoscopy. "I've got to go," she said. "The dogs will be expecting their dinner."

Melissa started. "But shouldn't you be expecting yours?"

"I can't, darling," she said, giving her daughter's hand one last squeeze. Kirk offered to call a cab, she accepted.

On the street, she said, "You know, it was very strange for me today. That man I had lunch with is more than just my partner in backing the car—you probably gathered that. But I haven't told him I have cancer; I'm afraid to. So I couldn't tell him about the test tomorrow, either."

An oil truck was stalled in the downtown lane, blocking traffic. Kirk considered Nona's thinness. "Would you like me to come to the hospital with you tomorrow?"

She held her elbows and looked at him. "No," she said after a while. "But it's kind of you to offer."

When Nona was seated in the cab they shook hands. "Least I know now who Lissy takes after. No wonder she's such a crack pistol shot."

Nona looked puzzled. He noted that.

"Maybe I've got that wrong. Anyway, good luck tomorrow." He shut the door, they waved, the cab lunged away.

Kirk decided to take a short walk before going back upstairs.

"What did Ehrler want?" asked Jeffrey, offering her the joint.

Melissa shook her head. She was setting the table and he was sitting at it. "Oh, nothing. He had the wrong number."

"What's the matter with you?"

"What's the matter with *you*? You're the one who started this wrong-number business. Who had the wrong number yesterday? Clarice? Or has she already been discarded, too?"

The napkin she had been folding was crumpled in her fist. Jeffrey exhaled at length, but the smoke did not rise. "Let's get this straight, Lissy: it's you who's having an affair—you and the dolphin."

She threw the napkin at his feet and started for the door. He caught her by the shoulder.

"As it happens," he said very quietly, "that was *not* a wrong number yesterday. It was one more person who'd read about you in the paper. She hung up when I asked her name. I thought I'd spare you that." When he let go of her, Melissa made no move to leave. "What did Ehrler want?" he repeated.

She told him. They argued about the summer, which they had planned to spend together. It would not be the end of the world if they didn't, Melissa said.

"You're pushing yourself too hard," Jeffrey insisted. "Can't you see your mother's dying, we're drifting apart, and that you . . . you're becoming more and more inhuman?"

"Jeffrey, don't—"

"You're *not* a human being anymore." He was stoned. He was shouting. "You're not even a goddamn human *being* anymore!"

Kirk came in. The kitchen floor was awash with beef daube and burgundy, and in the living room Melissa was writing things on index cards. The bedroom door was shut.

"Jeff go out?" he asked. She shrugged but did not look up.

Kirk scooped some of the stew off the floor with his hands, put it on a plate, and ate it.

Jeffrey woke up in darkness. He was alone, there were sounds. When he entered the living room, Melissa was sitting on the couch and the tape recorder was making dolphin noises in the feeble moonlight.

"Come to bed," he said.

"Soon," she said.

Black and silver. Black and silver. Black and silver.

BECAUSE he had not taken out his cab at all the previous day, because the favorable mention of his band in the *Times* had given him new resolve, because he found himself calmly in love with Nicole for the first time in months—for all these reasons, Diego decided the following morning to work a double shift.

He had already dressed and eaten when Nicole, in her coral-colored underwear, climbed down from the sleeping deck. She came directly to his arms, smiling sleepily, and he hugged her.

"You are feeling better?" he asked, pouring her the rest of the coffee.

"Mmmm . . . sort of." She took a single sip and handed the coffee back to him. They kissed. "Will I see you today?" she asked.

"I am going to work two shifts. But I will come back for lunch if you'll be home."

"I might not be." She put her lips against his shoulder. "What if I'm not?"

"I will come anyway," he said. "I love you," he said. On his way to the door he threw the keys once into the air and caught them.

Nicole studied the sprinkler heads on the ceiling of the loft. Then she telephoned Jeffrey. "You won't tell Diego, will you? About me still being pregnant? He's so happy now."

"Of course not, Nikki." He sounded tired, hurried.

"And Lissy either? Promise me."

"*Nikki . . .*"

"I'm sorry. You're being very sweet to me. I'll talk to you later."

Nicole looked at her hennaed hair in the pinking shears. The summer she had had her first period, she and Melissa and another girl had hennaed each other's hair in celebration. That was in Connecticut. On the jet back to Kansas she had, certain of her impending punishment, eaten a whole bag of candy corn and read a book with a maroon cover. She put the shears down on her sewing table. The cat had piled itself against the closet door so she had to wake it to get her suitcase down.

Laying the bag out open in the middle of the floor, she thought: When they find out at the ticket counter that you're married, they cut your pass to pieces with a pair of scissors.

She turned on the television and began to pack. Clothes were hung here and there about the loft as well as in the seven semicircular storage bins Jeffrey had designed. One thing was that she always knew what she wanted to pack even when she hadn't yet decided where she was going. Her morning sickness faded. On the television, housewives contested above a ribbon of little white letters that said the President would address the nation at noon. Sometimes the things Nikki saw on TV scared her, but a moment later she would forget about them.

Two books about babies; a portable white-noise unit; clothes both loose- and tight-fitting; a tiny folding camera; two swimsuits; all her essential oils; her design notebook; three disposable plastic pencils of differing blackness; goggles; cosmetics; several containers of krill paste and crackers; a necklace of industrial rubies; a shawl of iridescent silk. She zipped the suitcase shut.

In the taxi Nicole made conversation with the driver. It was a way of finding out what kinds of things strange women might say to Diego in his cab. The driver, a Vietnamese, showed her the machete he kept on the floor, and she thought of Diego's gun, of what Jeffrey had told her in the nightclub about his reclaiming it.

"Have you ever *used* that awful thing?" she asked the driver.

"Ever use? Ever use?" He chuckled, waving the machete around in an agitated fashion.

It was Nicole's opinion that men were smarter than they seemed, but that they didn't know it.

She watched the ticket clerk consult her computer. "That's one to Miami on Flight 417," said the clerk, and Nikki thanked her. It was always a relief when she got her pass back without incident.

The purpose of airport architecture, the reason it all looks the same, is to dilute the alarming wonder of flight, which might not otherwise be borne so casually and repeatedly and with such profit to the airlines. Nicole strolled about the terminal, wondering if she ought to call her aunt in Miami to tell her she was coming. When she found herself absently dialing Melissa's number instead, she abandoned the idea. Garlands of incompletely combusted jet fuel hung here and there in the sky, giving everything an exciting smell. After take-off, holding a copy of *The First Nine Months of Life* open in her lap, she peered out the window at her country.

Diego wiped the blood off the backseat of his cab with an old undershirt. This was the second time in a month that one of his fares had had an attack of information sickness, and he was getting tired of giving free rides to the hospital. It was noon. He turned on the radio. The President said he was dispatching the Secretary of State to Australia, where there would be an emergency meeting of world leaders to discuss the Antarctica situation, and for a moment Diego sat there behind the wheel, trying to decide if it was too early for lunch. Then he started the car.

The cat galloped across the loft's sunstruck floor. "Nikki?" said Diego, walking past soft bunches of gowns, a dressmaker's dummy, dirty dishes. "Nikki, you are here?" There was a faint smell of rosemary.

Diego cursed, shrugged, turned on the television. The President looked at him and said he was confident the issues could be peacefully resolved to the betterment of all nations, and Diego was glad he didn't have to drive the President anywhere. On the breakfast table, the cat had stuck its head into a glass to get at the last of the milk. There was a faint smell of burnt toast and rosemary. When Diego opened the refrigerator, a sheet of rice paper fluttered down, and he considered it there on the floor for a moment before picking it up.

Darling Diego: I've gone to Miami for a little while, where I can eat oranges and play shuffleboard with Auntie Bea. ¿Some fun, no? Don't hate me. You know when I get this restless it would drive us both crazy if I just hung around. And anyway it's only for a few days. I love you, Diego. I've been thinking some more about what you said in January about getting married. Maybe I'm ready to talk about it. I don't know exactly when I'll be back, but if I decide to go somewhere else first I'll call. I love you.

Nikki.

With one arm Diego swept the breakfast dishes off the table to the floor. He read the note again. Then he strode over to the wall of drafty floor-to-ceiling windows and looked into the street below, where the women were walking by in their skin-tight bluejeans, making plans, making their way.

He called his brother in Miami. There was no answer. He slammed the receiver twice against the table to knock some sense into it. He called Jeffrey at home.

"Nope, he's at school," said Kirk. "What's up?"

"That fucking TWA pass, man, that fucking pass."

"Nicole, huh?"

"Man, I'll kill that bitch!"

Kirk closed the diary of Admiral Byrd and sat up slowly in his chair. The sound of hurt in Diego's voice seemed momentarily to protect them both from the terrible things that never waited to happen, if they happened at all.

"She didn't say where she was headed?"

"Miami, man, but you don't know with her. She can fly all over the fucking *world* with that pass." In his mind's eye she was wearing sunglasses. She had been buying sunglasses when he had met her in Barcelona. "But I got a brother in Miami—maybe I'll go down there."

Kirk said, "Where you at now?"

"Home, man. We were going to have lunch together."

"I'll come over," said Kirk. When he hung up he realized he didn't know where Diego lived, and that Melissa, whom he might have asked, was not in the apartment. Without any difficulty, he found Jeffrey's address book in the bedroom.

Diego deep-fried six pig's ears at 365 degrees, trying to remember every word Nicole had said that morning. Then Kirk came in with a six-pack of Lone Star. "Your brother is my best friend," said Diego, giving Kirk a fierce and steady look.

"Mine, too," said Kirk. "He's a fine fella." They opened their beers. "Now what the hell happened? You and Nikki have a fight or what?"

Mashing up a few potatoes then, with the potato

masher, Diego explained there'd been no fight, but now he was going down to Miami to get her so they could have one.

"She wants it, my friend. She asks for it. When things go too good, it makes her nervous, and when she is nervous, she flies on airplanes." Diego spat a mouthful of beer into the sink, and Kirk thought about a woman he'd been getting too involved with in Houston, a wide-bottomed woman of great style and beauty who sometimes hid his car keys when he came to visit her.

"Of course, you *have* considered the possibility," he said, "that long as she does come back eventually maybe you're better off taking a little rest from each other?"

"No, *amigo*." Diego shook his head as he divided the pig's ears and potatoes between them. "No. She is playing with me."

Kirk admired the design of the table at which they ate and Diego explained that he himself had made it, that he did such things when he was angry or bored. A long silence ensued, and when Diego spoke again it was in a tone he had not till that point used. "You know . . . I wonder if it is possible she left because of the gun."

"Gun?" said Kirk, putting down his knife and fork.

"She was afraid of it," Diego said. He stared at his plate. It was unclear whether he was embarrassed at her fear or at his being the cause of it. "A few times I have . . ." He stopped.

"Guns do take some folks that way," said Kirk after a moment. Because his eyes were so blue, he could not look at people for very long without their feeling watched. When he had caused Diego to look up again, he went on. "But tell me now, buddy: what do you want with a gun anyhow?"

He shrugged. "I bought it in Barcelona. It is a beautiful weapon."

"You carry it when you work?"

"No, I leave it here. I will show you." He wiped his

mouth and got distractedly to his feet. "It is a 9 milli-meter Walther PPK. You know the gun?"

Kirk said that he did and refrained from adding that everyone his brother knew in the city seemed to own one. Diego rummaged through one of the semicircular storage bins. "It is because of her family that she is like this. She told me that one time she is in the hospital because she wrecked her car, and when she wakes up her mother is sitting there with the license plates. 'For souvenirs,' her mother tells her. I mean, man, that family is crazy."

Watching with interest now, Kirk swung the bench out from the table, the better to see Diego's movements, his quick, distracted movements. He recalled the way Melissa had smiled as she squeezed past him with the silver suitcase. It occurred to him suddenly that Nicole might have given the gun to her for safekeeping, and from across the loft came the sound of the cat landing on its feet.

"That fucking bitch," said Diego, closing the bin. "That stupid fucking bitch." He stood there stroking with two fingers the place where his mustache had been. Kirk grinned with relief for his brother and tossed Diego another Lone Star.

"What happen, *señor*? She hide it from you?"

Diego opened the beer and a geyser of foam shot out of it.

The green fiberglass chairs in oncology were attached to one another in rows so they could not be moved, but the patients who waited in them rarely conversed. Nona rummaged through her purse for a dime. Maybe it was a mistake after all not to have had someone come with me, she thought.

Air-quality-control devices hung inconspicuously from the ceiling, and five, six, seven patients wore hats to conceal what hair they had not lost in chemotherapy. Nona had lately noticed that even in her dreams she knew she had cancer now. She wanted to tell Richard this, in the middle of the night, in the middle of the world. Once, three years ago, she had woken up with her head on his chest, and the sound of his heartbeat had made her cry. She wondered suddenly if Melissa would understand that.

There was a dime on her palm. Everybody's eyes strained for a glimpse of white coat, stethoscope, file folder. To stop her hands from shaking, she leaned back in her chair and held her elbows.

When a nurse rolled in a television and turned it on, the President appeared. Goddamn him, Nona thought, *goddamn* him. She couldn't believe she was thinking about her husband.

At the drugstore, Melissa applied a new lipstick experimentally to the heel of her hand. Too red, she thought; and put it back. The cashier had already rung up the talcum powder, bath salts, and moisturizer when Melissa remembered she was out of spermicidal foam.

Of course by now he probably sees her whether I'm around or not, she thought, surveying the tiers of attractively displayed birth-control paraphernalia. Her back ached from lack of sleep, and she wondered what kind of ache it was to be pregnant. She felt another sort of ache then. It was Tuesday.

As she paid for the foam she thought: If I flew down there this afternoon I could still be back for Nona's bronchoscopy on Friday.

The plane to San Juan was not quite full, its passengers largely Puerto Rican families returning to visit relatives, or bury them, or make a new life. Melissa dozed much of the way. The man sitting next to her, a schoolteacher from Massachusetts, was reading a blue volume entitled *The Handbook of Unusual Natural Phenomena*. Whenever Melissa awoke he was on a new chapter.

" 'Glories, Broken Specters, Etc.,' " she read aloud over his shoulder. "What's a 'Broken Specter'?"

"*Brocken* Specter," he said. One arm of his glasses was fastened to the frame with a safety pin. "*Brocken.* It's a mountain in Germany."

She slept, and the sustained scream of the engines made dreams either impossible or unnecessary.

At the airport in San Juan, with an hour to kill before her flight to St. Thomas, Melissa dosed herself extravagantly with coffee and local fruits. Jeffrey had not seemed surprised when she had called him at school to tell him she was going; he had not even asked for how long, though she told him anyway. He had said simply: "Call Nona." But Nona's phone had rung on and on unanswered.

Tiny black-and-yellow birds streaked about inside the terminal, exuberant or panicked or merely exercising. Melissa bought a newspaper from a very young boy, and as he handed her the change, tears seized her eyes. What Jeffrey saw in her no one else had ever seen; she hadn't even known it was there herself, and with so many things changing hands it frightened her now to think she might have inadequately cherished it. Her flight was announced; she threw the newspaper away without having looked at it.

Ehrler met her at the airport in St. Thomas. His nose and cheekbones were newly sunburned, and his hands were nervous. "I hope the flight wasn't too awful," he said. Because the jeep had been parked in the sun, they had to drape beach towels over the seats before sitting. Melissa took her shoes off. "New York feels light-years away," she said, putting on her sunglasses.

The road stayed close to the coast, and as they drove, the smell and intermittent dazzle of the sea below soothed Melissa without diminishing her excitement. "I was up most of the night listening to the tapes," she said, half shouting to make herself heard over the engine. "I think we may have something with that moon business."

"Do you." Ehrler swerved to avoid a mongoose, but it misjudged the distance and ran right under the wheels.

"Yes, I do. The question is what." Melissa, who had not seen the mongoose, was adjusting her skirt to keep the wind out. She was glad she'd thought to wear her bathing suit underneath.

"But there's definitely a correlation between his vocalization index and the moon?"

"I think so. Yes."

The brilliant beach gave way to rocky coves and bays without bathers, then the road pulled higher into the woods. It surprised Melissa how comfortable she now felt with Ehrler, and she suddenly wondered whether, had they not been colleagues, they might have been friends. Four different kinds of wild palm grew here; the taller trees were choked with vines.

"It's clear he's missed you," Ehrler said. "Whenever I feed him, he says your name. Last night he woke me up with it."

Melissa pushed her dark glasses up onto her forehead, and in her eyes Ehrler saw a hint of delirium. He said no more. But Melissa found herself thinking strange words, words that as she considered them began to seem alarming. She thought: I've tried and tried and *tried*.

Ehrler parked the jeep in the scant shade of a poison-fish tree, and Melissa sat gazing for a moment at the flooded house. It was smaller than she remembered it, smaller and pinker. Memories are not permanent, buildings are not permanent, the sea is not permanent. Her toes were wiggling. In the hard light, in a square of newly broken ground, a black man with his hair grown out in dreadlocks was gardening. Melissa had not seen the man before.

"Knolly, this is Melissa," said Ehrler. She smiled at

the man and approached as though to shake hands, but halfway to him she stopped. His eyes were very red. "Knolly will be doing some grounds work for us." When Melissa said hello, the man nodded—half to her, it seemed, half to himself.

She entered the house through the dry area, Ehrler following, and in the dry bunk she put down her bag. One bed had a computer-parts manual next to it, the other a battered copy of Freud's *The Interpretation of Dreams*. There were clothes in both closets. "We do have that foldout cot in the storage room," said Ehrler, "and I can certainly—" Melissa looked at him. Then she unbuttoned her dress and pulled it over her head. "Has he had his afternoon feeding yet?" she asked, adjusting her bathing suit.

Sunlight shimmered off the water in the flooded area, off the water to the walls and ceiling. Melissa put her legs in it and splashed. "He's below," said Ehrler. "In the deep pool." She lowered herself down off the dry catwalk, and Ehrler reflected that once you lost your grace it was gone for good. She had hers.

And then it was as though she were alone. It occurred to her as she slogged slowly across the room, a face mask in one hand, that most of what one said to others was nonsense anyway; it was simply a way of sharing breath. Her heart contracted. "Peter?" she said, peering over the railing. When he did not appear, she fit the mask to her face and, holding it there with one hand, plunged feet first into the seawater below.

There were bubbles after plunging, and after bubbles, Peter—keeping his distance in the limpid green. He's not sure who it is, thought Melissa, waving a hand. With a flick of his flukes, Peter positioned himself eight feet below her and scanned her body with his sonar: a sound like a door creaking as it opened, or as it shut. I've scared him, thought Melissa, though it was her own heart that pounded. She surfaced to breathe, and the dolphin, ten feet away, surfaced too.

"Peter, it's me!"

He swam no closer, but sticking his beak in the air began to mimic the way Melissa was holding her head above the wash from the wave ramp. When she spoke his name a second time, he dived again.

There were yellowtail and lizard fish to-and-froing about the bottom, brought in by the action of the waves, and as Peter drove them toward her playfully, Melissa had a moment of panic. The sea's blunt fecundity frightened her; she swam blindly. Creaking and quacking, Peter streaked by, upside down, then wheeled and drew his length gently across her stomach. She made for the surface.

In his skin, he saw the woman swimming through water so deep there was no light there, so many body lengths from the surface there could be no thought of reaching it for respiration. In his skin, the woman had no hair or natural enemies.

"Well," said Melissa, "you certainly are playing hard to get, aren't you?"

Peter, several feet away, half leapt from the pool, falling lazily back on his side with a smash. He repeated the leap three times, alternating sides, then turned one bright eye to her and opened his jaws. "Ccxxxxxxxxxxxxxxx."

"Try English, Peter."

He dived. It was taught in the sagas that humans were without memory, that their starfish-shaped flippers took the place of memory, that the dry world was filled with monuments large and small to what had been forgotten. He was coming to sense that many objects could be named in the woman's language, each of them a monument, but that nothing held them together; more and more this confused him. Her energetically feeble movements as she swam toward him now sent a shimmer of sadness through his skin: the seawater that surrounded them both excluded her like a thing named.

He can't have forgotten everything, Melissa thought.

Peter glided over her head, out of reach. It's just a matter of him getting used to me again.

Ehrler, at the Plexiglas observation port, noted in his log Peter's unusual reticence, his low vocalization index, his restless movements. Then he drank all the iced coffee and tred to wipe the Plexiglas clean with his shirt. It was already clean. She's being too eager, he thought, watching Melissa shoot to the surface after holding her breath much longer than she'd meant to.

"Okay, Peter," she said between gasps. "Okay. Now, what's going on here? We were friends last time I checked."

Rolling over on his side, Peter squirted water from his beak in a gentle arc that touched down midway between them. Their eyes met, and in her mind Melissa saw herself splashing slowly forward to retrieve the yellow ball.

"Peter, you've got to try. It's very, very, important. Now say your name. Say 'Peter.'" Behind her, a wave larger than the rest crashed down upon the wave ramp, hung skied for a moment, and fell over her in a curtain. Peter emitted a series of very high-pitched whistles and made for the bottom. When she followed, he ignored her, swimming the perimeter of the pool, swimming its perimeter and tasting the disturbance of its salts. In deep water, dolphins pass into a meditative state caused by the weight of the water upon their skin.

Ehrler pressed the red button and spoke into the microphone: "Peter, Melissa: let's give it a rest for now."

Swimming quickly over to the port's plastic bubble, Melissa peered out at Ehrler (the dry world summoning her from a great height, from all sides, from within her straining lungs) and shook her head vigorously. He, just as vigorously, jabbed one thumb upward in the air. After a moment's hesitation, she obeyed.

No, decided Ehrler, it's just not possible she made the whole thing up. The ringing of his footsteps on the spiral staircase frightened a rat that had been resting there, and Ehrler made a mental note to pick up a trap in town.

"Why'd you do that?" she asked him when they met upstairs on the flooded observation deck. The sky was quickly clouding and a brisk easterly wind had sprung up. "We were just getting started."

"You need to relax," he said. "Both of you."

"Don't you think I should be the judge of that?"

"Three months is very different from three weeks, Melissa."

"But when you told me he'd been saying my name all the time—"

"I was rash. We've got to keep our expectations in check."

She tore the face mask off her forehead in a gesture that ended by being resigned, and they turned together to face into the wind with its featherings of salt and bird cry. "It's looking a little unfriendly out there," she said. "Anything on the radio about it?" Then, before he could answer, she set out across the flooded deck to where Peter's plastic feed bucket floated, bright and empty.

I could love her, Ehrler thought, watching Melissa pick her barefoot way down among the rocks to the feed-fish tank. And yet the thought was not important to him; that word which had once promised so much was now only one among others. He watched her netting butterfish one by one from the tank, the net's long aluminum handle striking the concrete sides of it with a dull, weightless sound, and it came to him that nothing about their work was as precious as the anguish it invoked: the exquisite pangs of one state of being glimpsing another.

Melissa slammed each fish she caught against the side of the tank to stun it before throwing it in the bucket.

*   *   *

"Ice?"

"Thanks."

"So how'd he seem to be taking it?"

"Well, he allowed as how they hadn't had no fight but he did say he was goin' down to Miami to get her, so I kinda figure they might squeeze one in." Kirk put his drink on the stove and began rotating his shoulder slowly forward, then backward.

"How serious was he?"

"Hard to say. Sure can cook a fine pig's ear, though."

"I'd better call," said Jeffrey, sitting down at the kitchen table. But when he leaned forward it was to turn on the tiny television on the counter. A map of Antarctica appeared, its immaculate expanse blossoming, as the commentator spoke, with colored Xs. "It's been a day for it. Lissy, too, you know: she's gone back to St. Thomas for a couple of days."

"Why, that girl don't care what she does," said Kirk. But there was no surprise in his voice. "You sure, now?"

"She called me at school. This guy she's working with on the dolphin project is pressuring her to agree to a three-month live-in, and it's getting to be a more and more attractive offer. For all kinds of reasons. So she's checking things out."

Kirk plugged in the heating pad he had wrapped around his bare shoulder, and for an instant the TV picture shrank back from the edges of the screen: a column of snow tractors laboriously circumventing a crevasse. "Did look like you two were having kind of a rough time last night."

Jeffrey shrugged. "It was time I lost my temper is all."

"Oh, I see. Y'all make a habit of that then—dining off the floor on special occasions?"

There was a pause while Jeffrey put the rest of the drink in his mouth. "Look," he said, flinging his ice into the sink from where he sat. "There's something about Lissy you have to know, something I'm just beginning to really see myself. She's obsessed with the dolphin. Not interested, not fascinated, not devoted: *obsessed*."

Kirk nodded slowly and leaned back against the counter, one hand holding the heating pad in place. While his own laugh lines were around his eyes, Jeffrey's were around his mouth. "You sound like you think that's a selling point."

"It cuts both ways. She knows how to want a thing. It's just that she hardly ever settles for anything so mundane as the possible."

"Yankee women."

"Horseshit."

"Whyn't you come on down to Rancho Penguin with me, give it all a rest?"

"Can't do it. Too cold for a boy."

"They say it's so quiet you can hear your blood buzz."

"That's all I need. Already hear everybody else's buzzing. What you trying to do, drive me deaf?"

There was a silence. Then Kirk began with some difficulty to roll a joint. "Think about it is all I'm saying."

"Okay." The TV showed frenzied young people in jeans shooting each other in the head with blow-dryers and laughing hysterically. "Here, let me do that. What the hell'd you do to yourself anyway?"

When the buzzer buzzed, Kirk immediately wished he wasn't so stoned or it was not who he thought it was or it was not necessary to be so constantly reminded of the power of natural events.

"Nona!" said Jeffrey. "Come in. How are you?"

There was a murmuring in the foyer, a murmuring, then Jeffrey brought Nona into the kitchen. "No, she's in St. Thomas until Friday," he was saying. "I thought for sure she'd called you."

"I was hard to get hold of," she answered hoarsely, looking at Kirk. He had turned off the heating pad, he had turned off the television, and, as their eyes met, her wide pupils widened still further to tell him all there was to tell.

"It's bad?" he said.

She nodded.

"What's bad?" Jeffrey almost said, himself a bit more stoned than he'd meant to be. But a preemptive look from Nona froze him. When she sat, fingers plucking vaguely at the knot in her scarf, it was as if, after one last assessment, she had turned her attention away from him forever. "Nona, you shit," he whispered. "You told us it was Friday."

"What they do," she said, "is stick one of their miracle machines down your windpipe and photograph the whole mess from the inside. A lot of blood, but I thought it would be worse." It was not her scarf she was plucking at, Jeffrey saw then, but her throat, the fear and insult there. "Anyway, it turns out there's a whole other tumor that the X rays missed. I saw the pictures."

Kirk extended a hand as if to protect Nona from her words, but it faltered and came of its own volition to rest on her shoulder.

"The doctor said with radiation I have one good year, maybe two." She closed her eyes. "I'm tired of doctors."

"Nona—"

"I'm tired of being *tired!*" She stood up suddenly and seizing Jeffrey's empty glass strode to the sink. Almost no one knew what made the water flow through the pipes, the greater pipes and the lesser pipes, into the fragile homes of men and women. In her hand, beneath the faucet, the glass brimmed. Nona put it down without tasting it and began quietly to cry.

"Nona, Nona, you mustn't shut us out." In his arms she seemed to Jeffrey out of scale with everything else, her body's very ferocity casting doubt upon the relative size and purpose of the refrigerator, of the table, of the chairs and floor. "The reason Lissy left this morning was so she could be back *in time* for this. Why are you so hard on yourself?"

Wiping her eyes, she put her head down on his shoulder, and in a way it was comfortable there. But only in a way. "Up until I was Lissy's age I thought I'd live forever. Then I had her. She *still* thinks she'll live forever."

Kirk turned off the faucet. He was thinking about the library, where that morning he had checked out, in addition to several books on Antarctica, a volume entitled *You Can Win Your Fight Against Cancer*. The man behind him in line had kept looking from the book's cover to Kirk's body and back again; the librarian had smiled at Kirk in a peculiar manner, the security guards had stared at Kirk. "What about that fella who's more than just your partner in backin' the car? I don't guess he's plannin' on livin' forever, too?"

Jeffrey felt her jump. "No, I don't suppose he is," she said, lifting her head. And with that gesture she found that she had exhausted what comfort Jeffrey's arms had offered: she turned away from him. "I'm exhausted," she said. "Do you have a phone number for her down there?"

OUT-OF-THE-BODY TRAVEL

As Jeffrey hands her the telephone, which has been mended with masking tape, Nona begins to cough. Although the pain is considerable, she has decided not to take the Percodan anymore; she now fears numbness more than pain. She dials.

With each successive click, the circuits open into a vaster space until the humming in Nona's ear seems the very sound of limitlessness. Selected sets of neurons begin tentatively to . . . rearrange themselves.

There are seven steps for proper use of the telecommunications network. The first is, hold your ear and mouth against the holes provided. The second is, count your message units. The third is, count your message units. The fourth is, you are not alone now, and the fifth is, this is a recording.

Nona hangs up and immediately dials again.

But consider the moment when, having borne the child successfully into its own life, the mother must staunch the tending impulse, or at very least divert it to a quarter where it will not be recognized for what it is, or was, or might yet again have been. This is the end of a long intoxication, and in its wake comes the hangover. But, after all, what is the number being dialed? being dialed from?

Nona can hear someone else's conversation, very faint and far away. The words *corazón, béisbol, más tarde* are all she can make out before another click annihilates the space and restores the dial tone.

She dials again. The tremor in her hand reminds her of her own mother, dead of a disease long since eliminated by science. She dials again.

Melissa, on the observation deck, closes the last of the galvanized-steel storm shutters just as the rain sweeps in off the cove in sheets. She is instantly drenched. Ehrler and Martin are carrying the Zodiac up from the dock, and when she calls to ask if they need help her words are lost in the wind and spray.

There is a bolt of lightning, a clap of thunder, the lights go out.

The four of them sit in candlelight—Ehrler, Martin, Knolly, Melissa. When she lifts the phone, it's dead.

"No answer?" said Jeffrey.

"Operator says there's trouble with the line." While Nona tried to decide whether she dared call Richard at home, Kirk idly inspected the phone. What the hell they *do* to that damn thing? he wondered for the dozenth time; play soccer with it? When it rang, Jeffrey was removing the pâté from the refrigerator, and it came to him that were it not for the others, with their expectant looks, he would not have answered it.

Handing a butter knife to Kirk, he accepted the charges.

"Jeffrey, you'll never guess where I am."

"I already know *where* you are, Nikki; it's the *why* that's got me." Carrying the phone with him, Jeffrey wandered out into the hall. "And I get the impression Diego has a few questions, too."

Nicole gazed through the glass of the phone booth to the line of artificial orange trees that separated the bar from the dining tables. A *charanga* band was playing. "Why, Jeffrey, don't tell me you never heard the term 'frolic and detour'? I swear I don't know what we're coming to when a girl can't have her little frolic and detour without the whole world having a hissy fit."

"Nikki—"

"Now here I am in the cutest little Cuban bar on Calle Ocho, waiting for poor Auntie Bea to get back from her Junior League meeting, and, why, you'd think the *sky* was going to fall—"

"Nikki, you know you're going to have to tell him sooner or later."

The men at the bar were wearing white shirts, tropical in cut, and their hair glistened with pomade. Nicole studied her short fingernails. "Yes, I know that, Jeffrey."

"He's talking about coming down to get you."

"Of course he is." And, looking up just as the bartender threw open a pineapple with one careless stroke of his machete, Nicole was seized by the enormity of the secret: flesh from flesh. She longed to hold and be held. "And you know I'll probably marry him once I've told him. It'll be sort of a trade-off: I'm not ready to give up my TWA pass and he's not ready to be a papa, but we're none of us getting any younger."

In his mind's eye, Jeffrey saw Clarice sitting down on

the bed with an expectant look, the door to the hotel room swinging shut behind him, the door to an apartment swinging shut behind him. "No," he said. "None of us are."

Nicole turned her back on two men at a nearby table who were making appreciative gestures at her. "What's the matter, Jeffrey?"

"Too much to talk about right now." Crescents were scribbled on the masking tape that held the phone together, but Jeffrey couldn't remember who was responsible: he or Melissa.

"I love you," said Nikki.

"We understand each other," he said. "When are you coming back?"

"That depends." There was silence and the sound of *charanga*, but they were both listening to the silence. "Maybe I could talk to Lissy for a moment?"

"Wrong number, sweet-cakes. She's back in St. Thomas."

"What?" One of the guitarists had begun to sing and Nicole pressed the phone tightly to her ear. "I thought she—"

"So did everybody else. She says it's only for a couple of days. You want the number there?"

She wrote it in pen on her palm, and in the pause that followed he asked her how she felt.

"Except for mornings, wonderful. Just a little tired."

"Travel's tiring."

"Yes," she said. "Travel is."

When she hung up, there were seven quarters in the coin return.

She ate a dried apricot and, inspecting the numbers scrawled across her palm among its stars and lines and fundamental motifs, reflected that destiny was a marvelous thing, one of the best things, almost as good as friendship. Then she dropped a few of the quarters in the slot and called Melissa. After three different kinds of silence, a recording suggested she try again. On her third try, the operator explained there was trouble with the lines.

Nikki sat down at a table near the bar, where she provoked so much congeniality that for a moment she considered returning to the phone booth. Instead, she ordered an apricot nectar, keeping one hand on her suitcase. There were certain things she had never heard Melissa say, such as: When the end of the world comes, when my baby comes, when you come to live with me in a coral-colored house by the oceanside. A man with a beard sat down across from her.

"You are very, very beautiful," he said.

"Yes," she answered, although this was not her opinion. "I am."

Leaving the seven quarters on the table, leaving the man with the seven quarters, Nicole swept out into the humid night where cars ranged up and down the avenue like fish. "I want to go to the airport," she told the cabdriver. Everything was one story tall and strung with lights. She settled back in the seat and tried to imagine what St. Thomas would look like: a place where night closed the flowers.

Melissa, poking with a spoon at the frozen lump she had placed in the pot, said: "Kallaloo. It's a sort of gumbo." The gas burner cast blue light, the candle on the catwalk yellow, and even here in the house the water was roily with sand and bits of palm frond.

"Sounds good," said Martin. He and Ehrler were sitting on either side of the candle, and Knolly, who had by now had ample time to notice and calmly absorb the significance of Melissa's restless toes, sat deeper in shadow.

"It's too bad we don't have a manual bypass for the elevator," said Ehrler, dangling one foot in the water. "Peter could join us."

"If he wanted to," answered Melissa.

The sound of the wind, the sound of the steel shut-

ters banging in the wind, the sound of the surf become
a single steady roar, the sound of the rain and of the
rain flowing from the water catchments on the roof to
the cisterns beneath the flooded house, the distant
sound of the pump: it was as though the sea had turned
itself inside out, and Melissa was suddenly, against her
will, grateful for the company of the three men. She
shivered.

"Maybe a slug of rum would warm you up," said
Ehrler.

Turning down the flame, she walked slowly across
the dry area, spoon in hand, and accepted the bottle.
Outside, the sea cared about nothing. She drank. There
was a movement in the shadows, and when she was
done she held the bottle out toward it.

"Knolly? Some rum?"

He let the candlelight catch the side of his face, but
made no move to look at her. He had seen the woman
climbing out of the jeep with her shoes in her hand; he
had seen her standing barefoot in the bristle grass, smiling to show she was not afraid of him; he had seen her
toes, dancing as if they belonged to another body.

Very gently, still without looking at her, he said,
"No, thank you, white lady." And Melissa handed the
bottle to Martin.

Halfway through the meal, the skylight began to
leak, and Melissa got up to spread a sheet of plastic
over the bed, which hung beneath it. "Tide's still over
two hours from full," said Martin, looking at his watch.
Melissa's reflexes were suddenly so good that when she
accidentally knocked a coffee mug off the bed's built-in
shelf, she caught it before it hit the water.

"You sure you don't want to eat something?" she
asked Knolly, sitting down beside him on the catwalk.

And although he was hungry, he did not know how
to answer her. He had come to believe what the Rastas
said, that eating the dead flesh of any living thing was
ignorance and fantasy, but this belief, like others, made

him edgy. A man could not know what his thoughts might require of him. Knolly looked away from the woman and acted as if something had happened to offend him.

"You know, I saw a funny thing down at Frenchman's Bay last week," said Ehrler, wiping his mouth. Melissa calculated that she had at most forty more hours on the island. "The trawlers were just in, still sorting out their catch, and there was a good-sized crowd waiting to buy. Now, I had always understood that barracuda were no good to eat—parasites, you know—so I wasn't really surprised to see these fishermen just throwing whatever barracuda they had right up on the beach, leaving them for the tide. Well, along comes this old woman with a handful of dimes. She goes up to one of the barracuda, puts a dime in its mouth, and waits. After a while she squats back down, looks at the dime, then picks up the fish and puts it in a bag. She moves on to the next one—another 'cuda, another dime. This time she leaves the fish where it is. It's not long before she's picked out half a dozen barracuda this way, always checking them out with a dime first. When I finally made up my mind to ask her what she was doing, she was gone."

Knolly stood up and, feeling his way with his feet, walked back to the dry area. The story reminded him of the woman he called his aunt—she often collected barracuda in that way—and of himself—he had often eaten the barracuda she collected. Just inside the storage room his fingers touched a flashlight, but he did not turn it on until he had closed the door behind him. His aunt had taught him that the world was full of signs, but what sign was there for the unfairness that was always upon a man?

He shone the light into the far corner where he had hidden his guitar. It was wrapped in burlap and lay across two coils of plastic rope under the cot.

His aunt would say that a woman whose toes danced day and night without her will was not a woman. She was the creature of the jumbie who had possessed her. She was a creature who at night could vomit her intestines into a bowl and fly through the air. She was a creature who at night knew all the languages of the natural world and in the morning knew nothing.

Knolly removed his guitar from under the cot and put it in a better hiding place, high on a shelf. It was modern times now, but a man still did not know what to believe. He switched off the flashlight. When he sat back down near the woman, but not as near as before, she looked at him. Everybody looked at him. The candle guttered.

"M'hear all kind fuckery 'bout barracuda, mon, but I don' have no confusion 'bout dat cas dose ignorances me investigate." He stared hard at the man with the glasses, then at the man who had hired him, then at the woman.

"What ignorances?" said Ehrler, glancing at Melissa to be sure she was listening. She tucked her feet under her and thought: What am I doing here?

"De fish is de fish, mon. Simple ting. Some barra no good ta eat: make ya blind, make ya hair fall away, make ya toot' 'n fingernail fall away. But some barra sweet-sweet, ya know. An' a mon can live on dat fish."

There was a splash, and by the candlelight Melissa could just make out the struggles of a rat that had fallen from one of the electric wires traversing the ceiling. Martin pulled the drawstrings of his hooded sweatshirt tight. "So how do you know which is which?" she said.

"Ya don' hear wha seh. A mon can *live* on dat fish, but him got to take *sign* first." Brushing his dreads out of his eyes, Knolly felt suddenly he was talking too much, mixing too many things together—things the Rastas said, things his aunt said—but he couldn't stop himself. "If de dime come away silver from dat barra mouth, den dat fish someting good ta eat, mon, an' me no care what fantasy talk people have ta seh. But if dat dime change green, den dat fish is corruption an' it make you blind so no medical man can help you. An' *den*, mon, den you die."

Melissa stared at Knolly. She remembered the soft, ruined scent of her mother's breath when she kissed her hello, when she kissed her goodbye. "That's fantastic," said Ehrler. "It must be some sort of enzyme released by the parasite." Martin gave what remained of his meal a slightly stricken look.

"John tells me you also know a lot about dolphins," said Melissa. She had asked the question too abruptly. She was the wrong person to ask the question. It was the wrong question. It was not a question.

Fumbling in his shirt pocket, Knolly removed a spliff and lit it. The woman was making him nervous. "Me an' de dolphin are from creation, an' science was just aroun' some rassclot corner, so what do us need from science?" When he offered the spliff around, no one took it, and Ehrler saw it was time to call it an evening.

Rain fell from a great height onto the deep part of the sea, onto the part of the sea that crashed against the rocks, onto the part of the sea that from the observation deck circulated through the flooded house, onto the trees and sand.

Melissa lay in bed. She had rigged one shower curtain to channel the water from the leaky skylight onto the floor, where it belonged. Clumps of phosphorescent sea-foam drifted slowly around this room, that room, and the other room, finally to disappear down the outflow fixture in one corner. It was very dark.

She thought about Ehrler and Martin, asleep in the dry bunk, and about Knolly, asleep in the storage room. The proximity of their sleep moved her very nearly to tears. Sometimes a person could feel as if she were in a big crowd of people, but without the people, traveling at a terrific speed, but without the speed. Sometimes a person couldn't be sure what it was she loved.

Then, in the darkness, through the keening of the wind and water, there was a sound.

Melissa sat up, put her legs in the water, and listened. She heard the sound.

Her underwater flashlight lay on the shelf, her face mask floated by the bed. 'I wish I could do something about my damn toes, she thought as she set out slowly across the room. The world was water, and everywhere around her water made a different noise. Her legs below the knee were numb. She heard the sound.

Even before she reached the railing around the elevator shaft, the upwelling of spray from the deep pool below had salted her eyes and soaked the top of her leotard. She looked at her watch. It was high tide. She had not turned on the flashlight.

"Peter?" she called down into the black heave and froth.

But there was no answer.

"Peter, are you all right?" she asked.

The world was water and her heart kept a different time. She struggled with the flashlight, its faulty switch. And she heard the sound.

"Peter, I'm right here!"

But the dolphin was patient, mainly; what else if not patient? He had again and again made the sound of the woman's name, he had picked her head out of the darkness now with his sonar, he had dreamed a dry dream in which that which was lost could after all be forgotten: the savor of the far places, the leaps and swims of the dead.

When the cold light came on, he thrust his blowhole from the water to say the woman's name, and Melissa (*trying to sleep, head between two pillows, hears the sound*) was so startled that she dropped the flashlight over the railing into the pool, where it shone a deeper and deeper green as it sank to the bottom.

She wrung her hands. "I'm coming down," she said. The whole pool was faintly illuminated now, and she could see Peter fishtailing about at a great speed. Fearful of hitting him if she jumped, she splashed over to the door of the observation deck, and, leaving the above-water portion of it closed, dived under it, into the storm.

Sheets of rain, salt lash, wind. The smell of sea and torn vegetation.

Wading across the deck to the spiral staircase, Melissa found it possible, in that blackness, to see the horizontal expanse of the cove—its churning, luminous foam—as a vertical wave about to engulf the house. This optical illusion she alternately entertained and dispelled. Her steps rang faintly on the steel stairs.

Her steps rang faintly on the steel stairs. She could hear the waves crashing in on the wave ramp. She put on the mask. Peter soared through green. She dived.

It was as though the violent agitation of the surface were a membrane through which she had passed to a place of great familiarity and quiet. This is how you enter certain rooms, certain embraces, this is what a recollection is. She swam downward, half thinking to retrieve the flashlight, but Peter streaked toward her and they met in the middle depths.

Reaching out to stroke his forehead, Melissa thought: But I forgot to turn on the tape recorders.

GLORIES, BROKEN SPECTERS, ETC.

It is immediately apparent to both of them, though in very different ways, that since the afternoon all of what they know and sense about each other has changed again in import. By noticing this change they have accepted it. Peter explores her fingers gently with his beak, then draws the length of his body quickly across her right palm. She swims a short distance toward him and he repeats the action, this time grazing the whole right side of her body. Melissa is alert, patient without expectation, and she is filled with tenderness both for the dolphin and for the creature she herself has become.

Above and below them are eleven feet of water. At the last possible moment the creature she has become shoots to the surface for breath.

Tumult. The dolphin beside her, on the right.

Is something wrong, Peter?

The sharply rising and falling whistle he emits is new to her. There are fragments of jellyfish in the tossing waters. A wave crashes in, she is stung at the base of the neck, they dive.

Distracted by the wound, Melissa momentarily loses her sense of direction and veers right, crossing Peter's path from above. He barrel-rolls over her, whistling as before, and when he is again on her right, he nudges her shoulder not quite gently with his beak. By the time they reach the bottom it is clear she is to swim only on that side of him.

Melissa does not ask herself what will happen next.

The dolphin tastes the water as they swim part of a circle. Without having to articulate the feeling to himself, he wishes to intervene between all that he has come to understand of the woman and all that he himself feels at what he tastes in the water. The details of her physical being—her hair, her fingers, her fragile limbs—remind him at every turn that there is a way of seeing him to which he can never be party. The desire to protect her and the desire to be seen in this way are indistinguishable. To confirm this, he tastes what is in the water. He shudders. They shoot upward. She is gasping and choking in the salt air.

Peter. You don't know how I've missed you, Peter.

As she lays her hand upon his back, the feeling of

tenderness wells over, making it temporarily impossible for Melissa to separate herself from the creature she has become. Together they dive.

Always, he is on her right. Always, she is aware of being protected, he of being seen in a way that allows him to bear more easily what he tastes in the water. They have made no claims on each other.

What are you protecting me from? she says. And yet she is underwater: she has not said it. Peter's eye meets hers.

It comes to Melissa that she is suffocating.

Two-thirds of the way to the surface, she begins to black out. With one hand she holds on to Peter and with the other, trying to maintain consciousness, she presses the burning red weal left by the jellyfish. They break water, she tears off the face mask.

Of the sounds the dolphin has constantly been making, the only one recognizable to Melissa is her name.

The shore. Melissa in the blackness, in the rain, trying to clear her head.

The wind slackening.

When she sees the figure sitting on the rock, silhouetted against the foam, she hesitates for only a moment before joining him. He stirs slightly at her arrival, then points out over the cove.

Mon, dem get sometin big like dat, dem never ease up! No have no fears, not anywhere.

Melissa is just able to make out a lesser tumult, vaguely circular, in the choppy waters. She hears a faint snapping sound.

I can't see what it is, Knolly.

Shark-dem. Fifty-sixty. An' dem all eat from de same fish.

The surviving whales continue northward past the cove, six days up from the Antarctic and its approaching winter.

The rain stops. Moon amid the clouds. Deserted beach.

* * *

Is it the case that at sunrise when a taxi pulls up before the flooded house and lets Nicole out with her suitcase she lingers for a moment beneath the poison-fish tree wondering whether to wake Melissa now or later? The sky is perfectly blue.

HAVING delivered the children to school, Clarice lingered for a moment at the gate to watch them disappear into their age group: a place she was not needed. Part of the age group was standing about talking and part was running after itself in sneakers that seemed from that distance to have soles of blue translucent plastic. As a test, she tried to imagine herself an old woman; the woman was wearing a hat, a rose, a wedding ring she couldn't push past her swollen knuckle. Then Clarice decided to walk around to the side of the building to see if Jeffrey was visible through the window of the teachers' lounge.

His back was to the glass, and a cup of coffee in his hand. There was a moment for everything and no doubt this wasn't it, but without turning around she could see a phone booth, and she knew the number.

"Hi. It's me. Are you alone in there or is it PTA time?"

"Hang on a sec." He vanished from the window frame and returned. "Sorry. Had to persuade a colleague out of the room. I miss you. I love you. I'm glad you called."

Sitting on the sill, he turned half toward her, but

there was a lot to look at in the city. Clarice put the phone between her ear and shoulder, her hands in her pockets. "Jeffrey, I've had a few thoughts since Monday. On the subject of us, I mean."

She watched him stand up again, plant a foot on what would be the radiator, run a hand through his hair.

"Don't sound so dire," he said.

"That talent isn't in me. Not a trace. It's just I don't think we should see each other anymore."

He didn't move, and for a moment she thought he'd spotted her. "You want that?" he said at last.

"No, darling. You do."

It was odd to see him lighting up a cigarette. She knew that Melissa smoked, and it was true that Jeffrey sometimes came to her, Clarice, with nicotine on his breath. But it was odd to see him with a cigarette.

"I think you'd better run that by me again," he said.

What ran by instead were hotel sheets, hotel pillows. I'm wavering, she thought; no wavering. "Jeffrey. It's even simpler than it seems. Whatever you may tell yourself, the truth is you want more Melissa. I've developed a sense for these things. And what you want you won't find with me. Nobody there but us chickens."

"So you're clipping our wings, is that it?" he said.

"That's it," she said.

"Punching our ticket, huh?"

"Punch, punch."

From her vantage it was impossible to tell whether the sudden movement of Jeffrey's knee, the movement which sent the teachers' lounge geranium plunging from sill to floor, was deliberate or accidental.

"Clarice, why don't you ask *me* what I want?"

"Because you don't know."

"I love you."

"Yes. But I'm right about you and Melissa."

"Are you right about yourself?"

Clarice touched the part of the phone booth that the

morning light had made lustrous: some of it glass, some metal. The woman was wearing a hat, a rose, a wedding ring. "Well, I meant you aren't trying to deny what I'm saying."

"Well, I mean you've got to give me a chance first." The smoke he exhaled against the window mushroomed back about his face. "I need to see you, darling."

"In that case, put out the cigarette, turn your head ten degrees to the right, and look down," she said.

"Oh," he said. She waved, the movement of her hand charging the air between them with a slight crinkle of physical inevitability that seemed to undermine much of what she'd meant. No wavering, she thought.

"No hotels," she said.

"Saturday?" he said. "At my apartment? Lissy'll be at the stock-car races with her mother. We'll have the whole day to ourselves."

Bells rang in the cavernous school building, and after bells, voices. "Jeffrey, it's no good."

"Things are changing, Clarice. You don't even know."

"No, they're not. Yes, I do." She traced a circle in the dirt on the phone-booth glass. "But I'll come on Saturday. Call me when she leaves—two rings, then hang up." He seemed to be trying to open the window. "Bye," she said and, leaving the phone dangling from its cord like a pendulum, walked away.

That woman does have a walk on her, thought Jeffrey, as he watched her go. Hip, slip: out of my life unless I slow things down around here unless I speed them up. He stirred the ribald geranium remains with a foot. Then he tried to call Melissa to tell her about Nona, but her phone was still out of order. What am I going to tell them about Saturday? he wondered. What am I going to tell anybody about anything? The coffee machine was empty, and in a room down the hall the state had once more gathered sixteen ten-year-olds with a view toward his molding them gently into shape. He picked up the sheet of paper he had been reading when Clarice called.

"In the light of recent developments in the Antarctic, the Board of Education has deemed it prudent to have ready a contingency evacuation scenario against the remote possibility of an outbreak of hostilities. Please have your students take home the forms attached so that parents may check the preferred plan: evacuation to the nearest in-city shelter, evacuation to a shelter in one of the outlying counties, or internment of the child at the school until a parent is able to pick him or her up. All forms must be signed by the parent and—"

I'm tired, he decided; that's what they call it, tired. He removed the top of the coffee machine and put the forms inside. Of course it was possible there was something in what Clarice had said, otherwise why hadn't he denied it immediately? And yet and yet.

Jeffrey decided to begin swimming three-quarters of a mile every day, in the afternoons.

While Kirk signed Jeffrey's name to the withdrawal slip, the teller, an interesting-looking black woman with little beads in her hair, complimented him on his change of look. "Now, baby, didn't I always say all you had to do was wear some shit that *fit* for a change? I don't know 'bout that hat but you gonna back your ass halfway into hip you keep it up with those boots and shirt."

"Honey, I do it all for you," said Kirk, hog-tying the drawl since it was hard to know whom his brother hugged or whether she was about to have a coffee break. Then she gave him several hundred dollars of Jeffrey's money and he drove, in Jeffrey's BMW, to the airport, where he bailed Diego out of jail.

"Ah, thank you, *hombre*. You are your brother's brother." Diego was looking a bit wrinkled as the desk

sergeant signed him out, and it was true these new airport jails had a reputation. Outside, the brilliant day
was full of microwaves and jets.

"Sure you got all the pieces now?" asked Kirk.

"The pieces?" Diego held his forehead with both
hands as he walked. "Only one of them I am missing.
Solamente uno, uno, uno."

They wandered about for some time on the parking
grid, thinking about the piece Diego meant and looking
for the BMW, which Kirk had momentarily mislaid.
Was it blue or sort of orange? Then they sped toward the
variously inclined city.

"Well, Diego? I mean I could turn on the damn radio
or somethin', but that was a fair bit of cash that Jeff
don't even know I took."

Without releasing his forehead, Diego used an elbow
to nudge the sun visor toward mercy. "Shit, man. Isn't
there any fucking aspirin in this fucking car?"

Kirk gave him a look. Diego settled back in his seat
and closed his eyes. "Okay, okay. So I'm going to
Miami to get her. I got my ticket, everything. I decide
to have a few drinks while I'm waiting for the plane,
and while I'm drinking I begin to have ideas. So I get
up and I call her aunt in Miami. It is eleven o'clock at
night, okay? Her aunt takes fifteen minutes to wake up.
Fifteen! That's a lot of quarters, man. And when she
finally comprehends what it is I am asking she says she
has not heard from Nikki in six months: no phone
call, no letters, no Nikki."

The BMW hit a pothole. Diego contemplated his lap,
where a can of windshield defroster had arrived. "So
the last thing I remember, man, I am smashing my stool
against the bar, and I am thinking of what it's like to be
a fool."

Kirk grinned. "Come to any conclusions I should
know about?"

To get a good look at Kirk without dropping his

hands, Diego had to tilt his face slightly upward. "Yeah, *hombre*. Now that you mention it, maybe I did."

Outside the electronics store, while Kirk used some more of Jeffrey's money to buy a telephone-answering machine, Diego tried to read the front page of the newspaper. A few countries had accused the United States of violating the Antarctic Treaty. It was not okay to produce plutonium at the McMurdo nuclear plant, they said. The BMW was double-parked, and when a policeman walked toward it, Diego drove it around the block. Kirk was waiting on the sidewalk with his package. Back at Jeffrey and Melissa's, hundreds of Styrofoam peanuts fell out of it. Diego ate some aspirin.

"Melissa's mother," he asked, "she's staying here?"

"Did last night. How'd you—"

Diego held up a child-proof bottle with an orange label.

"Yeah. She tested bad yesterday. Said she didn't want any more truck with that Percodan shit now she knows she's dying. Now she knows the doctors know." He stood up, switched on the answering machine, and slapped the butt of the screwdriver into his palm. "What kind of conclusions?"

Their eyes met and Diego sank into the nearest available chair. Its upholstery resembled the late paint rags of Claude Monet. Diego, for the first time all morning, was smiling.

"When I said to you in the nightclub that Jefe was a *guerrillero*—"

"I'm not real sure I knew what you had in mind, Diego. Whyn't you run it by me again."

"What Jefe wants is the future—not *his* future but *the* future. And because he wants a thing so big and far away, what he really wants is to want, no?"

Kirk leaned his back against the wall and slid slowly to a sitting position. "Yes," he said.

Diego smiled. "So Melissa is perfect."

They considered the idea of Melissa's perfection for a moment, then Diego added: "Now what I want you to know is I am a different kind of fool. I am not a *guer-rillero*. If I cannot get Nicole to marry me, if I cannot make her cut that pass to pieces with the scissors, then it is finished, I know that now, I do not want to be so alone in my life."

Kirk nodded. He was thinking about the Ice, as Antarctica is sometimes known. When Diego tossed the Percodan bottle up in the air, Kirk watched it tilt slowly over and fall toward his own opened hand.

In the park, Kirk explained that the two greatest enemies of the Antarctic photographer were the extreme cold, which made the film brittle, and the high level of static electricity, which could scar a whole roll of film in an instant if you rewound it too quickly. Then he put on three pairs of gloves and took Diego's picture, being careful not to touch the camera to his cheek. "Burn your damn skin right off in this kind of cold," he said. Because of his head, Diego tried not to laugh. Kirk winked. His hands in the gloves were twice the size of ordinary hands. Diego began to laugh. Kirk began to laugh. You had to advance the film millimeter by millimeter, and there were thirty-five of them per frame. Diego was in hysterics, gasping for air. Blind with laughter, Kirk bumped into a woman in shorts and caused her to drop the ice-cream cone she'd bought.

"But I mean you really are in love with her, aren't you?" asked Kirk.

"Oh, man, crazy in love. Crazy. She burns my skin right off me, *hombre*."

As they made their way south through the park, Kirk shot one whole roll of film with his gloves on and began another. In a sense he wasn't lonely but in another sense he was. He tried to remember the last time he had become so quickly involved with a group of people. His hands were very hot in the six gloves, and his shoulder still hurt from rolling out of the airplane. Diego was explaining that his mother believed the souls of the dead resided comfortably on other planets. She still talked every Sunday to his dead father.

"That scare you?" asked Kirk.

"No, man. That doesn't scare me."

"What scares you?"

Diego looked around. They were at the south end of the park. There were hotels across the street. A man was trying to touch everything. "I don't know."

Every time Kirk took a picture, he could see his gloves out of the corner of his eye because of the distance between his cheek and the camera. It was becoming annoying. He focused on Diego, then deepened the focus to take in the sidewalk cafe across the street. His heart flexed.

Nona sat drinking magenta on the rocks, one hand enfolded in the hand of a man in a gray-on-gray suit, and light was falling obliquely over them, car exhaust swirling up before them, and he was listening and she was talking and talking and talking.

"Click," said Kirk. And turned away.

When Ehrler came to tell her she had a visitor, Melissa, peering at his silhouette through the shower curtains, thought for one drowsy moment that he meant himself. Then she remembered it was not last month, it was this month. She stepped out of bed into the sparkling water with its particles of palm frond and sand. The electric clock had stopped; she remembered why. Visitor? she thought.

In the dry area she smelled tuberose. The sun shone through the screen door in such a way that she could not see who was sitting there, on the suitcase.

"Lissy, I swear I don't know why you can't keep the phones working on this two-by-four little island."

"Nikki!" Melissa's hand opened the door. "You insane creature! What are you *doing* here? *What*?" They embraced. "Tell me!" Her voice was louder than she intended.

"Aren't you glad to see me?"

She had never seen Nicole look so radiant, so self-possessed. A tiny green fly orbited her head and was gone. "Yes," Melissa whispered, shooing it away even so. "Yes, I am."

They walked arm in arm along the shore, the cove's glittering waters littered with copra husks and mangrove radicles. Melissa admired Nikki's necklace, and Nikki, all the while talking trash about Miami, took the necklace off and put it on her. They kissed. She even walks differently, thought Melissa, and lit a cigarette. There were little flecks of foam on everything. There were little dots of water.

"Anyhow, Jeffrey sounded kind of funny when I talked to him in Miami," Nicole went on. "Are you two fighting?"

"I think so, yes." She was keeping an eye out for whale bones.

"Well, that's dumb. What about?"

"This, I guess."

Nicole unhooked her sunglasses from the neckline of her carmine dress and put them on. " 'This'?"

"The dolphin. The project. The way I spend my time."

"He's jealous?"

"No, not exactly." She fingered the necklace. "Sometimes I even think he has a higher tolerance for my work than I do and that I push myself just to—" She smiled at Nikki, then shrugged, letting go the necklace. "But that's not really how it is." They parted briefly to avoid an overturned horseshoe crab that lay twitching in their path. Melissa flung it back into the water by its tail. "He thinks I'm becoming inhuman," she said. "Sometimes I think that, too. Mostly I don't. So we fight."

They both realized at the same moment that Melissa was trembling. She made no attempt to hide it. "Not that it helps much to know he's having an affair."

"Oh, Lissy, what does it matter? He loves you. Don't torment yourself."

Melissa stopped short in surprise at what Nicole had said, and Nicole did, too. She still had on her sunglasses, and they stared at each other. There was a lot of seaweed around. They began to laugh.

"Nikki, you know what? You're changing."

Nicole was beautiful. "Am I?" she said. Then she vomited behind a rock. Melissa asked her if she was okay and she said she was. While she rinsed her mouth out with seawater, they laughed some more. Nicole spit some water straight up into the air and got out of the way. They walked.

"Wait a minute," said Melissa, cocking an ear to the part of the cove they couldn't see from where they were. They were halfway back to the house. "That sounds like the—" By the time they rounded the promontory, Ehrler had already killed the engine on the Zodiac and seemed to be peering over the gunwales at a spot Knolly was pointing out with the grappling hook. The slight pitching of the craft, the concentration of the two men, the colorless glitter of the water—all served by their very timelessness to remind Melissa how little time left she had on the island.

"What're they doing, Lissy?"

"There's a whale carcass out there," she said simply. "They've found it."

At the house, she took Nicole down to the deep pool to meet Peter. He was amusing himself by herding together the various fishes that had been washed in by the storm, then splitting the school in two and running one part through the other. "I feel as if I'm introducing one half of my life to the other," said Melissa, scrutinizing Nicole for signs of nervousness. There were no signs. "You are," said Nikki. She does look lovely in that dress, thought Melissa, in that color. And for a tonic instant Melissa imagined herself swaddling her toes, which had not ceased wiggling, in its carmine folds. Then Peter burst, amid a storm of sea droplets, into the air before them.

"That's your name, Lissy! He said your name!"

He arced back down to the water and looped around again, thrusting his head above the surface to inspect them, first from one eye, then the other.

"Peter, this is my friend Nicole."

Nicole wished to know if he understood what Melissa had said, and Melissa said she thought so, in a way, whereupon Peter directed a stream of water at Nikki, soaking her dress, and she a stream of giggles at him, which he mimicked, and Melissa resisted the temptation to dive into the pool.

"Nikki, it's the same old story. Wherever you go, you're the center of attention."

"Why, Lissy *honey*," she said, leaning toward her in mock concern, "Fiddledeedee! Don't you know it's just my tits?"

They were still laughing when the wall of water which Peter had caused to hurtle from his plenum into theirs crashed over them both, but mostly over Nikki, so that she was nearly thrown off the rock ledge and into the pool.

"Peter, you shithead! You're frightening Nicole!" Melissa tried to bat him on the beak but missed. "You know better than that. *I'm* the only one you can frighten!"

But Nikki, when Melissa turned to her, did not seem unduly upset; she didn't seem upset at all. "A little water," she said. "What's that to me?"

Melissa regarded Nikki's unquenched glow. "He's trying to get you into the pool. He wants to swim with you." Nicole returned the look, and her smile went gradually abstract.

"What's he doing now?" she asked, turning back

toward him. Melissa turned, too, and their shoulders touched, remained touching. Peter had positioned himself in front of Nicole and, with his head well out of the water, his mouth slightly open, appeared to be nodding at her: long, slow scanning movements.

"He's checking you out with his sonar. That's what the creaking noise is; dolphins identify everything that way, and they're fantastically accurate."

Nicole looked down at their toes, twenty of them altogether, ten twitching almost imperceptibly. "Well, maybe later on I will," she said. "Swim with him, I mean. But not now." When she looked up, she was smiling again. "Besides, don't you and water baby here eat breakfast?"

From the top turn of the spiral staircase, Melissa could see Ehrler's head bobbing alongside the Zodiac, Knolly leaning toward it over the stern to listen.

Nicole changed into jeans and blouse, then lay down on Ehrler's bunk without buttoning the jeans. She put one hand on her stomach and the other around an apricot. "Is that all you want?" asked Melissa, bringing cereal. Nicole wanted to know whether Melissa was going through with the three-month live-in.

"I'm beginning to think so," she answered, sitting down on the edge of the bunk. "It depends on Nona. On how her tests turn out on Friday."

"What about Jeffrey?"

"I don't know. What about Diego?"

"I don't know." Nicole inspected the apricot, still unbitten. "I might marry him."

A few Rice Krispies leaped from Melissa's suspended spoon to her lap. "Marry him?"

"Why not? He loves me, he's dying to have me, travel's tiring."

Melissa put her bowl on the floor and stretched out beside Nicole on the bunk. " 'Marry him,' " she said experimentally to herself. Then she studied Nicole. "Does he know you're here?"

"No," said Nicole.

Out on the cove, the Zodiac had started up, the sound of its outboard coming to a slow crescendo as it returned. Melissa asked Nikki if she was chewing gum and, when Nikki nodded, held out an ashtray. The gum was not green; they laughed. "You won't marry him," said Melissa, getting up, and Nicole bit into the apricot.

From the observation deck, Melissa watched Ehrler tying up at the dock. "Baleen," he shouted when he saw her. "Nothing left of him." There was a flash at Knolly's throat as he stepped out of the Zodiac, and Melissa was sure he hadn't been wearing that bit of mirror the day before. As a child, she had sometimes for safekeeping put in her mouth the dime her father had given her for the ice-cream man; she distinctly remembered drying it on her skirt at the sound of his approach. "Nothing at all?" she said when Ehrler, alone now, reached the top of the staircase.

"A little bone and cartilage," he answered. "Must have been quite a scene."

"It was. I could tell something was going on but I wouldn't have known what if Knolly hadn't pointed it out."

"You mean explained it."

"No, I mean pointed it out." And she described Peter's behavior of the night before, from the moment he summoned her till the moment she crawled exhausted from the pool to find Knolly watching the sharks. She omitted only the carelessness by which she had nearly drowned.

"So Peter was treating you like a woman and a dolphin at the same time."

Melissa waded a short distance across the deck so that she could look at him from there. "Well . . . yes." It was evident to them both, though in slightly different ways, that he had said something interesting. "I hadn't thought of it quite that way, but, yes, of course. He kept saying my name, and yet he also kept giving me that rising-and-falling whistle business. Insisted I stay in protective formation, but knew when I needed to breathe."

Ehrler drew a hand through his hair, which the salt-water had made peculiar-looking. "Anything else?"

"Only what I've told you." She was trying to decide how to tell him what her own feelings had been, but there were too many of them. She repeated in a lower voice what she'd just said.

"This is the last time I'll mention it," said Ehrler, rubbing the back of his neck, "but I think it would be tragic if we had to abandon the project now. For all the reasons you know."

Melissa had no reply.

"I mean, if he really accepts you both as a human being and a dolphin—"

Melissa nodded, continued to look at him. She had no reply.

Halfway across the deck on his way to join Martin in the electronics room, Ehrler turned around again. "Oh, one more thing I wanted to ask you. Were there other whales last night or just the one?"

"We only saw the one, but it was very dark out there."

Ehrler began, as he waded on, to swing the face mask in a lazy arc that just grazed the water. "Yes. Because the thing of it is, if the migrations have already started, they're coming up early this year."

Melissa stood there fingering the necklace Nicole had given her. Then she went down to the deep pool and spent two more hours trying to teach the dolphin English. He behaved the same at high tide as at any other time, she decided; it was the *phase* of the moon that mattered. When she came back upstairs, there was still no electricity. Ehrler and Martin were sorting computer parts by the window of the electronics room, and Nikki was floating around the deck, face up on an air mattress.

"Lissy, I never knew you had such patience," she said. Her eyes were closed.

"You were listening?"

"It was incredible. All those repetitions. You'd make a wonderful mother."

There were ropes at the head of the mattress, and Melissa began towing Nikki in a slow circle. "Would I?"

"Absolutely. Hey, Lissy?"

"Yes?"

"Is it okay that I came?"

"Why? Is John being pissy? I didn't think he'd say anything now that I've got him so obviously over a barrel."

"No, no. I mean is it okay with you?"

One of the things about the heat of the day was that all the birds stopped singing, all the birds pretty much at once. "Well . . . yes. Of course it is, Nikki. It's just—I mean, there's a lot on my mind. I've never shared this part of me with anyone before." She pulled the air mattress in a tighter circle and let go, so that Nicole spun slowly away from her. "And how come you look so terrific?"

Nikki rolled off the mattress into the water and all the lights came on in the house. "We're on again!" Martin shouted through the window, but it was hard to hear what else was being said, because the radio was turned up so loud the dubwise bass rattled the speaker. Melissa felt something on her ankles: Nicole. Then they were both underwater. Melissa tried to laugh. That humming sound was very familiar, but what was it? Nicole didn't know how to laugh underwater either. Marry him? thought Melissa. When they surfaced, the radio had been turned off and Melissa remembered that what hummed was Peter's elevator, which was no longer out of commission.

"What's a little water to me?" she said to Nicole,

who was laughing, and Nicole suggested that among other things it was one way for her, Melissa, to get torn-up palm frond in her hair. Melissa shook her head like an animal. Then Peter came rushing out of the house onto the deck, squawking and squealing.

"How'd he get up here?" asked Nikki, touching his forehead. She was kneeling in the water and Melissa was too.

The only part of Peter not submerged was the tip of his dorsal fin, and he was pointing his beak right at Nicole, right at her stomach. He's totally ignoring me, thought Melissa. "That creaking is his sonar again," said Nikki. "Right?"

Melissa began to explain that since dolphins live in a medium whose density and sound velocity are comparable to those of their own bodies, they can presumably use their sonar as a kind of X ray to see *into* one another's body, perhaps to diagnose—

"Nicole!" Melissa was standing beside her in the knee-deep water. "You're still pregnant, aren't you?"

Nicole's eyes focused on her. Their look was that of a woman totally confident that, for better or for worse, she had just become incapable of being misunderstood. The tears which filmed them an instant later did nothing to disrupt this look.

"You never *had* the abortion, did you?"

Nicole shook her head. The dolphin's beak waved gently up and gently down, two inches from her womb.

"And that's why Peter—" One of Melissa's hands had wandered to her own abdomen, and she looked curiously down at it, then down at the dolphin, then again at Nicole. "Why didn't you *tell* me? Does Diego know?"

"Not yet." Water fell away from her as she stood. "Jeffrey's the only one I've told."

"Jeffrey!"

"I called you from L.A., Lissy, but you weren't there and he was."

"Jeffrey's *known* all this time?" She took a half step backward just as the dolphin swam between Nicole's legs, knocking her into a stagger from which Melissa reflexively rescued her. "He's *known?*"

"But that's why I've come here now, Lissy: to tell you myself. To tell you my news myself."

When Melissa let go of Nikki's upper arm there were red marks where her fingers had been. "Too late for that now," she said. "Peter's beat you to the punch." Her tone was petulant.

"Lissy, don't be angry with me, I love you."

"I'm hurt, not angry. Diego's the one who's going to be angry."

"I can handle Diego."

"Can you handle me?" The words seemed to have been given to her, their meaning to reside in repeating them. "Can *you*, for a change, handle *me?* That's what I want to know. That's what I've—"

Peter slammed the water with his flukes. The rain of variously sized droplets, as it caught the sun, suggested other possibilities, and Peter burst into a long string of humanoid sounds, suggesting other possibilities, and Nicole did not lean down to touch him as he drew himself slowly across her calves.

"Lissy? When I got to L.A.?"

"Yeah?"

"The first thing I did was rent this gigantic red car. I'd been thinking about it all during the flight, and I knew exactly what I wanted—how it should look, how it should handle, even how it should smell. 'A family-sized sedan' is what they called it at the rental agency, and that was perfect. So I buckled my little ass right in."

Melissa, as she listened, sat down in the middle of the air mattress; the ends lifted bluntly up on either side like wings.

"Until then I hadn't even thought twice about the abortion. But the more I drove, the more I felt I'd come there just to be in that car. I mean I delivered the costumes okay, saw some friends, all that. But, face it, what I really wanted to do was drive up and down, beating stoplights one after another in a car that could have held six people."

She smiled faintly at Melissa. Her breathing was labored; it was to catch her breath that she had paused. "Well . . . nobody's perfect, Lissy. Sometimes I'm slow to get my own messages. I mean, every day just goes so fast—one right after another. I hardly ever think about it."

Melissa was aware that her own silence was ungenerous; equally, that she could do nothing yet to undo it. The dolphin circled widely about the two of them.

"Well," said Nikki, and now there was a hint of anger, "we're not getting any younger, you know."

When Melissa stood, the air mattress shot away behind her. She imagined herself putting kohl around Nikki's brown eyes; she imagined herself talking and talking. "Nikki, I'm sorry, I just—"

The water between them, the plastic feed bucket floating in the corner, the families of spindly palms and bushes beyond, the sky, the cove, the biting flies, the farther islands—everything but the dolphin himself, now falling laconically back to the water on his side, now doing it again, seemed suddenly to be as it was by virtue of the pounding of their two hearts.

Melissa found Ehrler in the electronics room.

"I've decided to go through with the live-in," she heard herself tell him.

In one hand he had a number of solenoids and in the other a screwdriver. He put everything down to see what she meant. "Can we count on that? I mean, you may have some rough times ahead with your mother and—"

"Even so. I've made up my mind, John."

They embraced, and Martin, who had just looked up, looked away. For a moment everyone listened to the lawn mower: it was working well, from the sound of it. Then Melissa went back out to the deck to talk to Nicole about having babies. Was the sick every morning? Did she have crying jags? Fits of euphoria? Did it matter to her whether it was a boy or girl? What sort of dreams did she have? What physical sensations? Had she had herself checked for signs of information sickness? Was she more in love with Diego than before? Less? Did she believe in the future more than before? Less? Was she ever afraid?

When the phone rang and Martin leaned out the window to tell Melissa it was for her, Nicole pulled her feet up on the air mattress. Peter gave up nipping at her toes and flipped her over into the water instead. Not that I'm afraid, thought Nicole as she waded over to the spiral stairs, but if his sonar can really go right through me like that—

In the front yard, Knolly stood by the lawn mower drinking grapefruit juice. He watched her as she approached, and when she asked him what the mirror shard around his neck meant he hesitated. She saw that he was tired; she saw also, as he slowly drained the glass, that her question had embarrassed him.

"Is no big ting, nuh." He let the hand holding the glass fall to his side; he let embarrassment be masked by irritation. "Eh-eh, why you don' leave a mon do his work?"

"Sorry, I just—"

But he stopped her as she turned. "Me jus' know dat dere some eye aroun' dat don' like t'see demselve, ya know wha mean?" He touched the mirror, his own eyes fixed on hers. "An dat kind uh fuckery, dat obeah fuckery na can't—"

Melissa flung open the screen door. "Nikki!" She was running. "That was Jeffrey. I've got to go back!"

Nona wouldn't name her perfume when Richard, in the hotel elevator, inquired, because that morning she had at the last moment chosen Melissa's in preference to her own. I'll never understand what it means when she blushes like that, Richard decided. The room had a view of the park; the park's forking paths a way of touching off in Nona memories better left untouched. She tossed her skirt and underwear toward a chair, but they fell short; she unbuttoned her blouse without removing it.

Could she really have grown still slenderer since Monday? He could not be sure.

Had he always been so careful to hang up his suit as soon as he'd removed it? She could not remember.

Did she really, after all her insistence that he skip work, have something to tell him that would not be told by the touch of his hand here, here, and here? It was her unpredictability he loved.

In bed Nona had always surprised him with a bodily fleetness and vulnerability which afterward he would invariably remember as fierce and which, even in returning to her, he could never quite believe had again been entrusted to him. Now, as they sat upon the bed's edge, her lips avoided his, but so deftly he imagined he imagined it. She kissed his skin as he undid her gray and graying hair, as he undid her bra, and imagining suddenly that she might taste herself in his stirring, she took his cock into her mouth.

There was the movement of her breasts falling free, dipping to and fro.

There was the movement of his legs as he brought them up onto the bed and lay back, of hers as she swung slowly around to straddle his head with her thighs.

There was the movement of the years, which had thrown them together for a while, apart for a while, together for a while, creasing their flesh in the places where life had unaccountably been lived the most.

He had forgotten to remove his watch.

She had forgotten to remove his wedding ring.

The weakness that was always with her now warmed
and mixed with the other weakness, once familiar, and
had it not been for the sound of her own breathlessness
she might also have forgotten to remove her mouth,
herself from his mouth . . .

He rose, turned, entered her.

"Sweetest."

FREUD'S BULLDOG

Nona and Richard are lying side by side on the bed,
their damp bodies abandoned, his cock slowly slackening in her hand. There are magenta flowers on the
dresser, and a slight hum which in a moment Richard
will locate as coming from the television. Until now, it
has occurred to neither of them to turn down the bed.
As she does so, her hair brushes his shoulder without
tickling him.

It is noon. Richard discovers he does not care that he
is assistant commissioner of mass transportation for the
State of New Jersey. He chuckles. His mind is teeming
with the dates of trysts not yet arranged. A house acquired for the purpose. A divorce.

And yet it is once again true that their lovemaking
has not lasted forever. Nona investigates each instant
with the thought that surely this will be the one in
which she tells Richard she is dying. Now I will do it,
she thinks. No, now. This time. This.

She kisses him and tastes herself. What does he
taste? she wonders, reviewing the dozens of times her
mouth has evaded his in the last hour. And thinking
then of Freud's bulldog, she begins to laugh.

She has seen photographs of Freud's study; it is there
that her mind recasts the anecdote. Freud, exhausted,
cancerous, sits down upon his famous couch at the end
of the day, at the end of his life. Enough of the Vic-
torian age is yet preserved for his study still to be dec-
orated in that manner—warm, dark, soft. He is alone.
He picks up a sheaf of black-and-white photographs;

they are not like memories; he puts them down. The pain in his jaw is very bad tonight and he considers that life on the frontiers of human consciousness is not all it's cracked up to be. A man can learn everything there is to know about people wanting to sleep with their parents yet still be alone at the end of the day. And where is his bulldog Fritz?

He calls Fritz. Fritz, who adores him, whom he adores, gets up from the corner where he has been sleeping. He walks to within ten feet of Freud, then sits, looking at him.

Fritz! Come here.

But Fritz will come no closer.

Puzzled, Freud gets up and goes over to the dog. Fritz looks up warily. Freud bends down. What's the matter, Fritz? But as he speaks he coughs and the dog bounds away. It dawns on Freud that Fritz cannot bear the foulness of his master's injured breath, and indeed the dog never again comes close enough to Freud to be touched. Friends will later write that Freud was heart-broken at this desertion, but Nona, because of the absurd aptness of the anecdote, is laughing. She looks at Richard, who looks puzzled. She laughs harder. He touches her shoulder. Nona roars with laughter, she is choking with it, she is hysterical.

But none of this is true. Those are tears. She is weeping.

Richard, I have cancer. I'll be dead in two years.

Jeffrey stopped rubbing his eyes, which the chlorine had made very red. Then he drove to the airport to meet Melissa's plane. She had not mentioned anything about Nicole, but he had long ago learned never to be surprised at what plane Nikki got off and with whom. The pliancy of Melissa's kiss surprised him. The red-ness of Jeffrey's eyes surprised her. Can he have been weeping? she wondered, slightly panicked. When he kissed Nicole, both he and Nicole recalled her asking, exactly a week ago, exactly here, if he thought they would ever have an affair. Jeffrey said something, and Melissa, her left ear still congested from the plane's descent, said, "What?"

"I said there are an awful lot of military people here, don't you think?"

"Soldiers in airports, fish in water. Is Nona—"

"Out at the house. She's expecting us."

Nikki saw the way Melissa was biting her lip and Jeffrey saw the way Nikki was hesitating. He took her bag. "You come too," he said.

"Are you sure? Really, I can get a cab . . ."

But Melissa insisted. She and Jeffrey exchanged a look and Jeffrey said, "The necklace looks lovely on you."

She accepted the compliment and the observation it implied. It was like a moment of peace. As they walked toward the sliding glass doors, Melissa leaned across Nikki and, miming confidentiality, said to Jeffrey, "I think you're being paranoid about the soldiers." But that was not at all what any of them thought.

Nikki sat in the front seat and the country-music station played a song about driving around in pickup trucks whose beds had been illegally converted to giant gas tanks. For many minutes there seemed to be nothing to say. Even the smell of car exhaust was comforting. Then Jeffrey recounted something that had happened at school that day: a divorced father had tried to kidnap his own child, Jeffrey had had to intervene physically, the police had been called—unnecessarily, as it turned out, since the man had left before they arrived. Nikki wanted to know if Jeffrey had been scared. "I was angry," he answered. Melissa's left ear still seemed to be hearing everything from a great distance. She held up Diego's court summons, which she had found on the backseat, and said, "What's this?"

Nicole read aloud relevant portions of the document.

Jeffrey suggested the date of issue was also a relevant portion. "It's dated today," said Nikki.

There was a short silence while they traveled some additional kilometers. Then Melissa said: "Do you think he knows?"

Jeffrey's eyes met hers in the rear-view mirror and Nikki put a hand on his leg, the tender part just above the knee. "How could he?" answered Jeffrey, still looking at Melissa. Nikki gave his knee a squeeze, and when Melissa swallowed, her ear popped clear. At exactly the same time, for just a moment, they all smiled: it was as though they had celebrated Nikki's pregnancy.

SECOND RETURN POSTURE

There are trees, it is dark. Jeffrey is driving well, although at first the improved air quality made him sleepy. As they round a hill, the county art depot comes into view. Half a dozen semi-trailers are backed up to the floodlit loading platform, where men with hand trucks and hydraulic trundles pack the cavernous vehicles to road weight. Stacked bales of art await their attention—incredibly sophisticated arrangements of nothing in particular. Maybe the best arrangement would be for Nikki and Melissa to stay out at Nona's for a few days, thinks Jeffrey. All day long, in his mind's eye, Clarice has been walking away from the phone booth, the phone has been a pendulum. Are they asleep? he wonders. But by the light of a passing car he can see they are not asleep, they have both assumed full Möbius position, also known as single-surface posture, also known as second return posture. He switches off the radio, more static than song now. They are practicing Klein bottle-breathing as well.

Inside and outside slowly become a single surface.

He is thinking about the soldiers.

He drives.

Who do you love.

* * *

Every light in Nona's house was on, even those in rooms where no one ever went, and for some seconds the three of them sat there in the car contemplating all that illumination. Then Melissa pulled herself together: it would not be calm to let anyone know she had agreed to the live-in project, she decided, opening her door. Jill's shellfish-shaped sports car was parked by the gate. Melissa tried to keep the irritation off her face, but Jeffrey saw it anyway, by the porch light. The dogs came running around the side of the house, barking and wagging.

"I'm so glad you've come," said Jill, opening the door for them, and it was evident from the grip she had on her glass that she was. "Why don't you . . . I mean, we're . . . in the other . . ."

Melissa hurried past her, and when Jeffrey did not follow and Nicole stood there looking at Jeffrey, Jill sat down on the stairs. "Shit," she said. And drained her glass.

Because Nona was splendid. Melissa embraced her, confusedly scenting traces of her own perfume, and for a moment she did not know what to say. Because Nona was splendid.

"I'm drunk," said Nona. But that was not it.

"Jeffrey told me what the doctors said and I took the first plane I could. Did they—"

"I'm dying," Nona said.

They were sitting on the edge of the sofa holding hands. The sofa, five times recovered, was as old as Melissa, but didn't look it. The room itself was more than half as old as the country, but didn't look it. Nona was actually dying.

"Why?" Melissa asked.

She'd actually asked why.

Nona'ns eyes became almost amused and the hand not holding Melissa's reached out to touch the tears on Melissa's cheeks. Then the hand poured Melissa a drink. "You know, Jill said a funny thing about you the other day. She said she'd never seen you scared. 'Angry maybe, but not scared.' That's what she said."

Melissa said nothing.

In a quieter voice Nona said, "Do you know why all the lights are on in this house?"

Melissa nodded.

"Why are they?"

It was becoming hard for Melissa to look at her. "Because you're scared."

"That's right. And what am I scared of?"

"The dark," Melissa answered shyly. Nona nodded. Each knew the other was thinking about the moon-shaped nightlight Melissa had always insisted must be turned on by Nona and no one but Nona. At the window screens a few months beat themselves softly senseless.

The rest was brief and to the point.

"I never understood why he left me," Nona said. "I never understood why he left me." She looked at Melissa, whose widened eyes had no other place to look but back; Nona sighed and sat back deeper into the sofa. "Oh, I had plenty of time to rummage through our marriage in my head, lots of restless nights to think my way through A, B, C, D, E—and really I'm a very bright lady, I catch on quickly, you'd be surprised . . . But I never understood why he left me."

She looked at the place on the sofa where her hand clasped Melissa's. She looked at Melissa. "And what did you know about it? You thought we'd been hiding our problems from you for years. What problems? I *let* you think that. It was less embarrassing than the truth: that the marriage was happy, that there were no warnings, that you can live with someone for more than twenty years and end up knowing nothing, *I mean really nothing*, about that person.

"Because I never understood why he left me," she said and flung, while Melissa sat there on the sofa breathing, her empty glass across the wide, wide room to the hearth, where it shattered with a rueful, tiny tinkle.

There were crickets somewhere. And Melissa could not take her eyes off her mother because she had never before seen someone's skin smolder like that exactly; that is, she had never before heard her mother explain herself; that is, she wanted to know where she fitted in. But saying anything was beyond her.

"I've started seeing Richard again," said Nona in a tone that held nothing of bitterness. "It used to scare me how good it was between us—as if I was the only one in the world who knew more than I let on. But it's different now . . . Promising—if that's the word." She shrugged. It was the word. "So today I told him."

"You told him?" said Melissa helplessly.

"He was flattered, I think. At how I let myself go and at how obvious I made everything." Nona ran a few fingers through her hair's abundant and good-looking grayness. "Of course, there's no point in complaining, is there. I there? But I wish I'd spent more of my life being obvious."

Music came on loudly from another part of the house and was turned off almost immediately: some of that new music with rhythms too complex for the ear to seize upon. Melissa could hear Jill's whispered voice, Nicole's; but the footsteps were Jeffrey's.

"Let me stay with you a while," she said.

"That would be lovely."

"A couple of days. Until the race maybe."

"Yes."

In the distance the dogs had found something to bark about. "Was Richard . . ."

"Scared? I don't know, he didn't show it."

"We'll have melon for breakfast and the days together. A picnic on the afternoon of the race."

"That would be lovely."

"It will be obvious."

"Could you reach behind you and tilt that light out of my eyes?"

Jeffrey put Melissa's suitcase on the bed upstairs while Jill and Nicole put themselves in chairs by the window. Then Nicole saw he had brought her suitcase up, too. The backs of her thighs hurt from sunburn. Jill studied the ceiling, trying to determine how many squirrels were scrabbling around up there, in the attic. Of course, it wasn't very nice to hope her own children wouldn't turn out like Melissa, but that was what she was thinking as she stared at the ceiling and tied her scarf around her hair in a slightly different way.

"You must be exhausted," Jeffrey said to her. "Don't feel you have to stay the night."

"No," she said, flushing. "All right. I'll play it by ear."

Jeffrey waited to see if her ear was going to suggest some sort of hit-the-road music, but she continued to sit there underneath the ceiling, so he spoke to Nikki anyway.

"Let me talk to Diego and find out what's going on before you let him know you're back."

"Diego? Why, he's just a little aggravated is all. He'll get over it."

"But maybe you won't?"

Nikki fingered the curtains, midnight-blue muslin with white window mullions printed on it. "I miss him," she said.

"The best thing would be for me to call him tomorrow and then call you." Jeffrey's body still smelled slightly of chlorine, and he found he had decided to add sit-ups to his afternoon swimming regimen. "Besides, a day or two out here would do you good; it would do Nona and Lissy good to have you. Just let me check things out."

Drawing her feet up on the chair, Nikki gave him a look. Jill pretended to be absorbed in a back copy of *Real Time* magazine. "Okay," said Nikki. Jeffrey kissed her on the corner of the mouth, said goodbye to Jill, and was halfway down the stairs when he heard Nikki say something to herself. At least, it seemed she said it to herself. What she said was: "Boop-boop-a-doop."

Nona and Melissa were having a perfectly reasonable conversation on the sofa. Jeffrey looked at his fist, poised to knock on the doorjamb. The moon was poised on the horizon. When he turned the key in the ignition, Melissa came running out of the house. "Hey," she said, following him into the first point of his three-point turn. "Hey, *wait* a minute."

He looked at her through the window and cut the engine. A lot of times things were really normal, as if you were in a movie. She hesitated, then walked around to the other side and got in.

"Jeffrey, I have to ask you something."

He cut the lights. "Ask."

"How come you didn't tell me Nikki was pregnant?"

The house they were looking at was full of women. It seemed to Jeffrey that even if some of them left, it would still be full of women. "She made me promise not to," he said. " 'Insisted' might be a better word. So I promised."

Melissa's hand lit upon the gearshift, even though in her conscious mind she knew neutral was not a toy. "That's not what I meant," she said. The way she moved the stick from side to side caused them to look at each other and the way they looked at each other caused her to fall still.

"You know, it's a funny thing, Jeffrey. I mean how I found out about it? Not through Nikki. She hadn't figured out how to tell me yet, or even if she should. And you—well, as you say, you'd promised. No, it was Peter. Peter told me. He gave her one good scan with his sonar and that was it—he knew and I knew. And you know why? Because he's the only one in my life—male or female—who doesn't go through some elaborate bye-bye behavior as soon as the topic of babies comes up."

Jeffrey let his head rest against the headrest. "Lissy," he said, "you are an interesting woman, but you piss me off."

"Not one compliment but two!" she observed to the half rolled-down window on her right. "What *can* have possessed him?"

"I don't suppose it has ever occurred to you that Nikki has her very own life? And—wonder of wonders —it actually goes on without you?"

"Don't preach; it makes your face too symmetrical."

"But, baby, I thought you found bilateral symmetry irresistible. Or is that only underwater?"

Letting the necklace fall back against her breast, Melissa smiled the abruptly radiant smile with which she generally acknowledged his lapses of temper.

"Now listen to me, Lissy; I'm going to tell you something you already know. The reason I didn't tell you about Nikki, the reason she didn't tell you herself, is that there just isn't anyone home anymore: you live at the bottom of the ocean. Your friends may change, your heart may break—but you live at the bottom of the ocean. Now what I want to say is this: there's not going to be any second chance with Nona. I hope you don't misunderstand my reason for saying that; she's self-sufficient to a fault. It's just that someday you may want to come up for air."

Melissa took a deep breath and, sitting very still, let it out slowly. Maybe it was better when things were obvious, but the obvious didn't happen every day. "All that's true, Jeffrey. Those are my priorities that seem so cold, I'm the one they scare the most. So don't you think I know how it looks?"

She put her head in his lap. "It looks," he said, "as if you're running away." And as he smoothed her dress back down over her hips, he stopped short, repeated the caress, and began to laugh. He took his foot off the brake. Melissa was looking up at him and laughing. The car was rolling slowly forward. Jeffrey reached under her dress. Melissa laughed and laughed. A tree trunk was getting closer. Jeffrey said something about traveling light and Melissa tried to explain about her bathing suit still being too wet to wear but they were laughing too hard. Then Jeffrey saw the tree and slammed on the brakes.

"Oh, your hands are so *cold*," she said. But actually they both liked it that she wasn't wearing any underwear, and Jeffrey was still thinking about it as he drove back alone to the city.

In the elevator, a few movies were on. Ignacio was watching *One Million B.C., Two-Lane Blacktop, The Three Faces of Eve, Forbidden Planet, Five Easy Pieces*, and *Gidget Goes Hawaiian* all at the same time, by switching channels. "Is no trouble if you are used to the elevator," he explained. "In the elevator, *amigo*, you are used to see little pieces of everything." As Iggy let him out, Jeffrey saw a little piece of the evening's headlines:

IDENT DENIES MCMURDO REPOR
RCTICA TALKS THREATE

The apartment is dark; it smells faintly of wintergreen. When Jeffrey turns on the hall light he sees Kirk's hat hanging on the intercom. Muscle liniment, Jeffrey decides, remembering Kirk's shoulder.

In the kitchen Jeffrey pours himself a glass of refrigerated gin and looks at it without drinking. The world as portrayed in the headline is vast and, at the same time, minute. Melissa's parting laughter, the phone dangling in the phone booth, all the ice at the bottom of the planet: it occurs to Jeffrey that you can spend all your time stalking the future only to find that the future, a small place, has surrounded you. *And what*, he wonders as he pours the glass of gin down the sink, *does "Boop-boop-a-doop" mean?*

Stripped to his black cotton underwear, Jeffrey does forty-two pushups on the kitchen floor. He does sit-ups, but loses count. He touches his toes.

In the midst of a series of back-stretches he has designed for himself, Jeffrey finds his body drifting not quite inadvertently into memory-elimination posture. He thinks: It's not like a weakness exactly. He thinks: Sometimes a boy's just got to freshen his point of view.

When the phone rings, he is uncertain how much time has passed. It occurs to him that Kirk must have been awake after all to get to the phone so quickly, but on the other hand Kirk is awfully quiet.

Kirk is not quiet; the door to the study is closed, Kirk is snoring loudly beyond, and Jeffrey, in the hallway, stares down at the red light on the telephone-answering machine. As he watches, the reels stop turning. He is reminded of an animal freezing at the scent of an intruder.

It has taken him some seconds to find the rewind button, and then each message, run rapidly backward, becomes a short burst of chirps. There are more than twenty bursts, separated from one another by shallow silences. Jeffrey sits, hesitates, pushes playback.

Are dolphins smarter than humans? Are dolphins more numerous than humans? Do dolphins have houses? Does Melissa have an agent? Where do dolphins sleep? Do dolphins have a family structure? Is Melissa free for lunch next Thursday? Is Melissa an atheist? How is a talking dolphin different from a talking parrot? Are dolphins really smarter than humans? Are they warm to the touch? Are they warm in the heart? Are they afraid of death? Do they come from outer space? Do they mate for life?

Leaning over the machine, Jeffrey pushes fast-forward. The voices turn back into chirps. Dolphin-talk, he thinks. Chirp-chirp, he says. The machine's red light is like an eye.

IN the morning, in the bathroom, as Jeffrey
scraped his face smooth before the mirror
and silently rehearsed a dream he'd just had about his
father as body-builder, there came a sound from the
tub. He pulled back the shower curtain: Kirk, asleep
in Stetson and boxer shorts.

"Why, you damn Texas shit-kicker! You've started
sleep-walking again."

"Not me," he said without much conviction and, getting to his feet, blundered off to bed.

Jeffrey elevatored down into the wonderful day.
Sometimes, as now, the psychology of his twin brother
alarmed him slightly because of what it seemed to suggest about himself. Still, this was a world in which people were actually talking about a new emotion, one that
no one had ever felt before. Jeffrey crossed the street,
the better to read the T-shirts of the women walking
there.

He ordered another cup of coffee, he corrected another paper. Everything in America was getting lighter,
stronger, and more transparent. Jeffrey surveyed the
restaurant, with its Plexiglas appointments. One result

182

of coming here every morning was that he had been awarded his own table by the window, and another result was that Diego was motoring over toward it with a peculiar look on his face.

"Why the look?" asked Jeffrey as Diego placed a package between them on the table. Then he shifted his attention to the package, because the look together with the gesture had touched off little jets of adrenaline in his system, which had been doing perfectly well without.

"Go ahead, Jefe."

From the bag, Jeffrey removed a paperback book. *"Baby and Child Care,"* he read.

"I found it at home. Now, my friend: read the date on the receipt."

Their eyes met. "It's dated Monday," said Jeffrey.

"Is a funny thing, no? For a woman who had an abortion on Thursday to buy a book like this the next Monday?" Diego put the book very carefully back in the bag, which was shiny and pink and new and threatening, now that Jeffrey examined it closely. And Jeffrey found himself suddenly filled with tenderness—for Diego, for himself, for all the nights one spent in the dark with somebody else, waiting to see what might be born, or decided upon, or blundered into without delay.

"Yeah, Diego. You're right about that. It is certainly a funny thing."

"But maybe not a surprise, eh, Jefe? I mean, maybe not to everybody."

Jeffrey stopped looking at himself in his coffee spoon. "Maybe not to everybody. But don't call me Jefe."

There was orange juice there. And the waitress had said something that both of them ignored, but Diego's voice was very soft: "You should have told me."

"People keep saying that," said Jeffrey. Then he put down his coffee and went to a different part of the restaurant, the part with public telephones. "Hello?" he said, when even after inserting the proper number of quarters he could not get Nona's phone to ring.

"Jeffrey!" said Melissa. "How strange. I'd just picked up the phone to call you."

"Well, I'll be damned. Next thing you know, we'll be completing each other's sentences and looking like our dogs."

"Diego knows about Nikki, doesn't he?"

"Yes, actually, he does. But how'd you know that? I just found out myself."

"I don't *know* how I knew." She laughed. "I . . . uh . . . you know, get headaches."

"Better put Nikki on," he said.

"Do you believe in pre-natal influence?" Nikki said.

"No," said Jeffrey. "But I bet Diego does." And when he explained the situation, not neglecting to touch upon the influence of firearms and quick tempers, they agreed she should remain at Nona's for the time being. "Just until he calms down, though," he added. "You've got to talk to him. Game time's over."

"Game time's over," she agreed.

However, back at the table, Diego, who was smoking a cigar, offered Jeffrey a cigar, and it occurred to Jeffrey that game time did not end just because you thought a friend of yours might kill another friend of yours. On the contrary, that was when game time began in earnest. "I guess I say 'congratulations,'" said Jeffrey, accepting the cigar.

Diego's grin was not pleasant to look at. "You are a joker, Jefe." He struck a match, held it out across the table. "Really a joker."

"Used to be," said Jeffrey through the smoke.

"But you're wrong about Nikki. She's just a girl who travels. A traveler. Makes it up as she goes along. She's not scared of me."

"Well, maybe you two ought to have a talk, then."

"Oh, we will, Jefe, we will. Where's Melissa?"

"In St. Thomas."

Keeping his eyes on Jeffrey, Diego bit an inch and a half off his cigar, chewed it thoughtfully and swallowed it. The tobacco brought tears to his eyes; he grinned through them. "Yeah, that's when everything was going good, no? Back when everyone was a joker."

Jeffrey walked thoughtfully to school and Diego walked someplace else. The coffee in the teachers' lounge tasted like mimeograph paper. There was no one in the phone booth today; Jeffrey could see that without even looking. "Why the eye patches?" he asked the six children in his class who were wearing them, but they wouldn't give him a straight answer. The straight answer, the real reason they covered their right eyes day and night, was to stimulate their right brains. It was said that if you wore the patch long enough you began to experience your own thinking as a voice telling you what to do. "How many of you have heard your parents talking about Antarctica over the last few days?" he asked, and everybody raised a hand. After lunch he gave a spelling test. After school he swam three-quarters of a mile. After drying his hair and looking at himself in the locker-room mirror, he returned to the pool and swam another eighteen laps. What would I do in Diego's place? he wondered. Why would I do it?

Kirk put down the map and stared at the painting over Jeffrey and Melissa's sofa—a painting constructed entirely of broken Fiestaware. Then he received three letters from the woman who sometimes hid his car keys. "Thanks," he said to Jeffrey, who was looking through his own mail. Jeffrey's hair was wet. Kirk thought immediately of the blond woman they had seen in the restaurant. "Who's in the shower?" asked Jeffrey, tossing his keys onto the coffee table.

Kirk grinned. "Diego."

They all went to a Mexican restaurant.

"Only one thing's better than this *mole*," said Diego, pointing his fork at his plate, and his face at Jeffrey and Kirk. "Live brine-shrimp soup. Tomorrow I'll make some."

"You're inviting us to dinner?"

"No, man. I am moving in." He poured the rest of his beer. "This way, everyone will be happy. I can watch for Nikki, since I know she will come first to your place, and you can watch me, since you are afraid I will blow her away like in the movies." He emptied his glass in a single swallow. "I am a what is it you call that? Efficiency expert."

"Yeah," Jeffrey admitted. "You're an efficiency expert. You really are."

A waiter glided by. "*Cerveza fría!*" said Kirk, holding up three fingers.

Jeffrey, Diego, and Kirk sat around the tiny television in the kitchen and smoked a joint. Diego allowed his personality to merge with *Horror at 37,000 Feet*— an okay fantasy premise that disintegrates into a forgettable suspense drama of ancient evil aboard a transatlantic commercial flight. There was a quart of beer in the refrigerator. There was a fifth of scotch on the shelf. Kirk and the bottles followed Jeffrey into the living room.

"What s'matter, Jeff ole buddy—didn't care for the flick?"

"No, I liked it pretty well. I just got the feeling I'd seen it before."

"Well, of course you've *seen* it before, Jeff boy. We live in the land of the constant rerun. How else could so many owe so much to so little?"

"Let me have a slug of that."

"How else? Which reminds me: I've got a confession to make. I did you at the bank yesterday."

"How much?"

"I had to bail rock-'n'-roll man in there out of jail.

And I had to get you all an answering service before that phone rang everybody slap-silly. *And* I extracted a small service charge. Because of the peril to my reputation."

"All right, all right. Just don't look so damn self-satisfied."

"Who's self-satisfied? I feel friendly is all. This life of adventure's liable to do that to a fella."

"You like jumping out of planes, do you?"

"Hell no, I don't, I perfectly hate it. Hate it just about to death. I mean you would not *believe* how cold that wind can seem when you're the one that's makin' it. So what I do is, I think of it as practice. I say to myself, 'Kirk ole buddy; it's cold, but it's practice.' "

"Getting ready for the Ice, huh?"

"Well, let's just say I expect a general cooling trend. A long-range, deep-blue, gut-settling coolth."

"That bother you? As a prospect?"

"No, that doesn't bother me. All I want is to go someplace where everything is different. Someplace with no reruns, no facts, no used-up trash. Warm or cool—it doesn't make a bit of difference to me."

"Yeah yeah yeah yeah yeah. Someplace where everything is different. Now wonder you and Lissy don't hit it off—you're too much alike. Lemme have another slug of that bellywash."

"What's mine is yours. But hey, listen: don't speak to me of love, Jefísimo. I got the feelin' you were about to do that. But don't."

"Okay. But don't call me Jefísimo."

"Hell no."

"Who's Charmian?"

"Oh. Yeah. Well, she writes me letters when I'm away and hides my car keys when I visit her and—honest to God, she's such a crazy little thing I'm s'prised they let her run around loose. Her name's not even really Charmian. I mean her folks call her Mary Belle.

But I got an affection for her, come to that. Yes, indeed. That there is *love*. A field of fucking bluebonnets. Just sometimes it needs a rest."

"What does she think of your little trip south?"

"Aw, she don't like it worth a shit. 'I hate traveling and explorers' is what she says. Somebody wrote that. It's a quote."

"I know."

"Well, she says it all the time."

"Does she fuck other people?"

"Yeah, when I go away she fucks other people and says that about travel and explorers."

"It's a bitch."

"Yeah . . . Hey, what's so funny?"

"Oh, just that the guy who wrote that, about explorers?"

"Yeah?"

"He *is* one."

"Ah, he's just another asshole. But I'll tell you one damn thing. Not every asshole knows what we know."

"What do we know?"

"Which of us is which, ole buddy; who's Marco and who's Polo. Here, now—gimme a little of that brainbust 'fore you pickle your damn self in it."

The smell of pot drifting in from the kitchen was the only other evidence of Diego's presence. Kirk began to get very drunk. Jeffrey began to notice it.

"I'm seeing a lot of soldiers at the airport," he told Kirk. "A lot. And you can bet they all got their long underwear on."

"Yeah, soldiers. It'll come to that."

"I'm telling you it *has* come to that. It's just the way you said: things are getting cold. By the time you get down there, they're going to be shooting the place up with their ray guns or atomic slingshots or whatever they use these days. There'll be a lot to see. But you're going to have to take care of yourself."

"Yeah, well, I don't want to live forever; it ain't sophisticated."

"Sophisticated?"

"Yeah, you know, sophisticated. Real sophisticated. Which fork to use. *Sophisticated!*"

"Okay. Yeah. That'd be one way of putting it." Jeffrey felt his pockets for something, but even as he did so had forgotten what. "Only, a boy can get curious. That's my problem. I hate being distracted from my own curiosity, and there's not a thing I can think of more distracting than people dropping dead while I'm trying to concentrate."

"Nona distract you?"

"Yeah, Nona distracts me."

"You know," said Kirk, pointing the bottle meaningfully at Jeff's chest, "I'll tell you what. You're some kind of flyer, ole buddy. I'm a shit-kicker but you're up there in the air to me and I always admired you for it. But what I want to know is"—he paused to down a slug of whiskey—"what I want to know is, what the hell you see from up there."

"Hey, hold on—we're all land creatures here. And I see the same thing you do, the same thing everybody does: history's biggest snowball battle—biggest and last —all set up and ready to rock."

Kirk grinned. He put the top on the bottle and the bottle on his knee. When, in the middle of the night, Jeffrey got out of bed to investigate the sound that had awakened him, he found Kirk, eyes closed, one hand outstretched, walking peacefully into a closet in the hall.

"Hey, wake up," said Jeffrey.

"Don't it all make a picture," said Kirk. And opened his eyes.

In a hot spring sun, even the dog-bushes bloom. Nona, Melissa, Nicole, and Jill drove out to a house Nona was trying to sell. It was the next day, a Friday.

Melissa had a headache, although some of the time it was not a headache. Some of the time it was a tiny image of Jeffrey moving about the upper left-hand corner of her mind. Melissa pointed to a brilliant slice of space in the empty living room.

"Didn't there used to be a . . ."

"Wall there?" Nona held a blue yardstick. "We knocked it out."

Upstairs, the toilet flushed. Nicole was familiar with the house because one of Melissa's childhood friends had lived there during all the years that she, Nikki, had come East for the summer. Jill said, "We opened up the kitchen too. The kitchen could have been a problem but we opened it right up." Melissa found she had left her bag in the car. Certain open-ocean dolphins—the spinner, the spotted, the common—have so little concept of physical obstruction that if captured and placed in a tank they will batter themselves to death trying to swim through the sides of it. Melissa returned with her bag. Nicole walked carefully down the stairs. Jill began measuring things. Upper left-hand *corner?* wondered Melissa, lighting a cigarette and putting it out.

"I was the same way," said Nona. "When I was pregnant with Lissy I peed night and day for the both of us, God I was a mobile irrigation system. Then came the mood swings."

"Mood swings?" said Nikki.

"Highs and lows. Bursting into tears at traffic lights, dancing in the grocery. You'd never know to look at me now but my favorite color during my third trimester was black with pink socks."

"Black with pink socks isn't a color," said Melissa, hugging her. She noticed she could think about all kinds of other things and still watch the picture of Jeffrey in her mind. He was getting on a bus. And Melissa was feeling anxious, quick, improvisational, so she put away the aspirin bottle unopened and rehearsed aloud a little of the history of the house, recalling the time her friend's mother had been rushed to the hospital to have her third child, leaving Nikki and Melissa and friend behind to dose themselves with turned wine and release the entire family aquarium into the backyard pool— seventeen flashing goldfish on a rainy day.

"It was your idea," said Nikki.

"But it took the three of us to carry them out there," said Melissa.

"It was a boy," said Nikki. "She had a boy; I remember that."

Nona noted on a pad the dimensions Jill was calling out. And Melissa could not get over the light—the way it flattened everything, and brightened everything, and fell into the empty house from all directions. She walked over to a window that had been propped open with a stack of old *House & Gardens*. What's Jeffrey doing in my headache? she wondered. Jeffrey was offering his seat to a woman with shopping bags. Melissa raised the window just enough to remove one of the magazines and remind herself of a prose style in which house and home were interchangeable. She was trembling but it wasn't obvious. She was irritated but it wasn't obvious. She longed for the touch of saltwater.

"It was different for us, though," said Nona. "When I was pregnant, everybody was. We didn't think about it, we just went ahead and did it."

"I didn't think about it either," said Nikki.

"Recent mothers hazing new mothers, new mothers hazing the pregnant. We were all in it together. Unprepared together. It was a long stroke of lightning."

"Sometimes I try to imagine that," said Nikki.

"We were silly, actually. Ripe, silly, beautiful girls."

Melissa looked sharply up from her magazine to find Nona gazing at her with an expression in equal measures fond and fearful. Nikki swept her hennaed hair softly from her eyes and said, "But I mean, my mother actually used to tell me *bedtime* stories over the intercom. She really did."

The kitchen was not a problem. Melissa could still hear their voices, but the kitchen had been opened right up and it was not a problem. She closed her eyes. Jeffrey was walking into a restaurant she knew, he was sitting down at the bar. When the time comes to tell her about the live-in, thought Melissa, I'll know; it'll be obvious. She was surprised to find the kitchen phone connected. She called information, then dialed the number she was given and asked for Jeffrey.

"I'm sorry, there's nobody here by that name," said the bartender.

"Could you ask?" said Melissa.

"Hello?" said Jeffrey.

"It's me," said Melissa.

There was the sound of ice rattling in a glass, of the glass against the phone. "Hey, how'd you do that?"

She shook two aspirin from the bottle and swallowed them. "I don't know, you were on my mind. The upper left-hand corner of it."

"*Corner* of it?" Jeffrey coughed or laughed or just used up some time. "Sweetheart, I swear life gets funnier by the minute. Not better, just funnier."

Melissa let out a lot of breath. "Oh, Jeffrey, you know why I love you is you never shut your eyes. You never do."

"That's not totally correct," said Jeffrey.

"You see more than just about anybody but you never shut your eyes. For instance, if I had my foot on the accelerator while you were driving, it'd be obvious, right?"

There was a pause. "I can't help you with your father, Lissy."

Her finger traced a wavy line from one wipe-clean surface to another. "You coming to the race tomorrow?"

"There's a teachers' meeting. I'll try."

"I need you, love. I really need you." She was rubbing her temples because the image of him had vanished. Through the window a hummingbird vanished too. "Are we at war yet?"

"Who—you and me?"

"No, you know—the world. All the countries." She was trying to explain to him what the world was. "Each time I open the paper I—"

"Oh, Antarctica. No, as far as I know, it's still in one piece." Over the phone came the clash of crockery, the sound of silver being set down. "As far as I know, I'm just going to eat this bowl of chili and go back to school, you're just going to finish measuring out that carpet, then go take your picnic basket out by the pond. We're survivors, baby. We're swimmers and we're survivors."

"Hey," she said. "How'd you know that's what we're doing here?"

"Surviving?" he said. "Or swimming?"

"No, measuring out carpet. I never told you that. I never even said we weren't at Nona's."

There was a long pause. From Jeffrey's end of it, the sound of a distant car horn bloomed and faded. "I don't know," he said at last. "It's just that lately, when I think of you, it sort of makes a picture. If you know what I mean."

Nona passed out the wineglasses. Jill unwrapped the cheeses. Nikki was lying on her back with her head in Melissa's lap and Jill began to hum the song that begins: *The blue sky is full of stuff that we shot up there in rockets and forgot about.* That's true, thought Melissa, who could see the blue sky by looking at the pond, which was perfectly reflective. Nona was unable to find the corkscrew but nobody did anything about it because at that moment a large brown fish broke the surface of the pond, twitched once in sunlight, fell back to the water, and was gone.

"Did you see?" said Melissa. "That was one of them! Goldfish are carp and that was the biggest old carp I've ever seen."

Everyone peered at the pond, with its shivering bit of sky and moon. A tiny image of a dolphin rose into the corner of Melissa's mind. A tiny image of the moon rose there. On the hillside behind them, their shoes lay together in a colorful jumble.

A SHORT HISTORY OF FLIGHT

Okay, that's twelve and a half grand, says the jump-master, and motions Kirk forward. Kirk, who has a Nikon screwed to the top of his helmet, feels ridiculous. The jumpmaster, who is the reddest-haired woman Kirk has ever seen, is beautiful. Kirk's altimeter, which also says twelve and a half grand, is correct. A sixty-second freefall is really such an *unnecessary* thing, thinks Kirk; isn't it? The pilot cuts the engines; the jumpmaster kisses Kirk, peers clinically into his eyes, and kisses him again, this time using her tongue. That's better, Kirk hears himself say, and jumps through the open door of the DC-3 into the wonderful blue whatever.

1. In his loneliness and fixedness he yearneth towards the journeying Moon, and the stars that still sojourn, yet still move onward; and everywhere the—

2. Someone is shouting at Kirk to arch his back, check his stopwatch, find a reference point.

3. He does these things. He does them.

4. The horizon wheels into place, the swatches of green and brown, the enormity of blue. Kirk is laughing. It is he who has been shouting. But now he is a flying man. Bringing his knees up to his chest, he goes into a back flip from which he emerges with a vivid visual memory of Melissa smiling. He has discovered her with the gun. She freezes, she smiles, she's gone. And he is a flying man.

5. *Why no birds, baby?* Charmian's voice, even in his head, has always been a miracle of insinuation. *How come no birds?* And, indeed, it is true, there are none. Kirk takes a picture to confirm this.

6. Kirk looks at his altimeter to confirm that he is

falling. Far below, automobiles in unnatural colors are going places they've already been. It occurs to Kirk that things are getting comical. He takes a picture to confirm this. *Lately, every fucking thing's a picture.* At the thought of everything, his fear returns, but it too is comical: he is not sure where his legs are.

7. He is not sure where the birds are.

8. —and everywhere the blue sky belongs to them, and is their appointed rest and their native country and their own natural homes, which they enter unannounced, as lords that are certainly expected and yet—

9. It is the sound that catches his attention. He looks —not up, exactly, but toward the sound—and what he sees, shooting past him toward the sun—and upward, definitely upward—arms swept back like jet wings, back arched and legs extended, is—another flying man. They pass so close that Kirk can see his face; the man is grinning with an intensity that is distinctly horrible.

10. Kirk is shouting. He is flailing about in the air and shouting Jeffrey's name. Then he thinks: *Upward?*

11. He locates the horizon. He recalls that Jeffrey is on the ground. It comes to him that he is in a nose dive.

12. He pulls.

There is a brief sharp pain across his right ear, a vicious jerk as the chute deploys, and then—then everything is wonderful. *This is the sky,* he thinks; *we fly here.* Chutes bloom upwind, a half dozen at a crack. It is clear he will miss the drop zone by as much as a half mile, but the thin trickle of blood from where a connector link has grazed his ear seems to suggest that all is very well indeed. For a long while the silence astonishes him.

There is no exact moment when he decides to land standing up, he simply wonders what it would look like. *Not every asshole knows what we know,* he thinks as the scrubby ground presses up to him. He hears the crack before he feels the pain.

Lying in the dirt, waiting for help, Kirk wonders: Now what the fuck did I do that for? One of his feet is pointing the wrong way at the end of its leg. He unwraps a Snickers bar and bites into it. The sight of his foot makes him sleepy, but it is not to keep himself awake that he begins to laugh.

Looking up into the crowd the following day, Melissa saw—and she realized she had been seeing it repeatedly since joining the others in the pit—a tiny point of light rise from the stand's upper tiers, fall through the air in a glittering arc, and smash to bits on the track. "Ice cubes," observed Mason. And someone with a bullhorn was chanting something Melissa couldn't make out, something about Antarctica, but everyone in the pit was very excited about the car. "What *is* pole position, anyway?" Melissa asked Richard, who was leaning against a stack of tires, and he explained—even though she already knew—that their qualifying time had won them the inside track at the starting line. Then he saw her notice he wasn't wearing his wedding ring. "Doesn't Nona look great leaning there with her stopwatch?" he said, to fill up the silence, and it occurred to Melissa that it was going to be hard to stay ahead of all this on what little sleep she'd had the night before. She took two yellow pills from her purse and swallowed them, in the interest of staying ahead. "Yeah, she does look great," Melissa agreed in a confiding tone. "She really does. But that's us, you know? We like to sit where it's fast."

A man in a white Nomex jump suit was passing out cotton balls for everybody's ears. "Why's the crowd so mean today?" Melissa heard Jill ask someone as another ice cube smashed down upon the track nearby, but just then Nona gave the air wrench an experimental blast, drowning out whatever reply there might have been. "Just about ready to roll," said Richard and, excusing himself, joined Nona in back of the blind, curiously naked Chevy they had purchased in the interest of staying ahead.

"Isn't Jeffrey coming?" Nikki asked, drawing Melissa gently into a stroll.

"He has a teachers' meeting." She felt the first edge of the speed coming on and for a moment wondered if it would bring a reprise of the illustrated headache that had kept her up most of the night. "He said he'd get here if he could."

"I think I detect a note of disgruntlement there," said Nikki, stepping over a compressed-air hose, a compressed-water hose.

"Well, for one thing they don't hold teachers' meetings on Saturday," Melissa answered. A tiny image of the dolphin rose into the corner of her mind, then flickered out. You do this, Peter? she thought. You swim in my mind?

Steering them around a shiny new gravity gas tank, Nikki gave Melissa's arm a squeeze. "Why, sweet pea, I guess in that case we're just gonna have to watch the fine men burn up their tires all by ourselves."

Melissa started to laugh but ended up taking two deep breaths instead. Then the chief mechanic wiped his dark glasses clean, swung in through the window of the Chevy, and started it up. "What did you say?" shouted Nikki, but Melissa couldn't tell her just then because she was thinking about her father, because she was thinking about her father climbing through a window, because she was thinking about her father climbing through a window to rescue her when she had locked herself not quite accidentally in the bathroom the day after her third birthday and just eighteen years before she never saw him again. "I said, these things actually run on dinosaurs," Melissa shouted, cupping a hand around Nikki's ear. "That's what fossil fuel *is*: dinosaurs." But when the car shot out of the pit, leaving it fragrant with combustion, they could hear the crowd again and Melissa wanted to be very near Nona.

Richard's arm was around Nona, they were laughing. "Let's take a walk around the infield before the race starts," Melissa said and Nikki gave her a look that turned into a smile.

Pastel vans, sedans, and pickup trucks were parked every which way on the grass and mud. "It's like being at the bottom of a bowl," said Melissa as they threaded their way through the crowd, and it was true there was no boundary but the uppermost row of bleachers, nothing to be seen of the natural world but the sky, hanging over the bowl like God, if God were a color or a promising absence.

"Did you see that?" said Nikki.

"No, what?"

"That guy had a T-shirt that said 'Defrost Antarctica.' "

A line of teenagers on minibikes buzzed by and Melissa had to jump out of the way, but Nikki bent down to pick something up. "You know," she said, turning the rear-view mirror over in her hands as they walked, "I was talking to that guy who was mowing the lawn down there at the flooded house—what's his name? Noel?"

"Oh, you mean Knolly?"

"That's it, Knolly." She picked a shard from the mirror's broken face. "Anyway, he was wearing a little-bitty mirror around his neck, I don't know if you remember, and when I asked him what for, he said"—she handed the first shard to Melissa and began gingerly to pick another for herself—"he said, 'There's some eyes around that don't like to see themselves.' "

Melissa gave her a sharp look, but Nikki, having pried loose a second piece, had dropped the mirror's housing to the ground and was looking up into the stands like a farmer expecting rain. "I thought that was pretty good."

Melissa nodded. "It is. It's good." Her heartbeat was taking off on her—just off, up, and away. "I mean

Knolly's a pretty subtle fella. He—" She looked down at the mirror in her hand, caught a flash and took a breath. "Did he . . . say anything else?"

"Yes . . . But I couldn't really understand him."

Where they were walking now, lots of televisions were on; the surrounding track was too far away, the view of it too obstructed, for anyone really to see the race without a TV. "I don't understand him either," said Melissa, deliberately misconstruing Nikki's answer. She felt weak in the knees. *It's all these people,* she thought. And, a moment later: *It's the speed.* But she knew, even without thinking about it, that it was neither of those things, and as she and Nikki pressed on toward the number-one turn, she shook the bit of mirror loosely in her fist like a die.

"Why's it so much more crowded near the turns?" Nikki asked, and Melissa was about to say she thought it was because that's where the accidents were, when a woman sitting on the roof of a malachite-blue Mercury averted her face so suddenly that her braids wheeled briefly out behind, a flash of blond in the noonday sun.

"Pamela!" Melissa called. But the woman, still a dozen meters away, didn't turn around.

" 'Pamela'?" Nikki inquired and Melissa said, "I thought that woman over there with the braids was someone I know from the Aquarium." When she blinked, her eyeballs clicked, and she had a momentary mental image, incredibly tiny and precise, of Jeffrey walking in a white place. There were rules in the white place, there were elevators. "But maybe I was wrong," she added.

She was not wrong. "I didn't know we shared *two* enthusiasms," said Pamela, sliding to the ground. Her smile, while not unpleasant, was distinctly forced.

"My mother's part owner of the white-and-green Chevy," said Melissa.

"Isn't that odd! My husband's a mechanic for the Bonnett brothers' Oldsmobile, that red-and-yellow one they just took up onto line." She put her hands in the back pockets of her jeans and smiled again. "I suppose that sort of makes us competitors, eh? For the afternoon, at any rate."

Melissa shrugged and made a gesture of abundance. She introduced her to Nicole, and for a short time the three of them talked about Australia, where Pamela and her husband were from. They agreed the talks in Canberra were going very badly. Pamela thought war was certain. None of them could see much advantage in knowing about the situation.

"By the way," said Pamela, fixing Melissa with a look too sharp to be planned, "I saw the *Times* article on your work in St. Thomas." Her nostrils flared, the P-A system said some numbers. "Are things really going that well, then?"

Melissa was startled. She had not till now considered the possibility that Pamela might have a competitive side. "Yes, they are," she answered after a moment, and Pamela, no longer smiling, eased her dark glasses down off her forehead and over her eyes.

"They are, uh," she repeated tonelessly. "Well, that's good news, surely. For all of us."

"I hope so," said Melissa. She glanced uneasily at Nicole, who had been drawn into conversation with two teenage boys in Hawaiian shirts. "I think it will be."

The crowd roared. A very blond woman in fishnet stockings was being towed slowly around the track atop a float built to resemble an enormous red bird, an eagle perhaps, rising from a nest of oil derricks.

"Unfortunately, the news from the Aquarium is not so good," said Pamela. "In fact, I've been meaning to give you a ring."

"What's the problem?"

Pamela bent down and plucked a stalk of grass to chew. She looked at Melissa for a few fast heartbeats that got faster. She flipped her braids back over her shoulders. "Well, ever since the accident with—ever since Anatole's death, the other dolphins—I mean, I'm afraid they've taken it rather badly. None of them are eating well at all, and two of the girls—Liz and Ellie—are completely anorectic. I think we'll lose them both by midweek unless something changes."

One of the teenagers was holding up a can of beer and pointing at Melissa, but she didn't want anything like that. She shook her head. "Have you been giving them vitamins?"

"And antibiotics as well. Just in case, I mean. But really I think it's depression, don't you?"

Melissa felt her eyeballs click again. "I don't know what I think. It could be anything."

"Liz and Ellie were very close to him. Virtually all their observed sexual activity was either with him or with one another. Or with Oliver, who's nearly as badly off now as they are. They played together, they were never separated. It's obvious, really. Anatole's gone and they miss him."

From over by the boys, Nikki's voice said, "No, but my husband would," and the crowd burst into applause.

"Nothing is obvious." Melissa's chest felt hollow. The loudspeaker was introducing the drivers, and to be heard over all those names and numbers she nearly had to shout. "We don't know *what* they feel. Have you tried force-feeding them?"

Pamela shook her head with a precision that Melissa took as a rebuke.

"Well, there's force-feeding." She tried to think of words that Pamela would like, but things were getting fast and odd. She saw Nikki trying to catch her eye, she saw two bright Hawaiian blurs trying to illustrate something. "Listen, Pamela. Why don't I come out there tomorrow. If it's all right with you, I mean. Maybe together we can come up with an idea."

"Maybe together we can. But I doubt it."

"I'll call you tomorrow morning," Melissa said, the white place flashing once more through her mind like windshield glare. Then she turned, seized Nikki by the hand, and together they hurried off down a zigzag row of cars.

"What was that about?" asked Nikki.

"It's all my fault. I knew what I was doing. I let the first one die and now the others are going to die."

"What are you *talking* about? What's going on?"

"I can't handle this," Melissa explained. Abruptly, she was crying. "It's just too fucking much."

"*What* is?"

Melissa stopped and looked at Nikki. They were standing beside a black van with star-shaped plastic windows. "Last week there was an accident at the Aquarium. Only maybe it wasn't an accident and maybe I let it happen. Anyway, one of the dolphins was killed. Now the other ones won't eat and they're going to die." She tried to keep the tears out of her voice. "From grief. You know? Grief? They're going to die from grief."

Nicole put her arms around her. "Don't be so hard on yourself. Not everything is your fault."

"I can't accept that." She stepped away from Nikki's embrace. "I can't and won't. And anyway, what do you really know about it? You don't even know about me and Peter."

"Lissy, I know what your work means to you. I was down there. I saw how you changed."

"Did you?" Melissa wiped her nose on her sleeve. "Nikki, you know, it means a lot to me that you and I are close, but I have to tell you, there was something down there you *didn't* see." She had stopped crying. "Want to guess what it was?"

Their eyes met. Nikki shivered, and at the same time so did Melissa.

Melissa said: "Peter and I are lovers."

There was some smoke there. A man nearby was burning beef over a charcoal grill, but Nicole continued to fan the air in front of her face even after the breeze had shifted. She said something that sounded like, "Pray thee," and Melissa said, "What?"

Nicole shook her head. The way she was looking at Melissa made Melissa feel very lonely.

"I don't know, Nikki, is it really that weird? He seduced me. It was like a hole opening up in the sky, and what am I going to say, 'Please, sir, I'd like to go home now'? We were already flying through it, already flying, it was more than curiosity, I just didn't want to stop."

Nicole smiled faintly, a lopsided smile. "Nobody wants to," she said. "Me, either. It's the times."

"Fuck the times," said Melissa.

"Gentlemen," said the P-A system, "start your engines."

The crowd let out a prolonged roar, and on all sides people were getting to their feet or climbing atop their cars or pressing transistor radios to their ears. Nicole's eyes went moist as she brushed her hair back from her face, and Melissa had the sense, very strong and frightening, of time running out, of circuits switching off one by one as they counted down toward an ending.

"Nikki—" she began, but Nicole, putting one hand on her shoulder, her lips close to Melissa's ear, cut her off.

"I've got to go," she said.

"Now?" said Melissa. "Where?"

On the track, the cars cruised by on their first parade lap, bunched tightly two by two behind the pace car.

"I said, I have to *go*!" Nikki shouted.

"No, I heard you. But *where*?"

Drawing back to look at her, Melissa saw a dent of stubbornness alongside her mouth, a beauty so sudden and elegant it was alarming. "I've got to find Diego,"

Nikki's lips said, and Melissa leaned close again to hear. "I said I've got to find Diego and tell him I'm pregnant."

The field of cars passed by a second time, still picking up speed behind the pacer.

"Whatever's right," said Melissa, turning half away from her. There was a viewing stand built into the bed of a pickup truck nearby and children were swarming up it as if it were a jungle gym. It occurred to Melissa that she no longer knew why she was doing whatever she was doing; she didn't even really know what it felt like. She wondered if it felt anything like needing to find Diego to tell him you were pregnant. Nikki touched her shoulder.

"Bye," she said.

"Bye," said Melissa, and turned to give her sunburned cheek a kiss, but Nikki, flushed and fleet, put her arms around her and pressed her lips so quickly to Melissa's that there wasn't even time for astonishment: a lover's kiss. The phrase "blind faith" crossed Melissa's mind. Her own eyes were open. She didn't know how to respond but she responded anyway, a little—it happened so fast.

"I'll call you," Nikki said. "Be sure to . . . you know, take care of yourself."

"Right," said Melissa, just as the pace car quickened through the third turn, pulled away, and darted down the pit road.

"They comin' now," somebody said, and the cars seemed for a moment to pull back, a single enormous animal coiling itself to pounce. *Why'd she say that?* Melissa wondered. Then the green flag fell, the rasp and rumble of the engines became a single roar, and the cars shot past Melissa down the straight in an explosion of blue smoke, sound, and power. Everyone around Melissa was shouting, but she couldn't hear a single voice. She looked for Nicole, but Nicole was gone.

Melissa made her way through the crowd. She was

thinking about commitment, but it was hard to keep her mind on any one topic. Her limbs did not feel fully connected to her body.

At the center of the infield, two trailers had been set up to treat information sickness. Three people were admitted as she watched, but no one was released, even though she stood there for a long time. *Bang*, she said or thought, *right in the head*. She wondered what Peter was doing, but there were no pictures in her mind just then.

Neither Nona nor Richard noticed her return to the pit. They were sitting side by side on a Styrofoam ice chest, drinking beer and watching the race. "I wish I could do it over the phone," Richard was saying. "But of course I really can't."

There was a truck parked right behind them. Melissa climbed up on it. From up there, she had a better view of the track.

Nona said no, he really couldn't.

The cars had not yet fully strung themselves out around the circuit. Melissa saw there was another car, a brilliant-blue Pontiac, just inches behind her mother's green-and-white Chevy—in "drafting position," as Melissa remembered it was called. Once, Nona had explained to her how the second car rides the wake of the first, matching its speed while only using two-thirds the throttle. She had said that sometimes the vacuum grew so intense all the windows in the second car were blown out.

Melissa took another pill from her purse, bit off half, and swallowed it. After a moment she swallowed the other half. She'd seen so many more people's windows blown out than she'd ever thought to see.

Looking back out over the track, Melissa had the impression that her memory for the events of the last eight days had become absolute. From the moment she had seen Peter's yellow ball flying at her until now, not one funny little thing had passed her by. She remembered exactly what it had felt like, cranking the dolphin up over the pool at the Aquarium; she remembered just how much she had wanted to see what it looked like up there.

Directly below her, Nona was shouting into Richard's ear. Melissa continued to peer down at the two of them until the cars entered the backstretch and the din diminished sufficiently for her to hear a snatch of the conversation.

"But I mean she won't put up a legal fight, will she? When she finds out it's me you're marrying?"

Richard said no, he was sure she wouldn't.

Melissa felt a sudden coolness across the inside of the fingers of her left hand, and looking into her palm, she found the mirror shard smeared with blood.

Somebody threw a handful of ice cubes out of the stands, down toward the cars' blurred colors.

Returning from the hospital, unlocking the door, Jeffrey discovered a booklet wedged against the jamb. It was entitled "Home Care for Information Sickness" and had a rained-on look. There were other copies at the other doors, up and down the hallway. It was illustrated and indexed, a printed insert suggested it be memorized and passed along. Well, thought Jeffrey, good.

In the kitchen, he turned on the TV and radio. In the living room, he lay down on the couch. Seeing Kirk in traction had induced fatigue, no, it had frightened him, no, it had reminded him why people were embarrassed by the thought of their own deaths. He called Diego's name once just in case, then got up and dialed Clarice's number, let it ring twice as agreed, and hung up. All the messages on the answering machine were for Melissa and all of them concerned the dolphin.

"It's invisible," offered the television; Jeffrey automatically looked at his watch. When he opened the refrigerator door, the soup there smelled of shellfish and was faintly mobile: live brine-shrimp soup. He watched it for a while, then returned to the living room and went patiently through Diego's leather duffel bag for the gun. Not finding it caused a curious thought to pass through his mind, one he associated with cigarette butts flying through the air: he was glad to be alive.

Clarice arrived looking beautiful, frightened, defiant. She was wearing a hat, she was out of breath. "I took the stairs," she said.

"No need," he answered, kissing her. "The elevator man's a friend."

She smiled at him for the first time. "Not of mine," she said. She was examining what she could of the apartment in a series of short glances, each a fraction shorter than the last. "You look tired. Are you okay?"

"I'm fine," he answered. "I'm glad to be alive." Raising her hands to remove the pin from her hat, she gave him an inquiring look, then preceded him down the hall to the living room as if it were she who lived there. All right, he thought, it's on wheels now. He felt the fugitive's fascination for the what next. No more hotels.

"Did you hear about Antarctica?" she asked.

At the mention of Antarctica, Jeffrey nearly fell asleep standing up. He sat down in the middle of the sofa. "Yes," he answered.

She had removed her coat and was walking slowly around the living room, inspecting it. "We're sending troops to McMurdo. It's very scary. I cried."

Jeffrey considered this. *"Sauve qui peut,"* he said.

Turning around, Clarice looked at him very hard, then sat down beside him. "Something else is wrong. What is it?"

He let out a lot of breath. "Oh, I don't know, my brother's a fuck-up. Or maybe he's not, maybe that's just . . . Anyway, now he's gone and smashed his ankle all to shit, and they don't even know if they're going to be able to put him back together again." He looked at her. "I just got back from the hospital."

Clarice blinked and eased her head back against the sofa. "Oh, Jeffrey. That's hard. How did it happen?"

"Skydiving."

"*Sky*diving?"

"It's not as dangerous as it sounds. Unless you're dumb enough to think you can land on your feet."

From the kitchen, the TV's movie sound track wandered briefly into the same key as the music on the radio. Then Clark Gable's voice said, "Why didn't you take *all* your clothes off? You could have stopped *forty* cars." Clarice was watching the ceiling with something like expectation, and it seemed to Jeffrey, watching her, that his own desire to live would be unendurable were it not for—not for what? He sat suddenly forward.

"It's like this: when you land you're supposed to do a certain little somersault, right? To absorb the shock? Well, Kirk decided to land standing up—why?" He smiled at her and eased back into the couch. "He wanted to see what it looked like."

"What it looked like?"

"That's what he said."

Without raising her head, she turned and gave him a look of such knowing calculation that Jeffrey wondered briefly what it was he had communicated. Their affair had offered many such moments, had even, as it seemed to him now, been built upon them, and he did not take it lightly that Clarice had seen fit to come so far on the strength of what she saw, on the evidence of how it looked.

"I think maybe your brother's too imaginative to be a skydiver," she said.

Jeffrey laughed a little. "No such," he answered. "Kirk's just like those kids with the eye patches. He wants to hear voices telling him what to do."

Clarice had not heard about the kids with the eye patches, and when Jeffrey explained, she affected to be shocked. "And whatever happened to a good wholesome game of pirates, I'd like to know."

"Modern times, sweetheart."

"Yes," she said. "Modern times."

They looked at each other, and there was an awkward moment when the news came on the radio but they couldn't hear it very well because of the TV.

"When's Melissa due back?"

"Not tonight."

Clarice had shifted slightly away from him and, in raising an elbow to prop against the sofa back, had caused one wide sleeve of her loosely knit black sweater to fall bunched to the shoulder. A shadow of irritation passed over her face. "Don't they miss you at these gatherings?"

"I'm trying," he said, "to become less necessary."

She closed her eyes and shook her head. "Don't, Jeffrey."

"Okay. They miss me. But I'm here." A taste rose in the back of his throat like the anticipation of citrus. "When are you due back?"

She inspected the floor. "I have to make dinner later."

"Want some tea?"

"Maybe brandy." She looked suddenly up at him and smiled. "Jeffrey, you're so full of crap. I mean it— you're a bad guy."

He was not offended. When he returned with the brandies she had kicked her shoes off and was examining "Home Care for Information Sickness" with what seemed to be attention.

USE OF THE FIRST RETURN POSTURE

She accepts the glass without looking at him and begins to read aloud from the pamphlet. What a careless and disorderly lot we are, he thinks, how easily injured. The practical tone in which Clarice is reading suggests an authority—in the text, in her, in the moment—that is, for all its fragility, quite beautiful, maybe even moving. He puts down his glass and watches her, watches her lips. Survivors, he thinks. Swimmers, he thinks.

Without moving, he assumes the first return posture, or sea breather's pose. Through his mind, like a stream of bubbles, pass the 9,017 names for the taste of water. Thus, he thinks. In such a world he too might have cried about Antarctica. Under the waves.

Clarice falters, meets his gaze, tosses the pamphlet to the ground.

Caresses never failed to bring to Clarice's features a look of closure, as if she were retreating, with the faintest suggestion of a taunt, into a cave precisely the size and shape of her body. This look, which Jeffrey thought of as the exact inverse of the one she had given him earlier, never failed to excite him: he longed to see this look transformed, he craved to reveal her to herself. And as she moved against him now, warming fully dressed to his kiss, he saw, with a suddenness that stunned him, how thoroughly desire might be compounded of fear—fear of being left or unreachable, fear of being unable to unseal the sealed, fear, at bottom, of being so thoroughly at the testy mercy of disorderly events.

He froze before the vividness of the insight, his lips a few bright inches from hers, his hand on one of her breasts. She looked at him from her cave. They stood together and walked toward the bedroom.

In the hall, she stopped and began to undress. When she was nearly naked, she looked at him impatiently and said, "Here."

He stripped, adding his clothes to the pile she had made of hers. Here: it was the only space in the apartment that was not a room, the only space that did not belong to what had already happened in it.

He kissed her neck. He drew the flat of his tongue

across her nipple. She moved so that his cock, as they stood, was between her legs.

Here. The word caused him a dart of loneliness as they sank together to the floor.

I never close my eyes, he thought, looking at hers, which were sealed. And then, oh my goodness, he did: Melissa, in the upper right-hand corner of his mind, sitting on a truck and looking at a mirror. No, he thought, certainly not, and opened them again immediately. He had only blinked, Clarice moved beneath him, he entered her.

They made love slowly and without tenderness, though it was not the less loving for that. He held himself slightly up off her, because of the floor. When the phone rang, less than a meter away, her eyes fluttered open in alarm, met his, and were held.

The phone rang again. He saw the alarm was sexual.

Her lips began to swell, she threw her legs around him, and, in the second's fraction during which the two of them acknowledged, each silently in the other's helpless gaze, that it was the phone that had excited her, she began to come, and he, a moment later, followed after.

There was a puzzled *bing* and a nearly inaudible click as the tape recorder answered the call.

Afterward, though neither Jeffrey nor Clarice spoke of it, it was as though something had been settled between them.

In the phone booth Nicole waited for the beep. "Hi, Jeffrey," she said, although it was Kirk's voice on the recording, "Melissa finally convinced me to face Diego." She hesitated, uncertain what it was she wished to say. "I'm in the city now. I thought I'd let you know." But, giving the phone a slightly puzzled look, she hung up without adding the truth: that for the first time she was frightened of the chain of events she had set in motion. The necessity of announcing her pregnancy to Diego— though she regretted nothing—was a humiliating reminder of how she had put herself at the mercy of the world. In telling Diego, she would begin the process by which that world would inevitably claim her child. She pressed a thumb against the phone's chrome and stared at the print it left.

The sudden, urgent sound of metal on glass startled her so badly that she bumped her head. For a moment she could not understand what was wanted of her; then she apologized and turned the phone over to the woman with the quarter.

It was a day in middle spring, warmer in the city than in the country. There were an unusual number of people on the street.

Nicole knew, because she had called, that Diego was not at home, and the idea of returning there to wait for him seemed ludicrously at odds with what it was she had to tell him. It was not their menage but the notion of return itself which had become paradoxical. She decided to walk to a nearby fabric store to buy the material for a dress she'd had in mind.

It did not surprise or frighten her that the groups of people she passed on the sidewalk were talking of war. Though she gave little thought to politics, she assumed war was inevitable, even if she doubted the present events in Antarctica would be the occasion for one. What astonished her was the notion, oddly confirmed by these knots of people, that *it had come to this*. Her love for Melissa, like her love for Diego, had been a series of mounting surprises which, having finally surprised itself, *had come to this*. She pressed her palm to her abdomen, a little below the navel. What frightened her was the likelihood that there was no one with whom she could share her own, possibly infinite, curiosity about this state of affairs.

In the shop, which bore no sign of having for nearly thirty years housed a ticket-printing concern, Nicole felt momentarily insulated by the bolts of fabric. The bolts were on racks, and the racks made aisles. As a small child, Nicole had sat under her grandmother's sewing table in Wichita, watching scraps of fabric fall from above for her to arrange. Now, she and her unborn child were themselves scraps; they had fallen from the jet-fouled sky to this place where thousands of thicknesses of cloth temporarily separated them on every side from what in the world was coming next.

A salesman asked her if she needed help. She said not yet. The sound of her heels against the hardwood floors seemed about to remind her of something.

She stopped before a bolt of pearl-gray silk. The dress she had in mind was one she had long imagined making for Melissa, and always she had imagined it in silk of this grain and color. Pulling perhaps a foot of fabric from the roll, she ran her fingertips across it, trying to envision the dress as it would look on Melissa's body. Instead, and with a jolt, she saw the pearl-gray dolphin leaping from the water, she heard its high banjo voice pronounce Melissa's name. Maybe the blue's better after all, she thought, and catching the salesman's eye, she selected three and a half yards of brilliant cerulean silk.

She put the purchase on her account. Pausing by the door, she put a dot of hibiscus oil on either wrist. The kiss she had given Melissa was simply one more reiteration of the obvious: *that it had come to this* changed everything.

In the streets, the sun made her dreamy. With each breath she took for herself and her child, her own childhood seemed to recede.

She had gone only a couple of blocks when she noticed a commotion up ahead: a taxi driver and his fare arguing in a cab. The passenger seemed to be refusing to get out. As she watched, the driver opened his own door and marched around the cab to drag the passenger from his seat. It was Diego doing the dragging. It was she doing the running. "No charge," Diego was saying as she arrived just in time to see the passenger, a young man in a suit, deposited ass-first on the sidewalk.

"Get in," Diego told her.

Not till then did she realize she had been the cause of the scene. She got in.

Staring through the open window at her, Diego made as if to place his hand gently over her nose and mouth. Her eyes met his unwaveringly. Then he locked the door and hurried back around to the driver's seat. As they shot away from the curb, the man in the suit bounced his attaché case angrily off a fender.

"¿Qué tal, chiquita?" Diego looked at her in the rear-view mirror. "It's a nice day for a walk, no?"

"I was just waiting for you. I called you at home but you weren't there."

"How was Florida?"

His tone of voice encouraged silence. She recalled that silence was not what she had come back for, so she would have to live with questions and tones of voice. "I didn't stay there," she said. "I mean, I was going to, but I changed my mind and went on to St. Thomas. To see Lissy."

"To see Lissy," he repeated, throwing the cab into a sudden right. For the first time Nicole saw the bruises on his face and she began to feel afraid. "You missed her so much so soon?"

"I had to tell her something." The whole cab smelled of hibiscus.

"Bueno. And I have to tell you something." He turned, in a motion very like a swerve, onto a crosstown thoroughfare. She remembered the gun. There were games she had encouraged in Diego, games of physical violence and threat, of which she was now, before this third person taking shape in her womb, deeply ashamed.

"Diego, where are you taking me?"

He drove for a block in silence. "Hey," he said, turning around with false brightness to look at her. "Why don't you ask me what happen to my face? Don't you care anymore about my looks?"

Nicole's hands searched for something to brace against. She had never been afraid of him before and now she was. This fact seemed almost as important as what she said next.

"Diego," she said. "I love you. I always have."

"This is how it is," Diego said, putting a dead cigar butt between his teeth. "1961, Sunday afternoon, hot for Havana in April. My brother Chalo and I, we are walking back from the baseball field and I am pissed off. He says I am too little to play first base. All the way home I call him names but he says nothing. Then we get to the house."

Diego sighed, shrugged, mocked himself in falsetto:

" 'What is it, Mama? Let me in. Why are you crying so?'

"But she doesn't answer, she doesn't even open the bedroom door."

Nicole had become unpleasantly aware of her heartbeat. She clutched the package in her lap, and when Diego, who was driving a good deal faster than the traffic would bear, did not immediately continue, she said, *"Entonces?"*

He nodded. *"Entonces*, I follow my brother out to the back yard. There they are, sitting in their chairs under the cedar tree: my uncle and my father with their white suits, my cousins and . . ." Diego turned fiercely around to Nicole; she looked in terror at the truck ahead of them.

"And two yanqui children I have never seen before! Never!" He swerved, changing lanes to avoid the truck. "My uncle stands up and says, 'Chalo, Diego, these are your brothers.' I look at them: brothers. I look at my father: a man who has been crushed like a lizard, a man who will die in less than five years from too much work.

" 'But where is their mama and papa?' I ask, and my uncle says, 'Their papa is your papa.' I look at Chalo and he says, 'But their mama? Where is she?' "

"So everybody turns to look at my father. He is sitting in his wicker chair, and there are day lilies all over the place, sunshine—I remember it all. And he says—these are his exact words—he says, 'Their mother is a *norteamericana* who came every night to the club. She is a traveler, a lady who travels. But now she has grown tired of us and she has gone away. We will never see her again.' "

Nicole stared at the back of his head. Having never known this story about Diego but discovering it now, she had the sensation that it was becoming increasingly possible—moment by moment by moment by moment —to discover everything. Her fear confirmed this sensation. Her exhilaration confirmed it. Her hand on the strap above the door, the package in her lap, the bright blur out the window, the hairs at the base of Diego's neck, the small lump to be felt in her abdomen just below her navel—*it was coming to this*.

"Diego," she said. It was like the whisper of someone in a darkened house urging someone else to hurry. But the taxi was in no way a house and it was not darkened.

"You cannot know, Nikki, how I have always hated that woman."

They sped past a truck. "You cannot know!" She touched his shoulder. They hurried. He was shouting in Spanish. He was shouting in English. He was saying, "Marry me! Marry me, Nikki! Marry me or leave me alone!"

"*Okay!*" she said.

Diego's eyes in the rear-view mirror.

"*Okay!* I'll marry you." She swept the hair from her brow. "But I have to tell you this: I never had the abortion. I'm still pregnant. And I'm having the child. Our child. I'm having it. I'm having it! Whether you marry me or not, I'm having it. *Because that's what I have to do*."

She found herself talking to the rear-view mirror. It appeared Diego had begun to weep.

"You see," she was saying through her tears. "You see."

He had slowed the cab and was crying and shaking his head no as he drove. It was unclear to both of them to what, if anything, he was saying no. Ahead of them was the tunnel, recently renovated, which led under the river to the rest of America.

It is possible that Nicole, from the moment she acceded to Diego's command to get into the cab, had expected in some way that what she had begun must lead unavoidably to her being shot to death by him. If so, her fear must have been a mounting awareness which, like the being taking shape in her womb, could have no meaning until, as now, it quite suddenly existed for someone other than herself. On the other hand, it is equally possible that, until she saw Diego's hand reach for the glove compartment, she simply saw no need to anticipate the cirumstances of her own death: it would, as it had, *come to this*. In either case, there can be no doubt as to what happened next: seeing Diego open the glove compartment, Nicole opened the door of the moving cab and, still holding the package of silk she had bought, stepped delicately out into traffic.

The first car to hit her, a panel truck labeled with bright-red words and yellow pictures, threw her perhaps fifteen feet into the air. Turning a slow, lopsided somersault, she saw, because she was unable to close her eyes, the yards of blue silk coming undone. The fabric wrapped itself around one arm and between her legs in an improbable manner. She believed this fabric to be the sky its color claimed it to be. That she could fly seemed to her not at all improbable. That her baby would be born in this sky did not surprise her in the least.

By the time Diego got to her, she had been run over several times and a minor collision had occurred as the traffic slowed to avoid her. There was an enormous amount of blood and silk. His hand, which was still holding the photograph he had removed from the glove compartment, became a fist and remained one for a time that was long and, at the same time, not long at all.

THE hand that fed the dolphin: the main thing was, it was not the woman's hand. He sonared the butterfish it held out, then accepted and swallowed it.

In the sagas it was said that humans dream with their hands, only their hands, and so have cities rather than sagas, monuments rather than memories. He had reviewed in his mind every movement and gesture the woman's hands had ever made within reach of his sonar, he recalled every dream their touch had caused his skin to dream—but still he did not understand what made her come and go come and go from dry to moist to wet and back again, and what his name meant in her language and what his language meant in her ear and where her offspring were and what hair was for and why she was so afraid of the shortness of life.

The man with the seaweed-shaped head held out another fish. In the dry area, a box the man had touched with his hand sang human music. Lifting his body partially out of the water, the dolphin accepted the fish and the music, though he was uncertain of the music. His back was peeling from the air and sun. The woman was not here. She was in a dry place—a city. When the dolphin dreamed of cities, they were like enormous coral reefs—half alive, half dead, growing insensibly in all directions. If the woman were here, she would have put a cream on his back. He accepted another fish. In his head, the changing musical replica of the world included the human music even though he was uncertain of it. He accepted another fish. He said the woman's name. He (and there was watching going on, and the man who wore transparent discs over his eyes was two and a third body lengths away, and he was getting closer) breathed.

"Okaynollyweeralmostreddynow."

There was the sound of the lizard fish moving to and fro ahead of him in the shallow waterwash, but now so suddenly still. There was the sound of a length of kelp drifting by, the sound of the shape of a crab claw on the hard flat bottom, the sound of the shadow of a bird passing over his skin. There was the sound of the moon, growing slightly fainter. There was the sound of the breathing of the two men, there was the sound of the hearts of the two men, there was the sound of the last butterfish dying in the bucket, drowning in air. There was the sound of what it was like to miss the woman; she lived an unfinished life in air forever. There was the sound of the man-who-watched splashing closer, the sound of the shape of the thing he was holding, the sound of the man's heart speeding up, the sound of the dolphin's heart speeding up, the sound of the man with the bucket falling down, knocked over by the dolphin's flukes, the sound of the sound of the sharp quick pain as the watcher pressed the metal thing against the dolphin's skin and made soothing sounds with his flexible lips.

When the dolphin swam away from the men, there was something electromagnetic attached to his skin. It hated him. It was not alive. He tried to scrape it off where the water was narrow, there where the sunshine stopped and the house began, but it could not be scraped off. It was an electromagnetic barnacle, but it was not alive. The dolphin swam into the house, singing a distress call though there were no other dolphins to hear. He swam into the elevator's harness and pressed the button with his beak. There was no pain. There were no other dolphins. The woman was not there. As the elevator lifted him up over the shaft to the deep pool below, he imagined for a moment a set of hands— not necessarily those belonging to the woman, but some other single set, moving about both the wet world and the dry to patiently undo everything that hands have ever done since the first fish slapped its fins against muddy banks and dragged itself out of the waterwash. The elevator lowered him, with a long hum, with its mechanical sequences, into the waterwash.

And he dived.

Ever since the woman's departure, the dolphin had been turning over in his memory a certain story from the sagas. He had replayed it in every sequence, reviewed it from every perspective, and still it flashed through his mind like a double-headed mackerel, taking directions that could never be expected, leading him again and again to thoughts he did not know how to finish.

Nor did he know why the man-who-watched was watching him now, peering at him through the dry bubble in the side of the deep pool, touching with dreamy hands the skittish machinery of dryness and hyperdryness. The woman would never have allowed the man to put the thing-that-was-not-alive on the dolphin's skin. The thing hated the dolphin. The woman knew how to love the dolphin by seeing him in a way to which he could never be party, and the desire to be seen in this way had become indistinguishable from the desire to protect the woman. But the woman, who was not here, knew nothing of protection.

The lapse of the dolphin hero Nel Nu was perhaps not a lapse; the sagas allowed for that possibility. Elsewhere the sagas slyly but repeatedly celebrated his melancholy disposition; seldom, even after the lapse, was he referred to as anything but a hero. And because the story belonged to that cycle of stories whose action always continued to the present, generation after generation for the instruction and betterment of all, it was impossible to avoid participating in the story by knowing it, impossible, once a participant, not to influence its outcome. So perhaps the voluntary exile of the dolphin hero Nel Nu was not a lapse—although it certainly seemed to be one. And the dolphin had always thought of it as one. And it was always referred to as one. In the sagas.

He swam the perimeter of the deep pool. In passing the dry bubble he saw the watcher communicating with the man-who-mated-with-machines. The man-who-mated-with-machines had teeth that were always visible and a hyper-dry machine that displayed a squiggling line of cold green light. The dolphin ignored them both. He swam another perimeter. Then he performed the movement in which his tail thrusts, which would normally have pushed him forward, were counterbalanced by simultaneous backward movements of his flippers. He had performed his movement, the movement of recollection, in exactly the same way ever since it had been taught to him by his mother, immediately after she had initiated him to sex. He experienced every occasion for the movement of recollection as though it were simultaneous with every other such occasion. He experienced himself as simultaneous with the dolphin hero Nel Nu.

It is remembered: that long after the Great Return from land to water, long after the moon had all but forsaken the praise of dolphins, a certain group of dolphins, Nel Nu among them, became aware that creatures from the dry world had succeeded in building structures with which to venture safely forth on the surface of the waterswell of the waterwash of the tides.

These structures, it was observed, were growing ever more congenial to the sea's touch, and would soon be able to cross the oceans with little difficulty. Further rumors had it that these dry creatures carried devices by which to praise the moon with measurement, and that in return for this attention the moon guided them safely across the waters. At length, it was decided that the dolphins should send one of their number to make contact with the creatures so as to discover what they were like and what they knew of the moon's intentions. The dolphin hero Nel Nu was chosen for this task.

Despite his melancholy disposition, which was already well known and already recorded in another part of the sagas and already itself the subject of rumors of several different salts both congenial and uncongenial, the dolphin hero Nel Nu was chosen for this task.

Nel Nu swam to the mouth of a river.

He swam up it so far as to let his belly be tickled by the long grasses of it and his taste be dulled by the saltlessness of it and his skin become hallucinated by the relentless current of it, which after all flowed in only one direction. He passed many of the dry creatures, in cities and villages; he passed many of their seagoing structures, large at first, then smaller. But still the dolphin hero Nel Nu swam, for he had determined, in his melancholy and delirium, to penetrate to the very heart of dryness, there to discover he did not know what, but perhaps along with it his own lost feelings of dryness, those thoughts and feelings which belonged to him in some way, and to all dolphins in some way, but which neither he nor any of them had ever found before.

The water grew so shallow that it did not cover him. The skin on his back grew cracked and dry; gravity began to weigh on him. The more he entered the dry world, the more everything divided up into . . . *things:* separate, disconnected.

The dolphin hero Nel Nu wriggled up onto the

muddy bank. There was a human there, a woman. She lay down in the mud with him and put her arms around him, her . . . "hands."

"We want to know how it is in your world," communicated Nel Nu.

"Petercanyuheerme? Aryuallrite?"

Startled by the sudden intrusion of the watcher's electromagnetic voice, the dolphin shot to the surface and (but the thing-that-hated-him was still on his skin and the moon had not yet risen and the woman was in a metal thing that traveled) breathed.

"Aidontnomartin, maybeenuthing. Buteeseemduh-beeinsumsortofconvulshuns."

He could see the men watching him from the dry bubble, watching him and communicating. He swam right by them two times. Humans ate water through their mouths because their bodies longed for the sea, which they did not remember. They never urinated but wrapped their genitals in fabricated skin and knew nothing of how to taste each other in the sea, where they did not live. It made him lonely to see the man-who-mated-with-machines eating colored water without knowing why. Sometimes water came out of the woman's eyes. He did not know why. She wasn't there. It made him lonely. He swam deeper.

It is remembered: that when the dolphin hero Nel Nu wriggled up onto the muddy bank, there was a human there, a woman. She lay down in the mud with him and put her arms around him, her hands.

"We want to know how it is in your world," communicated Nel Nu.

The woman held him close in the warm sun. She breathed more frequently than a dolphin, and there was hair. Her lips were flexible. "We live up and down upon the earth, wherever there is land to rest upon and air to breathe. We will be everywhere."

The dolphin hero Nel Nu wriggled further up the bank in his effort to understand, and the woman wriggled with him. In the air were tiny creatures that bit their skins, his skin and hers. The woman breathed against the skin of the dolphin hero Nel Nu. There were tiny flecks of blood—his and hers. "But what it is like?" he communicated.

"We have hands with which we make things. We have sleep in which we dream, and afterward we are rested and may forget the dreams. We walk upright on our feet, but that is only the beginning, for always we are finding new ways to travel farther and faster and with greater ease. We fear death, but to distract ourselves from the fear we make things. We are not really distracted, but it is better to pretend, and better to have things that you have made. We have more emotions than thoughts, and more needs than emotions. We believe in different things at different times; our memories are short and will grow shorter. I will not tell you what hair is for."

She drew her hair back and forth across the skin of the dolphin hero Nel Nu and made a sound like shallow water. "We have laughter," she communicated, and made the sound again. "Nor have I told you that we are able to lie." And, as he lay with the woman in the warm mud, high on the bank, it came to Nel Nu that he no longer knew which way lay the waterflow of the tide, he no longer remembered exactly what it was he had been sent to discover. "Moon," he communicated, and the woman put her legs around him.

"We care nothing for the moon, a dead thing. We have fire instead."

Her lips touched his skin.

In his dream, the dolphin hero Nel Nu was able to swim in air. He had become small, the size of a mackerel, and he floated three ordinary body lengths above the woman. She was making a fire. "I have not told you yet that we are able to lie," she communicated. The fire was bright and ate dry things. It could make water dry. The moon had risen. "We will be *everywhere*," she communicated, placing a hand on her belly and looking up at him.

There was a splash at the surface of the deep pool and the dolphin (but the watcher had disappeared from the dry bubble and the thing-that-hated-the-dolphin was still on the dolphin's skin and the lapse of the dolphin hero Nel Nu, which was perhaps not a lapse, flashed out of his mind—even, like a double-headed mackerel, before it had arrived) streaked to the site and breathed.

"Peeteritsmee."

But the dolphin did not want to swim with the man-who-watched. He snapped his jaws together several times in warning and sang the threat call. He butted at the man's legs with his head. Nothing about the man's way of seeing him provoked in the dolphin the desire to protect, or the desire to communicate, or the desire to continue to be seen in that way. Nothing in the man knew how to draw things to the surface and keep them there with impossible thoughts.

"IziturtingyooPeeter? Duziturt? LetmeeseePeeter. Aiwonturtyoo. JustcalmdownPeeter. Letmeesee."

The touch of the man-who-watched was not soothing, and the lunging swim of him was not congenial, and the dolphin made rush after rush at him until he had driven the man out of the pool again and back to his waterless postures and attitudes. Only when the watcher had reappeared in the dry bubble was the dolphin able to calm himself, and ignore the men. He swam two slow perimeters of the pool. He went deeper.

It was possible, if there was a lapse, that the dream of the dolphin hero Nel Nu was the beginning of it, if there was a beginning. Certainly the sagas did not recount how the dolphin hero Nel Nu managed to find his way back down the bank to the waterwash. They did not deny that the woman helped him, and always much was made of his melancholy temperament, which was perhaps not melancholy but something else instead. So perhaps that was the beginning of the lapse.

Ignoring the men, the dolphin swam deeper. He performed the movement.

It is remembered: that the dolphin hero Nel Nu returned the way he had come, down the saltless river to the ocean. There he reported to the other dolphins what he had learned, and his news was received with much disappointment, since not even the most shore-wise or tattered-fluked among them had imagined human beings to be so careless of the moon as to consider it a dead thing. All thought of further communication with humans was abandoned for the time being, all hope that the moon's return might be hastened was set aside. And there was much belly-to-belly swimming that night. In the flood of the tide.

But the dolphin hero Nel Nu had changed. He was melancholy, of course—what else if not melancholy?—but his swim grew more and more restless and his movement of recollection more and more violent. Moon gave way to moon gave way to moon. And though he had never been more amorous, never more tireless in pursuing the moody swims of females, or in raking sensitive female skins with his teeth, or in swimming belly-to-sensitive-female-belly, it was during this time that he ceased to father. He chose to mate only with sexually immature females, or barren females, or females who were already pregnant. This preference was noted.

This preference was noted but it was not condemned. And so the dolphin hero Nel Nu became bit by bit lost to dolphin society.

Increasingly, he swam by himself. Each time he set out by himself, the swim grew longer. There was no actual moment when he decided to return to the woman, to what she had hinted of the dry world.

He swam to the mouth of a river. It was not a river. He swam up it.

There was no actual moment when he reached the city of canals. Nor could there be any numbering the canals themselves, interlocking, interweaving—channel after channel after channel of controlled water. There was no actual moment when he became lost among those canals. He is lost among them now. The moon waxes and wanes. He has not ceased longing for the woman, who is there in a sense but only in a sense. He has not ceased swimming.

There is no actual moment in which you did not know the story of the lapse of the dolphin hero Nel Nu. The moon waxes and wanes. There is no actual moment when you did not favor the moon. You, most of all. It waxes and wanes.

The dolphin (rising slowly to the surface of the deep pool) breathed. He swam to where the waves spilling gently over the ramp from the cover beyond might wash his back. On the night of the storm, he recalled, the woman had forgotten to breathe like a woman.

Swimming over to the elevator, he became aware again of the thing-on-his-skin, but he made no attempt, while entering the harness, to scrape it off. It hated him, but it was only an electromagnetic barnacle. He pressed the elevator's button with his beak.

On the second floor, in the shallow water, he swam rapidly and purposefully about the house. His rubber rabbit he found by the sink; his floating ring and striped dishrag had become caught beneath the place-where-the-communicating-machine-rang; his yellow ball, as always, was orbiting the outflow fixture. He took these things one by one out onto the flooded observation deck and tossed them over the wall. Back inside, he splashed a few things off their hooks—the pieces of wood that were different shapes, the ones that were the same shape but different colors, a few other things that floated and had purposes. Taking them out onto the deck, he tossed them also over the wall. He made several more trips. And yet, when he was done, when he had rid the water of things that woman had given him or utilized with him or attempted to explain to him, he found that his longing for the woman herself had only grown more intense. And he began to swim systematically about the shallow waters of the house.

He swam rapidly and systematically with no allowance for legs. When the men appeared on the dry catwalk, he ignored them. This place was a place of controlled water, of tideless water, of canals. And though it was a small place, the dolphin had come to understand that he was lost in it. The man-who-watched attempted to walk in the water, but the dolphin was swimming without regard for the man's legs and knocked him over.

If it was true that the dolphin had become lost in this place of controlled water, and if his story had become simultaneous with that of the dolphin hero Nel Nu, then it was up to him to determine the outcome of that story. The woman was present in a sense but only in a sense, and the outcome of the story had not yet occurred.

Pausing before his mirror, examining himself first in the wet part of it, then in the dry part, the dolphin decided to eschew the deep water until the woman returned. It seemed to him that it was the sagas that had made this decision, the sagas through which now rippled this sudden sense of—acceleration. He swam.

The woman was in a city. She had gotten out of the metal thing that traveled. Water was coming out of her eyes. And in her hands, in her fingers, there were dreams that transformed almost everything.

So the dolphin swam. He would swim this way a long time—at high speed, in shallow water, with no allowance for legs. Until the woman came back. Or until he found his way out of these channels of water that was controlled and tideless and confusing. In either case, he would know now what to do. There was no actual mo-

ment when he had not. And the desire to be known by
the woman and the desire to protect her had always
been indistinguishable.

In shallow water, a dolphin will sometimes fall to
dwelling on the shortness of life and will seek to make
the best of it with amazing feats of attention.

TWO weeks later, three rights and a left down the spotless hospital corridor, Jeffrey forgot whether he was following the blue arrows or the orange ones. "The green ones," said a passing nurse. Jeffrey became lost. The information-sickness ward was much larger than he had ever thought, much larger than the press was reporting, so large it injured hope. At first, there were signs warning visitors of the penalties for smuggling in unnecessary information—whether printed, photographic, or recorded. Then there were no signs at all, no messages of any kind. Jeffrey could hear the patients murmuring in their beds, behind their palpation screens. When he turned around to retrace his steps, a tiny picture of Melissa rose into the upper right-hand corner of his mind: she was cracking eggs with one hand and talking to Nona.

"*Chiquita*," Kirk was saying as Jeffrey walked in, "I swear since I been in this place I seen every *manner* of shit." The woman sitting on the edge of the bed was wearing a black T-shirt with pink letters that said TALK NORMAL. She was very pretty. The room was very crowded. Kirk had a new roommate and the roommate had visitors. And the TV was on.

"Hey! Jeff, ole buddy! I won't even tell you how glad I am to see *you*. Charmian, this is my brother Jeff, who, I fondly hope and believe, has come here today to release me from this disinfected Disneyland. That *is* why you're here, Jeff?"

"That *is* why I'm here." He put down the single cowboy boot he had brought with him and smiled at Charmian, who was beyond all doubt a sight worth breaking an ankle for. She had beautiful shoulders, three little parenthetical lines to the left of her smile, and hair seven shades blond. It became necessary to look at her yet again.

"Charmian here came all the way up from Texas just to see about my bone structure," said Kirk, winking at Jeffrey. "And I told you how she feels about travel."

"Ne'mind 'how I feel 'bout what, big buddy," she said, standing up and looping the strap of her bag over her shoulder. "You just call me up later on tonight. You know where I'll be."

"Ain't no tellin' where you'll be," he said. "I'll call," he said.

"Bye," she said. Then, giving Jeffrey a laughing smile and a long once-over, she swept out the door like a fugitive bit of Gulf Coast weather, humid and spiky-eyed.

"Mother of God, what an armful," sighed Kirk. He looked down at his cast with what seemed to be a measure of weary companionability. "It could make you weep."

"How'd the X rays turn out?"

"They say I got forty–forty-five percent alignment. I'll be okay." His eyes met Jeffrey's. "How 'bout you?"

"I don't know." He put Kirk's empty duffel bag on the bedside chair and unzipped it. "I mean, I don't know too much about alignment right now. Next to nothing."

Feeling looked at, Jeffrey glanced across the room to where the other patient's visitors sat, two women and a small boy. They were silent. What he had taken for conversation was actually the delirious mumblings of the man in the other bed.

"Yeah, well, I been talkin' to Diego," said Kirk as Jeffrey tossed a razor, a sweater, a half-finished six-pack of Snickers bars into the duffel bag. "I know all the music and I can sing the words. And I know what tore up *is*." He produced a nearly empty pint of bourbon from under his mattress and studied it. "You think I don't?"

"I think you do." He caught the bourbon bottle with one hand and dropped it into the duffel bag. "But I'll tell you one thing. I don't have the shit-fuckingest idea what getting run over eight times is. Or what stepping out of a moving taxicab to do it is."

On the TV, a snow-goggled news personality was doing a human-interest story on the garbage at Mc-Murdo Station. Part of the human interest lay in the fact that the Antarctic Treaty of 1959 specified that all garbage must be flown off the continent for disposal. The personality pointed to a plane full of garbage about to take off. Another part of the human interest lay in the fact that the planes that were landing behind him were full of soldiers. The personality recited the clause of the treaty that forbade military maneuvers. Then the personality arched an eyebrow and said some names—first his own, then the network's.

"You're blaming yourself," said Kirk.

"I didn't do enough. I could've done more to protect her."

"From what? Radial tires? Don't be an asshole."

"There were things going on."

"Like what?"

"Like guns. Like he used to threaten her with a gun. I was supposed to protect her."

Jeffrey, lowering one of the cameras into the duffel bag by its strap, was turned half away from Kirk. The fact that he was being discharged from the hospital today had encouraged Kirk to aspire toward a reality in which people did not threaten each other with guns or secrets or planes full of garbage. It occurred to him now, recalling the kind of smile Melissa had given him when he had surprised her with the gun, that actually she understood the both of them—Jeffrey and himself —very well indeed.

"Jeff," he said, "nobody gets protection."

Jeffrey did not turn around. He was crying. "We lost her, man."

"Yes," Kirk allowed, "we did. And sooner or later you and I are going to be just as dead as she is. Now listen to me, I'm your brother. You think you know better than me? You don't."

Jeffrey turned slowly around. He didn't have anything in his hands, so they fell to his sides and absorbed his grief. It shocked him how much room that left.

"You can't protect other people from their lives, you fuckhead. It can't be done. Why do you try?"

Jeffrey took an uncertain step forward. "Is that what I do? I try that?" In a moment he was pacing up and down beside Kirk's bed. He was no longer crying. "Okay. Maybe I try that. Maybe I do. But even now, even with everything as fucked up as it is"—he stopped, glared at Kirk, and pointed at the TV—"even with shit like that going on, isn't there, I don't know, something people do for each other?"

"Sure there's something." Kirk lifted his cast-encased leg in both hands and swung it around so he was sitting upright on the edge of the bed. "They stay alive."

"That's all?" said Jeffrey. "You think that's all?"

Kirk looked at him for a long while, his eyes going slowly to discs. Then he shrugged and said, "It's not as simple as it sounds. Ask Diego."

Jeffrey used a pair of scissors to slit one leg of his brother's jeans to the knee. The two women looked away while he and Kirk managed the business of the hospital gown, but the little boy looked on. At times it was possible to hear the murmuring of the man in the other bed, but at other times it wasn't. Nobody was watching the television.

In Jeffrey's mind, the image of Melissa was stirring a pot of gin fizz with a soup ladle. He resolved to see what she and Nona were drinking when he got there.

"So how are you and Lissy doing lately?" Kirk asked, tucking in his shirt's checkered tail.

"Me and Lissy?" Jeffrey repeated, a bit startled. "I don't know, really." He put Kirk's battered-looking copy of *The Antarctica Catalogue* into the duffel bag and scanned the area for other overlooked artifacts. "I've stopped seeing Clarice, though. That must mean something."

"Clarice?"

"The blond woman in the restaurant."

Kirk laughed a little. A nurse came in and said a few pleasant things in an unpleasant way but everybody ignored her so she turned up the TV and left.

"Lissy decided not to go ahead with that dolphin project then?" Kirk asked, inspecting the stitching on the sharkskin boot Jeffrey had handed him.

"I don't know what she's decided."

"But you only got a couple of weeks of teaching left anyway, right?"

"Less."

Kirk nodded. He put the boot on the floor and his foot in the boot. He began carefully to pull it on. "Want to go to Antarctica tomorrow?"

Jeffrey looked sharply up from the duffel bag. More and more frequently these days, he found himself waiting to see what he would feel next. His curiosity, over the weeks, had become quite genuine. "I thought that was off now," he said, watching the teeth of the zipper mesh as he pulled it to.

"Well, yeah. For me it is."

Their eyes met, and Jeffrey had the sudden vivid sense of being in a crowd—a crowd that, had there actually been one, would surely have been composed of creatures very like himself. He felt as if they were all traveling together at an incredible speed, harmonious and oddly without movement. It was a peaceful feeling, and for a moment the image of Melissa in his mind grew very vivid—he could actually hear the words she was speaking—and then, just as suddenly, he felt nothing at all.

"You're saying you haven't told anybody at *Newsweek* about your ankle," he said.

"Everything's all ready to go: I got the equipment, the press clearances, the plane tickets. Seems like a shame to let it all go to waste."

Jeffrey smiled at him. "No weapon? You were gonna go out in that terrible cold weather without a weapon?" He began to pace again. "How about that."

"All you have to do is talk like a shit-kicker and sign your name a little different. Only three or four guys actually know me, and they're up here on this end. Once you're on the plane, it's all you, Jeff buddy, any way you want it." He looked closely at Jeffrey. "Just keep on shooting pictures, show the folks how it is. And it's all you."

Jeffrey stopped before the corner where Kirk's aluminum crutch was leaning. Not till that moment had he remembered the dream about the Indian in the back yard, the dream in which Kirk had been in a wheelchair. He shook his head and began quietly to laugh.

Kirk grinned. "You like it."

"Yeah, maybe so," said Jeffrey, handing him the crutch and shouldering the duffel bag. "I don't know what I like." Melissa was answering the apartment door, she was greeting Richard. "Let's just get the fuck out of here."

When Kirk was halfway to the door, the little boy's voice stopped him. "Hey, mister," the boy said. "Are you twins?"

"Yeah, I am," said Kirk, turning around. Jeffrey was

already in the hall. "I'm twins." His ankle hurt him very much. "Now you take care of your daddy, hear?"

As they shot out of the hospital parking lot, Kirk rolled down the window of the BMW and stuck his head out. "Hot *damn*, it's good to be out of there," he said.

They drove straight to Diego's. Jeffrey had decided to pick him up on the way home because otherwise Diego could not be counted upon to show, things being what they were. He asked Kirk if he wanted to wait in the car, things being what they were. Kirk said no, he'd hate that.

The elevator was out of order, and by the time they'd reached Diego's floor they'd already separated the sounds coming from his loft into two categories: country music and other. "Some sort of machine?" said Jeffrey, pressing the buzzer.

"Uh-uh. Sounds more like—"

"*It's open*," yelled Diego from within.

"Crickets?" said Kirk. They looked at each other. Jeffrey opened the door. The loft was completely dark except for a single clip-on automotive lamp at the back. "But Daddy never let it worry him," sang the amplifier. The other sound seemed to come from everywhere at once. "Yeah," said Jeffrey, with a shrug. "Crickets." The door swung shut behind them. "And I ain't a-gonna let it worry me." The singer was a woman, her voice very beautiful in the dark.

"Hey, Diego, it's us. Where y'at, man?"

"Back here."

He was sitting in an easy chair, smoking a joint and staring at the wall. Actually, he was staring at the ellipse of light made on the wall by the automotive lamp. There was a foot-long blue lizard in the middle of the ellipse. It moved.

"People say there will be war," said Diego. "They say this is the end of the world."

"Probably it just feels like that," said Kirk, accepting the joint.

"No, *compañeros*. Really. It *is* the end of the world. Look how fucked up everything is."

"Well," Kirk admitted. "You can't rule it out." He dragged deeply on the joint.

"What's that blue thing?" said Jeffrey. "I mean, I've seen rats before, but that doesn't look like them."

"Cristóbal?" Diego was so deeply settled in the chair that his elbows were higher than his shoulders. "I did not tell you about San Cristóbal?" He sighed. The crickets chirped. And with pedal steel coming in behind, the woman on the amplifier allowed as how some folks said she wasn't free. "I know I told you about her cat, though. I tell you about that, man?"

The woman said that didn't worry her.

"Yeah." Jeffrey sat in the string hammock in the corner. He kept his feet on the ground. "You had to give the cat away, right? Because it kept reminding you of some conversation you had with Nikki?"

"Right, right. But what I did not remember was that the cat, she used to do nothing all night but kill the cockroaches. Stalk, pounce. Stalk, pounce. All night long. So with no cat, it's very quiet, okay? But it's also very fine for the cockroaches, and in one week, man, they are back." He waved away the joint, and Kirk, taking it with him, sat carefully down on a nearby stool. A cricket hopped off into the darkness. Legs, thought Kirk.

"Anyway, last week I read in the papers that geckos are very good for the cockroach problem because they love especially to eat them. They *live* on those *cucarachas*, man. So I bought Cristóbal. What happens? It turns out he has a special diet: he hates cockroaches. Won't even look at them. Cristóbal eats crickets. Ten dollars for a hundred." Diego looked at the wall and shrugged. "Yesterday they escaped."

Jeffrey and Kirk peered around at the dark into

which the hundred crickets had fled. Then the radio announcer came in over the end of the song to voice a few opinions about the right of every individual American to keep on rolling down the road, and Diego said something in a quiet voice.

"What?" said Jeffrey.

"I said: 'She just opened the door and stepped right out.'" He stood up. The gecko turned one amber eye upon him and moved a few steps up the wall. "Why'd she want to do a thing like that?"

Jeffrey looked at his feet. Melissa was reading part of a recipe aloud to Nona, and Richard was ladling himself a drink.

"Oh, man. Things just . . ." Kirk waved the joint vaguely in the air. "You know . . . escape."

"*Qué vida,*" said Diego.

When they left, the radio was still on. In the car Diego turned to Jeffrey and said, "I lied about the crickets escaping. It was me. I let them out."

Jeffrey flicked the turn signal on and shivered. He'd been thinking about the cold weather. "How come?"

"That sound is what keeps me going." He smiled. It was almost infectious. "Really. It keeps me going."

Every light in the apartment was on. And there were lilacs, irises, baby's breath, and daisies. "I think that's them now," said Melissa's voice from the kitchen. She sounded drunk but didn't look it, rounding the corner in her turquoise pumps.

"I didn't know ya'll were havin' a party," said Kirk. "I—"

"It's for you," she said, kissing him on the mouth. She kissed Diego on the mouth too. Richard wandered in from the living room, looking sheepish and confused. "I'm Richard," he said. Gin fizz, noted Jeffrey, taking a sip from Melissa's glass. She smiled at him in a slightly wicked way, shrugged, and kissed him on the nose—or rather, put his nose in her mouth, for part of a second.

Nona came out of the living room, weaving slightly. Then music did. "Welcome back," she said to Kirk, and hugged him. "We missed you here in the closet."

"Closet?"

"We closet skydivers."

"Shit." He glanced at Jeffrey because Jeffrey always blushed at the same time he did and Kirk wanted to see how noticeable it was.

"Okay, it's 7:25," said Richard, holding out his wrist and continuing to look at his watch even though he had just said what time it was. "You wanted me to tell you when it was 7:25, right? That's what it is now."

Melissa put the duck back in the oven. The tureen of gin fizz was in the living room. At first Diego didn't want a drink, but after Nona came over and introduced herself, he realized that the vivid way in which the women were dressed had been making him nervous, so he had one after all. Then everyone sat down, because of Kirk. Coming in from the kitchen, Melissa dunked her glass in the tureen and said, distinctly but to no one in particular: "Quack." She sat down opposite Jeffrey, who was sitting next to Kirk on the sofa. She concentrated.

"Prize money?" Richard was saying. He chuckled. "What prize money? Third place gets you the price of your tires—thirty-five hundred, give or take." Pausing to reflect on the give and take, he looked soberly at Nona, seated beside him. She nodded almost imperceptibly, and his features expanded in a grin. "As it turns out," he said, finishing his drink, "neither of us was in it for the money."

"Why, then, I just bet it was the thrill of competition," offered Kirk, looking from one of them to the other. His foot was up and he was feeling good. "That it? The sweet thrill of competition?"

"Actually," said Nona, looking nervously at Melissa, who was concentrating, "Richard and I are getting married."

Jeffrey jumped, spilling a bit of his drink. It was not what Nona had said that startled him, but the sudden proximity of Melissa's voice, whispering urgently in his ear. Or rather in his head, since he had been watching her and was certain she had neither vaulted over the table from her chair and back at the speed of light nor indeed opened her mouth at all.

"I think that's great," said Melissa. "I really do." She had stopped concentrating. "Congratulations. We need a toast."

"How 'bout a larger world?" said Kirk.

"We need that, too."

"No, I mean how 'bout that as a toast. 'To Nona, Richard, and a Larger World.' "

Jeffrey let out a lot of breath. "Yeah, okay," he said, raising his glass. "I think that just about gets it all." And as Melissa, smiling widely, raised her glass too, the décolletage of her blue-and-white wraparound dress parted just enough for Jeffrey to see what he had till then failed to notice: between her breasts, on a silver chain, she had hung a single flashing shard of mirrored glass.

"Anybody mind if I roll another joint?" asked Diego, when they had drunk the toast.

"Larger world," mused Richard, rattling the ice in his glass. "What's that mean? How come larger?"

"Oh, Richard. You never miss a chance," said Nona.

"God yes, roll another one," Kirk said. "Roll two."

"Chance?"

"To tell us what an old fart you think you are," she said, hugging him.

"I fell here out of the sky," Kirk said. "And I am full of self-confidence and I am ready for another joint."

Diego flashed the TV on then, just to get the picture, and Melissa got up to turn the record over. The picture showed an actor dressed like a cowboy; he was trying to ride a mechanical bull in a bar in Texas.

"You know later maybe we could play some poker,"

said Jeffrey. He'd been studying the backs of Melissa's legs as she leaned over the stereo and he had been thinking about no help. No help took some getting used to, as a concept. "I mean it's a very good game. Nikki liked it."

"Nikki did not *like* poker," said Diego as he laid a line of grass across the rolling paper. "Nikki loved poker. She believed in it. You think I'm wrong?"

"No, you couldn't be."

"I couldn't be," said Diego with satisfaction. "I could not be. And I am not."

"Richard, you a poker player?"

"Sure."

The music came back on, a little louder than before, and Melissa sat back down opposite Jeffrey. All things considered, that was the position she had always occupied in respect to him. It pleased him to remember that that was why he loved her. Reasons had become somewhat scarce, and with the weather threatening to turn so chilly, it was good to know a few coordinates. He saw that she had painted her toenails red, and when he looked up at her, she gave him a slightly wasted smile.

"I know what you're thinking," she said, "and you're right."

"What I'm thinking?"

"You do have my number."

"Hey, aren't you all gonna pass me any of that fine-looking cheese?" Kirk asked, but just then the oven timer beeped and Melissa announced that dinner was ready. Jeffrey carved. He tried concentrating on something of his own, something in an urgent whisper, but when the joint came by, he forgot what. There was asparagus and wild rice. Richard had brought the tureen into the dining room, and though there was wine, everyone continued to drink gin fizzes. Diego looked at the unlit joint he had placed beside his plate.

Then his mind returned to the thought that occupied him now whenever nothing else distracted him—the one about opening the door and stepping right out. The Nikki thought. Somethings he thought the same thing through in Spanish—but not often, because of the loneliness.

"I'll tell you one thing I wasn't prepared for, though," said Jeffrey, "and that's Nikki's mother. I'd forgotten what an eccentric little item she is, with that long black scarf and all."

"The Isadora Duncan of Kansas," said Melissa.

"One second here," Nona said, wiping her mouth with her napkin. "Emma may be an acquired taste, but she's all right. I'll defend her. We mothers have to stick together."

Diego struck his forehead with one hand and began slapping his pockets with the other. "Man, I almost forgot."

"Forgot what?"

He half stood, produced a dog-eared photograph from his back pocket, and handed it to Nona. "That's you at the left, no? You and Lissy?"

The phone rang then, and Jeffrey, who had placed a hand on Melissa's thigh under the table, felt her stiffen. "It's okay," he said. "The machine's on."

"I can't believe it," said Nona, looking at the photograph. "Where on earth did you find this?"

"But what if—"

"It was in Nikki's sewing basket," Diego said. "Right there on top of everything."

"I told you," Jeffrey whispered. "The machine's on. Please." And, as the phone stopped ringing, Melissa looked at him. She nodded. She put her hand on top of his, and it occurred to Jeffrey that, things being what they were, he could very easily fall in love with her all over again. Never mind the telephone. All he required was a little encouragement.

"I have the feeling," said Nona, handing her the photo and reaching for the wine, "that Lissy will remember this."

After examining it a moment, Melissa looked up at her mother. "Oh, my God. Nikki's party."

"I think you were seven. Maybe six. You'd just met Nikki at camp."

Jeffrey smelled pot again and saw out of the corner of his eye that Diego had lit up the second joint. Richard was trying without much success to reassemble his look of polite interest. "What was it—a birthday party?" he asked.

Melissa handed the photo to Jeffrey. She didn't look at him. "Not exactly. But you're close."

"Emma—Nikki's mother—invited Lissy and me to stay with them in Kansas City for a week," Nona began. "I think Nikki's brother and father were off hunting in Louisiana or someplace. Anyway, they weren't around, and it ended up being a pretty female few days."

The picture in fact showed fourteen females—seven little girls and an equal number of young women. Nona, always photogenic, was looking at the woman next to her and laughing, her chin thrust gaily forward. A lock of hair had fallen half across her face, and with the hand not holding a cigarette she was about to brush it back. It took Jeffrey a moment to identify Nikki; he would not have guessed her to have been so nearly fat as a child.

"How come Daddy didn't come?" Melissa said. "Where was he?"

"No, thanks," said Richard, looking first at Nona, then at the joint Diego held absently out to him.

"Oh, I guess he was out with the other men, flying around in his Superman uniform and earning us a living." She laughed, the register of her laughter veering from fondness to scorn and at least partway back again. Richard accepted the joint, after all.

"It's some kind of dress-up party," Jeffrey said.

"Right," said Nona. "But the interesting part is, *what* kind?"

Melissa, exchanging a look with Kirk, lit a cigarette. When her first puff drifted across the table toward Nona, she immediately put it out.

Jeffrey had always had something of a problem with photographs of Melissa as a child; they tended to stir up in him a vague dissatisfaction which he knew she read in him as a sort of retrospective love, a yearning for what might not be had of her. In fact, it was something altogether different and more promising. He felt it now, studying this array of girls and women, among whom Melissa, despite her makeup and high heels, was instantly identifiable—by the generous cut of her mouth, by the feral exuberance of her stance, by the way she had rolled her eyes upward toward Nona and the ceiling. And at the same time that Jeffrey saw the premise of the party and photo, he understood the nature of his dissatisfaction. It wasn't dissatisfaction. It was fear. He was afraid of everything that stopped.

"Was it Nikki's idea?" he asked, turning to Melissa.

"Of course."

"Nikki's idea to *what?*" yelled Kirk, pounding his crutch on the floor at his end of the table.

"Have a party where all the girls come dressed up as their mothers," Jeffrey yelled back. He passed the photo to Kirk. "You and I probably wouldn't of had a good time."

Diego gestured with the drumstick he'd been gnawing. "Don't kid yourself, *amigo*: we were not invited. She looked at that picture every time she opened her sewing basket, but me, I never saw it until yesterday. I found it, that's all."

Nona said, "It was a good party."

Drawing on the joint, Melissa seemed to Jeffrey pale and inward, newly fatal. He could tell she was thinking once again of the three of them together on that humming hotel bed, a stack of quarters in Nikki's hand, and he wondered, as she met his glance, how much she knew of his own thoughts. He remembered the words her voice had whispered in his head, if it had; he re-called the touch of her hand on his. This, he reflected, was a whole new ball game.

"Jeff, there any more stuffing in that bird?"

"Sure. Pass your plate."

"What about you?" said Nona, looking at Kirk and taking off her earrings.

"You mean, what've I got left in the way of stuffin'?"

"I mean, what do you do now? I don't suppose you'll be going to Antarctica like that."

Kirk gave Jeffrey a look of such sheer bonhomie that Melissa turned to look at him as well. Okay, thought Jeffrey, I can do it this way, I know this one too. He experienced a curious surge of total optimism—for himself, for all of them—and he saw to it that Melissa noticed. Kirk nodded twice in the manner of one disin-terestedly admiring a bit of handiwork. "Well now," he said, turning to Nona, "one thing you should know about temporarily unemployed flying men. We may sit around on our asses all day and night, but when we wake up in the morning, we are full of plans. And let me tell you I mean *full*."

Diego chuckled tolerantly and shook his head. "This fuckin' guy," he said to Richard, indicating Kirk with his thumb.

"Now I got a woman friend down in Houston hates to travel. *Hates* it, you understand. But she come up here to visit me in the hospital 'cause that's the way she is. And you know what? She don't even realize it yet but she's havin' one helluva time. I mean she likes me pretty well, but what she *really* likes is night life—clubs with live music and whatnot. So I give her one of my cameras, showed her what an *f*-stop is, and told her to by God *document* it." He laughed a little over his stuff-ing. "She's good."

"Hey then, *hombre*—you ought to have her document me and my band. We're talent, right? You heard us."

Kirk paused to watch Diego toss the wishbone he'd been picking at to his plate. Then he smiled and poured himself some wine. "You know, I may just take you up on that, buddy, I may just do that. Because the other part of what I've got in mind is that Charmian and I move in with you."

The record player had turned itself off a long time ago. Everybody looked at Diego. He blinked once. "Okay," he said "*¿Por qué no?*" He grinned. "Sure."

"I mean, I'm gonna have to persuade her first."

"That's all right." Diego took another joint out of his pocket and tossed it the length of the table. Kirk caught it. It was a key. But nobody gets protection, Jeffrey thought, watching Melissa get up from the table. He assumed she was going to put on another record until he heard the faint garble of the answering machine being rewound in the hall.

Picking up the last piece of asparagus, Jeffrey surveyed the gathering. They were stoned.

"Star Wars," he told them.

Melissa no longer found it surprising that when she left Jeffrey's physical presence, his image rose instantly into the corner of her mind—there by turns to be scrutinized or lived with or temporarily ignored. In fact, she found this particular development enormously reassuring. In a world about to go to war over the South Pole, she supposed it meant she loved him. Lighting a cigarette, she replayed Ehrler's message, then took the phone into the kitchen and dialed the flooded house.

Martin answered. He said that Ehrler was very anxious to talk to her. She said she knew that.

"Hi, Melissa," Ehrler said through the general static. "How are you?"

"A little deranged."

"You're stoned?"

"That too."

He sighed. "I know you've got your hands full up there, and the last thing I want to do is add to your troubles. I mean, you'll be down here in a week anyway . . ."

Her toes, even in her turquoise pumps, were wiggling. When she looked at them, she thought: Toenail polish. "I'm not going to run out on you, John. Is that what you're worried about?"

He hastened to assure her that it wasn't. "But," he continued, "there've been some developments I thought you should know about."

"Developments?" she said. "*Developments?*" The cigarette had begun to bother her and she put it out. "John, please stop talking shit and just tell me what's going on."

During the brief pause that ensued, she fancied she could hear splashes over the phone. She was reminded of what it had been like to discover Nikki's voice on the answering machine the day after her death.

"A couple of weeks ago," Ehrler began, "Martin came to me with a finished prototype of that radio electrode the three of us had talked about—you remember?—and he'd solved the attachment problem so prettily that I saw no reason not to give it a whirl."

"Sure. Why not."

"Okay. Right away we started getting some very interesting results—completely different from what we got when we had him all hooked up in the lab. Not only was there a great deal more electromagnetic activity than we had supposed, going on right there in the epithelium, but it tended to follow an overall wave conformation—similar to, but different from, brain waves. So much so, in fact, that metaphorically speaking, the integument as a whole might be seen as a kind of secondary brain."

Nona and Richard came wobbling in with the dishes.

Melissa pointed to the sink. "Terrific," she said to Ehrler. "Maybe it's even true. So what's the problem?" Fucked, fucked, fucked, she thought, trying to clear her head. Richard couldn't find the dessert plates. "Wait a minute," she said into the phone. "Upper right-hand cupboard," she said to Richard. Nona had taken the chocolate cake into the dining room, and Richard, giving Melissa a snappy little wave, staggered out with the plates. Melissa closed her eyes. "So what's the problem?" she repeated.

"Well, we don't know exactly. Right after I attached the electrode, Peter made for the deep water and started in on what we've been calling his 'rocking-horse behavior'—you know, kind of seesawing back and forth in the water—but so violently that really it amounted to an entirely different category of movement. At first I thought he was in some kind of convulsion, but when I went in after him he stopped long enough to push me back out. So I figured it was voluntary."

"Maybe he was trying to shake off the electrode. What exactly was he doing?"

"Swimming in place, he's done it before. But never so persistently or violently. He'd propel himself forward with his flukes and rotate his flippers backward at the same time so that he stayed right where he was."

"I've never seen him do it quite that way either," she said. People up here do that all the time, is what she almost said. She opened her eyes again. "Then what happened?"

"Well, actually it was Martin who noticed it. As long as Peter was moving that way, the electrode showed all that epithelial activity to be falling into what was basically an alpha-wave pattern. Like what happens to human brain waves during meditation or daydreaming."

"Or TV watching."

"Right, right—or TV watching. Of course we have no way of knowing what it indicates in dolphins, and, what's more, it's their skins we're talking about rather than their brains, but still . . ."

Melissa went into a slight glide over that last phrase —"their skins rather than their brains"—but she recovered nicely. "John, that *is* exciting. It really is."

"We just might be on to something. Who knows? But first we've got to figure out what to do with it."

Feathering a cuticle with her teeth, Melissa wondered whether he had called simply to make her jealous —he had succeeded—and thus more manipulable, but almost at the same time she realized she must be wrong.

"That's the good news," Ehrler said. "The bad news is more complicated."

Melissa fought down another glide. "Something's fucked," she said at last. "Something's really fucked for you to be talking like this." Her free hand drifted to her throat as if to monitor the passage of air within, and her voice simultaneously rose to a whine she could not control. "*Where's Peter? What've you done with Peter?*"

"He's right here, Melissa. He's okay. It's just—" She heard him take a deep breath. "Look, take it easy. I'm telling you everything. Just hear me out."

There was a tiny crescent chip missing from the corner of her thumbnail. "All right," she said. Or thought she said. Without having said anything, she waited.

"Okay. So Peter kept up this rocking-horse behavior for about twenty minutes. Then, quite suddenly, he swam over to the elevator and went up to the second floor. By the time Martin and I got up there from the observation port, he'd systematically thrown all his toys and training equipment over the wall of the sun deck, out of the house." Ehrler paused, and again Melissa thought she heard water splashing in the background. "I don't remember him ever doing that before, do you?"

"No. He never has."

"That's what I thought."

Melissa smelled dope again and waved her hand as

though to disperse the smoke. In her mind, in the living room, the image of Jeffrey performed the same gesture twice as fast and half as wide to indicate he didn't want the joint. Did you take the electrode off? was what she almost asked. Her heart was pounding. She said nothing.

"Well, maybe you can tell me what you think it means," Ehrler went on, "because after that happened ... Well, after that, he changed. He hasn't been down to the deep water once since then, even at night. He just keeps swimming around upstairs, moving from room to room in a kind of circuit—very regular, very fast. What's more, we're getting no humanoid vocalizations at all now, certainly no words. He ignores us completely—even physically. If we're in his way, he runs right into us. If we try to catch him, he doesn't struggle. We're just not a factor."

"Maybe," Melissa suggested, "he wants a vacation."

"That's what I thought too at first, something like that, but then a week ago he stopped eating."

"He *what?* I thought you said he was okay. Why the fuck didn't you—"

Ehrler cut her off. "He *is* okay. We're force-feeding him. As I told you, he doesn't struggle."

Melissa was silent.

"But naturally," he said, "I'm concerned. Soon we're going to have to think of something better than shooting fish purée down his throat every eight hours." He paused, and through her mounting panic Melissa saw suddenly that it was not pride—not discretion or even manipulativeness—that had caused him to delay a week in calling. The discovery embarrassed her, and embarrassment took the edge off her panic without diminishing it. "You have any ideas?" it seemed he had asked her.

"What about the electrode?" she said numbly. "You junked that, didn't you?"

"Right away. As soon as he came upstairs."

She had taken the bit of mirror from between her breasts and was testing its edge against her thumb. "John, this isn't happening, right? I'm just stoned and tired and all disinformed, right?"

When he said nothing, she put a hand over her face and began to cry. "It's too much," she said. "Just one thing after another."

A moment later, she added, "It's like with Anatole."

"Anatole?"

"You know—Anatole. That dolphin I told you about, at the Aquarium."

"You mean," said Ehrler cautiously, "you think Peter's trying to commit suicide?"

"No, no *no*," she answered impatiently, wiping the tears from her eyes. "No, poor Peter. I mean it's like what happened to the other dolphins after Anatole died." It occurred to her that by this formulation she had cast herself in a peculiar role, though actually it wasn't really she who was doing the casting, and in the end it was only a role.

"Tell me about that," Ehrler said.

"They wasted away from grief. Two of them—his most frequent lovers—died. Pamela and I tried force-feeding them, and finally I think that's what saved the others, but with Liz and Ellie nothing helped. Complete anorexia. It was horrible."

"And you think Peter's grieving?" His voice was genuinely, openly curious. "Over what?"

"He needs me, I need him. It's a stupid arrangement, and I'd undo it if I could. But I can't." As soon as she'd said it, she realized she'd been caught.

"In that case," Ehrler said, "maybe you'd better think about coming down sooner than we'd planned. Maybe you should think about coming down tomorrow."

The thought of coming down tomorrow made Melissa sleepy. She was, for the first time since Nikki's death, very tired. "Yes. Okay, I'll be there tomorrow." Probably, she reflected, Ehrler was a genius after all. Certainly he had always seen her for what she had only recently discovered herself to be.

"There's a direct plane out of Miami tomorrow at noon. Martin and I will be in San Juan buying some hardware for the computer, but I'll have Knolly pick you up."

"I haven't told my mother yet. I haven't told anybody yet."

"You'll do okay."

Melissa said nothing.

"So I'll see you tomorrow."

"Yes. When you get back from San Juan."

"Thanks, Melissa."

She hung up, fingering the shard around her neck. There were voices in the other room and she listened to them without trying to make sense of them. It was always possible to go back to where they were—now, or in a few minutes, or in a few days.

She was the scientific method continued by other means.

"Lissy, you've got to wake up, baby." Jeffrey's hand was cool on the back of her neck. "Everybody's leaving and they want to say goodbye."

She lifted her head from the kitchen table. "Goodbye?" she said drowsily.

"Come on, sweetheart."

Ah well, she thought, slipping back into her turquoise pumps, this I can do. I know all about it. Jeffrey's smile reminded her that there was something she wanted to ask him, but she couldn't quite recall what. Yawning convulsively, she followed him across the hall into the living room, where everyone was indeed standing about, ready to go. They looked as though they'd had a good time.

"I'm sorry," she said, wrapping her loosened dress a bit more decently about her. "Must be my blood sugar."

"How could it be *your* blood, sugar, when it's right here on *my* shirt," said Kirk, twisting one arm around so he could see the elbow. He peered in mock puzzlement at the small patch of red there.

"You can see about how much you missed," Jeffrey said to her.

"Looks," she said, watching Richard gulp down the last of a cup of coffee, "as if I missed a lot."

"Hey, we can make up for it now," said Diego. His shirt was out and he had a joint behind one ear. "Come on down to the corner with me an' Kirk an' have a *cerveza*. We'll let your boyfriend here get his beauty sleep."

She shook her head sadly. "Too late for me." Nona was standing by the light and Melissa had to squint to see her. "You two really driving out to the country tonight?"

"Sure. We'll be okay."

"And, Kirk, you're really going out and try to break that other ankle your first day out of the hospital?"

"Thought I'd practice getting around is all. It's Saturday night."

Melissa sighed. "Well then," she said, looking about the room, "I guess this *is* good night." She went over to Diego and kissed him. "Don't you get yourself in any more trouble now," she said, taking the joint from behind his ear and handing it to him.

"No," he answered soberly. "Of course not."

"Night, Kirk. Richard."

They thanked her.

"And you," she said, hugging Nona. "Congratulations. I'll talk to you later."

"Yes," she said. "Call." Her voice was hoarse.

"I'll call," Melissa said.

Jeffrey, holding the door open, said that he would see

them all out to the elevator, and Melissa, in the foyer, found herself staring at the door as it swung shut behind him.

"All right," she said. But it was not all right.

ABANDONMENT WALTZ

Closed, the door seems quite perfect to Melissa—a thing from the movies, a dream door. She stares at it without wanting to, feeling addressed by it in the most literal way. *Oh, I don't know*, she explains silently, *it's just all these people disappearing on me, I can't help it.* The door offers nothing further, and with a shrug she turns away.

In the living room, she begins to collect the coffee cups and brandy glasses that are scattered about. The television is on, picture without sound, and she finds that as the only other thing in the room that moves she feels a certain kinship with it. On the screen, a man at a podium is shaking his fist and shouting, while a ribbon of words snakes by beneath: "Live Coverage of the UN Emergency Session—Antarctica." It occurs to her as she adjusts the antenna that the television is like a baby except its demands are fewer. She holds her hand over it, marveling at the warmth. Then, suddenly angry, she uses the same hand to switch it off. *What a disgusting idea*, she thinks.

The bedroom is stuffy and she opens the windows. There is moonlight. She undresses in it.

When Jeffrey first entered her life, it did not take him long to discover her weakness for dwelling on the circumstances by which he might leave it. Don't holler before you're hurt, he would tell her. Now, pulling the sheet up over herself, she reflects that loving him has caused her to become acquainted with an unusually wide range of hollers, not all of them her own, but that she continues to think of hurt as being silent.

She puts her head between two pillows, thus causing

the image of Jeffrey to grow smaller and brighter in her mind's corner: Jeffrey waving goodbye as the elevator closes, Jeffrey putting his key in the lock. When the door slams shut in the foyer, the image vanishes at once and Melissa flings the top pillow to the floor. A light goes on in the kitchen. She resolves to stay awake for him.

Over the years, Melissa has used a single sentence both to stand for and to explain her father's departure from her life. It is on this sentence that she was concentrating earlier in the evening and she wonders now whether Jeffrey really could have heard it in some way. The words of the sentence, which often pass through her mind of their own accord, threaten to do so now.

When she closed her eyes, the kitchen is very distant.

I've tried and tried and tried to understand, but sometimes a person just never comes back.

There seems to be a moment when anything at all could happen. It fades. She sleeps.

They woke together in a confusion of touch, bed linen, and near-darkness to find themselves making love. Jeffrey, in sleep, had entered her half from behind, straddling her far thigh with his knees, cradling her near one with his arm. Melissa, in sleep, had received and held him. Each half believed that the other, in some barely imagined afterward, would know exactly how they had arrived at this moment, and neither, therefore, had the slightest inclination to question it. Melissa lifted her leg from his arm's embrace, held it in the air over his head for a long moment, then brought it, with a sigh, back down on the other side of him. He moved deeper in, holding his weight up off her with his hands. Her eyes fluttered open on his, then closed again, and as they came, he first and she immediately after, it seemed to him that she spoke to him.

They lay like that for some time before Jeffrey gently disengaged himself. There was a small lamp by his side of the bed, and he turned it on. Melissa lay looking at him, her legs doubled over above her, knees to breasts, in a way he hadn't seen till then.

"What are you doing?" he asked, ashamed at the lameness of the question.

She laughed with her mouth open, as though in surprise. "I don't know. This."

He stretched out beside her. "Lissy, I want to have children with you."

She waved her legs a little in the air, first one, then the other.

"It's something simple but I didn't know it before," he continued. "I want to marry you. I want to have children with you. I'm afraid of things that stop and I don't want to be one of them. I don't want us to be one of them."

When she spoke, it was so softly he almost didn't hear her. "Nothing stops." She seemed to be addressing her legs. "It all goes on for a million years."

He said nothing.

"I love you," she said. "I want to marry you and I do want to have—try to have—children with you." She turned to face him. "But I can't right now. Not until I finish what I started with the dolphin. I have to see that through. Whatever it takes."

"So you're going ahead with the live-in."

"Yes. I'm leaving in the morning."

He sighed. "I knew all along that's what you'd do."

She touched his face. "I knew you knew."

For a long time there was nothing to say. The moon, all but full and very distant, could be seen through the open window, framed by a pair of dilapidated water towers. "Well," said Jeffrey, "Kirk's asked me to take his place on the Antarctica trip, and things being what they are, I think I'd be dumb to turn him down."

She stared at him. "When would you leave?"

"In the morning, assuming I can get someone to carry the last week of class for me."

Again there seemed to be little to say, "Maybe you'll be around when I get back," Jeffrey offered. It was not a question.

Melissa was crying again. "Yeah. Maybe I'll be around."

Later, when she got up out of bed to call Nona and tell her about the live-in, Jeffrey started to say something about their being able to read each other's minds, but then he thought better of it.

Melissa misdialed twice before getting the right number.

At the Miami airport, between planes, there was an awkward moment with the luggage. Melissa had forgotten to bring sunglasses and was in the process of selecting a new pair when, through a break in the background music, she heard herself paged. A gravelly male voice requested, first in English, then Spanish, that she report as soon as possible to airport security. Attempting nonchalance, she bought the pair of sunglasses she happened to be holding, put them on, and left the store without her change. For several minutes she considered ignoring the summons. The terminal was very crowded and her flight was due to board in twenty minutes. Finally, however, angered by her own violent trembling, she sought out the security office, walked up to the man at the counter, and identified herself.

He seemed genuinely relieved to see her. It developed that her luggage had not been checked through to St. Thomas as she had requested, but had instead revolved unclaimed upon the Miami baggage carousel, there to be picked up by a man known to airport security as a suitcase thief. When challenged by an official to produce his claim check, the man had dropped Melissa's bags and bolted. Because of the crowd, he had escaped.

"Frankly, miss," the official said as Melissa signed for the bags, "we do what we can, but me, when I travel, I always take as much of my luggage on board with me as I can. That way, you *know* where it is, understand what I'm saying?"

"Sure," she answered. "Thanks, I'll do that." She gave him a great big smile and accepted the bags. At the airline counter, however, when the attendant asked her if she had any luggage to check, she put both bags on the scale.

The plane was full, and the stewardess seated Melissa next to a middle-aged man, tanned and athletic-looking, in a neck brace. "Bad back," he explained. Because he could look neither at her nor out the window without turning his whole body around, Melissa became acutely aware of his attention as something waiting to be engaged. He began, in that way, to remind her disturbingly of Peter. And, after takeoff, after refusing the slim flask of rum the man had sportively offered her, she felt compelled to dispel the effect by making conversation.

"No, no," he said. "I wish it *were* vacation." He took another slug of rum and shifted his body far enough around in his seat to see her out of one eye. "But it's a goddamn funny way to live, I'll say that. Never knowing whether they're going to up and burn the place down on you. On themselves, for that matter. Not that it's so different anywhere else, really—I mean, Christ, look at what we're doing in Antarctica." He put the flask away. "Way things are going, there won't be any place to move the business *to* by next year." He chuckled grimly. "We'll *all* be on vacation."

There was a pause, then Melissa asked him what he did.

"I'm a developer," he said, easing back into his seat. "Real estate."

"A developer," Melissa repeated. "Doesn't that mean you sort of have to be an optimist after all?"

"Well, I guess it does." He stared at the tray folded

into the back of the seat in front of him. "But I gotta say, my optimism took a nasty beating last week when those four tourists were murdered up in Mafolie."

"Oh. I didn't hear about that."

"You will." He grimaced. "Where you staying?"

"Nazareth Bay."

"Oh, yeah?" The answer seemed to interest him and he turned around again to look at her. "That's right where that dolphin house is. You know about the dolphin house?"

She hesitated. "Yes. I mean, I think I read something about it."

"Talk about optimism!" He leaned back in his seat and began to laugh. "In this corner, you've got tourists getting sprayed with semi-automatic rifle fire during cocktail hour; in this one, a dolphin that talks English and lives in an oceanfront property." He started to shake his head but was reminded by the brace not to. "It's a very weird world."

"Pure madness," Melissa agreed.

From the sky, St. Thomas was breathtakingly green, and while they were waiting for the health officials to finish spraying the plane's interior, Melissa experienced a sense of place so complete that it constituted an insight. To check herself, she referred to her mind's corner, where Jeffrey, his mouth partially open, sat asleep in a jet en route to Christchurch, New Zealand. He woke up. She sneezed. The insight was that things assumed their proper shape only when one was moved by absolute necessity. No necessity, no shape. Drawing the glinting mirror fragment absently up from inside her dress, Melissa reflected that as far as necessity went, and destiny, Nicole had, for all her quirkiness, been right on the money.

The tarmac radiated back the air's clear heat, and by the time Melissa reached the concrete terminal, she was sweating. Knolly was not at the gate. In the baggage area, she had to wait quite some time for her second suitcase to appear on the carousel, but when it finally arrived she removed the bit of mirror from around her neck and put it in her purse. Without exactly knowing why, she felt she didn't want Knolly to see it.

He was waiting for her at the taxi stand, leaning against the rail in his jeans and jersey. "Hello, white lady," he said loudly, taking one of her bags.

She was conscious of the drivers' interested gazes. "Hi, Knolly." The sunglasses she had bought were very dark, and she lowered them off her forehead, over her eyes. "Professor Ehrler and Martin still in San Juan?"

"Only me an' de dolphin here, sister. Jus' de two of us." He smiled, not exactly at her. "But, like, everybody miss you, nuh."

A jet engine started up not far away, its scream strangely birdlike in the soft air. "It's good to be back," she said, as they walked around the corner to the jeep.

They took the coast road through town, skirting the harbor's wide blue semicircle—submarines at one end, yachts at the other—then continuing on along the open ocean. It was all very familiar to Melissa: the shimmering pink of the beach with its double line of palms; the jagged rocks and black-brown reefs; the coves; the little bays; the shattered spray. And yet, as the road pulled higher into the hills and forest, leaving the sea sound behind, she felt again what she had felt so strongly upon landing: that she had never before seen all this for what it was—an island, a locale, a place given shape by its limits. She wrapped her dress more snugly about her thighs and lifted her sunglasses. The road they were on was like a tunnel of green.

"So you don' bring you friend wit' you this time?" said Knolly, leaning his head toward her as he drove.

She looked at him. The string visible at the back of his neck ran beneath his jersey in front. "My friend is dead," she told him.

It seemed to her he said, "Hmm."

"She was killed in an auto accident."

He said nothing.

The trees through which they drove—both wild palm and softwood—were choked with creepers and pencil-thin lianas; sunlight touched the road only in patches. Melissa had the impression that the growth had become noticeably more luxuriant over the last month, obscuring many of the brightly painted tin signs—for soft drinks, for ice cream, for tobacco—that she remembered being able to read upon arriving for her previous stint in the flooded house. And now she found herself wondering for the first time about the trails and unpaved spur roads that intersected the main road every two or three hundred meters; it began, in that obscurity, to seem they could lead somewhere.

"It's very green," Melissa said. "You must have had a lot of rain."

"Not so much," Knolly answered, slowing the jeep.

Thinking he might be braking to avoid an animal, Melissa peered at the road, but when he turned left onto one of the spurs, she looked at him. "Where are we going, Knolly."

He appeared slightly embarrassed. "M'have to pass in on a friend, nuh."

"Not far, I hope." The road was rutted and she had to brace herself against the sun-baked doorframe.

"Oh, y'know: never-see-come-see. Everyone like that these days." And then, as if recognizing that he had answered a different question from the one she'd asked, he added, "But today is business, nuh. It won't take long."

She looked at him again, noting for the first time the red, black, and green wool tam he wore to conceal—perhaps to protect—his dreadlocks. But she made no further objection. The detour was something to be surrendered to because it was exactly that; it made her eventual arrival at the flooded house, her ultimate return to Peter, seem that much more inevitable.

The tires of the jeep raised a red dust from the road;

it filmed her sunglasses, she could taste it on her teeth. With the heaving and pitching of the jeep, conversation was impossible. Nor, for now, was there anything left to say. Tiny green flies circled without biting. Melissa held fast to her seat with the hand she had burned on the doorframe, and glancing from time to time at Knolly, she waited.

They came quite suddenly to a clearing—earth without grass, a few chickens scratching about, two dusty motor scooters parked beneath a wild banana. Not until they had pulled up beside the scooters did Melissa see the building itself. Half set back into the bush, it was long and narrow, with walls of ocher-washed concrete and a sagging roof of corrugated metal. There were two separate entrances, and over the far one a sign in Day-Glo pink: "Desmond's Rest."

"You know Jah music?" Knolly asked, reaching across Melissa to open the glove compartment. His eyes were hooded: again he appeared ill at ease.

"Of course. I love reggae." She watched him remove two reels of audio tape from the otherwise empty compartment. "Are you a musician?"

He didn't answer.

They got out of the jeep and separated without speaking. She watched him walk to the near entrance, where he was greeted by someone she couldn't see and immediately admitted. With assumed idleness, she wandered over to inspect the blood-red blooms of a lone hibiscus. Then, made bold by the movement, she continued around the edge of the clearing to the entrance of Desmond's Rest and stepped through the open door.

It was dark inside but no cooler. Taking off her sunglasses, she saw she was not alone: a small boy, six or seven years old, was sitting on a wooden crate next to the jukebox, and at the far end of the square-built counter which served as a bar sat a man in white-rimmed shades. There was no bartender.

She took an uncertain step forward, twirling her sunglasses between thumb and forefinger. "Hi," she said.

"Hello, sister," said the man in the shades. "You would like to use something cold to drink?"

"That would be lovely," she said and, smiling at the boy, took a seat midway down the bar.

The man got up and began to fix her a rum punch.

"Are you Desmond?" she asked him.

He laughed. "No, sister. Desmond and Desmond brother inside playin' de big record boss-dem. All de day long: star is born, nuh." He laughed again as he put the drink down in front of her and picked up the two dollars she had placed there. "All de day long."

"But they don't really work for a record company?" she asked, taking a sip.

He shrugged. "De sweetness is all up by Kingston, eh. Everyone here know dat." Drawing a cigar box from behind the bar, he put Melissa's money in and picked out her change: four quarters, which he laid one by one in front of her, the last daubed across its face with scarlet fingernail polish. "But sometime Jamaica seem damn far, y'know. Desmond understan' about dat. An' his brother have connection."

She watched the man walk back around the bar to his seat. Then, glancing behind her at the boy on the crate, she picked up the painted quarter and went over to the jukebox.

It was an old model, very ornate, with colored lights and the vegetal, almost Deco-ish forms that Melissa remembered from her adolescence. Except for two Ray Charles offerings, all the titles were reggae and nearly all the groups unknown to her—Tapper Zukkie, Big Youth, Boney M. She put the quarter in.

"Yeah, positive," said the boy, who had stood up to watch her make her selections. "Play I some music." He was wearing green-and-yellow-striped pants. Melissa smiled at him, and when she had pressed the glow-ing buttons he ran barefoot across the concrete floor to a place behind the bar.

The jukebox continued to glow but gave no sign of having registered her choices. She pushed the coin return. Nothing happened.

"Hey," she began, "doesn't this thing—"

Music burst from two speakers at the back of the room, skipped, then stopped again. She turned around just as the boy, biting his tongue in concentration, lowered the needle onto the record a second time; he was holding her other selection carefully aloft with his free hand.

She returned to her seat. Her drink, though made with raw rum, was very cold.

> *If you are the big tree,*
> *We are the small axe*

She took two long swallows from the tumbler.

> *Sharpened to cut you down*
> *Ready to cut you down, oh yeah*
> *These are the words of my Master.*

In her mind, the image of Jeffrey on the plane was awake again and playing cards. She could, at certain moments, see his hand—he was drawing to a full house —and it occurred to her that someone more practical-minded than herself might contrive a way of turning this new talent to profit.

But could it be, she wondered, *that Peter somehow knows I'm coming?*

The man in the shades and the boy stared past her at the door's bright rectangle. Above her head, a fly flew into a gleaming spiral of gummed paper; she could see it struggling to get loose. The music grew louder. And all at once there was nothing left to say or do. She got up and stepped out into the heat without finishing her drink.

Knolly was sitting in the jeep. When he saw her coming, he started it up.

"Today it's business," she said, sliding into the seat beside him.

He threw the vehicle roughly into reverse and grinned. "It don' take long. M'seh dat before."

They did not return the way they had come but plunged on from spur road to spur road, continuing around the hill's folds and draws toward the coast. Each time they came to a fork in the road, Knolly chose their route without hesitation, and little by little Melissa came so completely to entrust him with her progress toward Peter that, in the heat and haze of the rum, she had the intermittent illusion that the two of them shared the same aim. This impression was reinforced by the frequency with which Knolly turned to look at her: that repeated look might, with very little misunderstanding, have appeared to an outsider as a look of collusion.

The forest palms thinned, the jeep eased down onto asphalt.

And then they were gliding along the edge of the mangrove lagoon.

"So did Desmond and his brother listen to your tapes?" she asked him as they skirted the yellow-green water—its stand of mangrove, its smell of salt and vegetable decay.

"Dem take de tape to Kingston, nuh, to de studio. An' dem listen to m' music in de studio." He frowned slightly and shrugged. She saw that he was very pleased. "Music is music, ya know wha mean . . . Material tings . . . me don' really understan' plenty wha people have to seh . . . is so much tings people have to seh. But every day I grow bigger in de world. An' simple ting about it is me have to have sumting to do. Music is music. It continues, ya know. An' a man don' have noting to do, him useless. De world go on witout him."

"Yes." She did not look at him. "It's the same with me."

"Wit' everybody," he said.

They crossed a small iron bridge painted silver. It was impossible to tell whether the brackish stream it spanned was flowing to or from the lagoon.

There is a quality to a woman's movement through the world, through her life in the world, which, even as it urges her to become more and more bound up with the lives of men, keeps her sense of direction forever distinct from theirs. One way to talk about this quality would be to say that women move with less sense of interruption than men—a man, for example, would have viewed Knolly's detour as an annoying hiatus in his progress toward the flooded house, whereas Melissa saw it as ensuring that progress. Another way of viewing the difference would be to invoke the analogous distinction between a woman's walk and a man's—the roll of a woman's hips, which are as they are by virtue of her capacity to bear children, ensures that her forward movement is complicated by a lateral one; a man, by contrast, walks in a straight line even when he doesn't know where he is going. It was perhaps both these circumstances which caused Melissa, in crossing the tiny iron bridge, to feel for the first time the full impact of what she had told Jeffrey the night before: she wished to have a child by him.

The tide was going out. In places, the water's retreat had left dark tangles of mangrove root exposed.

As they continued on around the lagoon, Melissa leaned back over the door of the jeep to see the way they had come, and her sunglasses, which she had propped atop her head, fell soundlessly to the roadbed. She turned back around to Knolly. He responded in no way.

And then, as the road pulled one last time into the bush before skirting the marina, before dipping down to Nazareth Bay and the flooded house beyond, Knolly slowed the jeep quite suddenly and pointed off into the indeterminate tangle of sun-blotched green to their left. "Look at it, white lady!"

She peered in the direction he indicated.

"You can see it?" he said.

"What?"

"Where I point."

"I don't see anything," she said, but at the same instant she did. On a short stake, flies buzzing round it and a bit of red rag tied to the tip of one horn, a goat's head was impaled. Before it, in a square of dirt scratched clean of growth, stood two pint jars of yellow liquid, their tops screwed tight.

"Oh, my God. What is it?"

Knolly looked at her to be sure she had seen, then accelerated again. The marina came into view. Its several vessels, with their faintly gesturing masts and tipped-in outboards, seemed, like the olive swathe in the sea beyond, to propose the absurdity of the tableau she had just witnessed. It seemed beyond probability that so much order and so much chaos could have been compacted within so small a compass. It was to re-establish the probable that Melissa again asked: "What was that?"

He wrinkled his brow as though offended, and for a while he said nothing. Melissa looked at the high white bank of cumulus clouds forming in the distance over St. John. Then, as he downshifted, Knolly said, "Plenty people talk about jumbies an' obeah workin' an' all de old ways, but ya know . . . is modern times now. Obeah against de law. An' only de old people know all de ways of takin' sign an' cleanin' de soul like dat back dere wit' de billy goat."

He was fingering the mirror shard through his jersey

as he drove, but when he saw Melissa watching him he stopped. It occurred to her that since her arrival at the airport the two of them had shared a variety of feelings, but that neither was capable of explaining those feelings to himself. For the first and only time, the question *Why am I here?* offered itself to Melissa. Then there was the sharp crunch of gravel as Knolly turned off the road and onto the long winding driveway that led to the flooded house.

He parked beneath the poison-fish tree. The pink of the house's concrete walls—even when she wasn't looking at them—seemed more vivid that the blooms of bougainvillea, oleander, and hibiscus. She got out of the jeep. The only sounds she could hear were the pulse of the pump in back and the lapping of the waves.

"Thank you, Knolly," she said.

He looked closely at her, then nodded and moved off toward the toolshed. She removed her bags from the back of the jeep.

There are moments—often they involve a lover's return to the site of a rendezvous—when the world of things seems so charged with one's own past intentions and future hopes that the desire to move through it seems identical with the desire to live. Melissa carried her bags to the dry entrance of the house in precisely the same manner that the lizard on the tree behind her, startled by her movement, froze against its gray bark.

She put her suitcases on Ehrler's bunk and stared at them. She listened. Her ears were ringing. From the flooded rooms it seemed to her she now heard the sound of splashing.

Bending over to unbuckle her sandals, Melissa saw that Ehrler's bedside copy of *The Interpretation of Dreams* had sprouted place markers—a dozen strips of pale blue typing paper, curling in the heat. For a moment she was curious, but she did not stop to see what had captured his fancy.

She stepped carefully out of her dress. She opened both suitcases.

Just as, on her previous visit, she wore her bathing suit underneath her clothes to facilitate the transition from dry world to wet, so she has this time packed it away in one of her bags. Melissa has foreseen her need —however short-lived—to undress completely. Reaching behind to unhook her bra, she glances at the picture postcards Martin has taped above his bunk: his sister is on vacation in Italy.

For a moment Melissa stands before her suitcases naked, her arms folded over her breasts as if out of modesty. From where the water is, there comes a sound like a human being with a cold. *Okay,* she thinks. Then he says her name. *"I'm getting dressed,"* she says. It is hard for her to speak.

She removes a leotard from her suitcase and puts it on. Then, slinging her waterproof tote bag over one shoulder, she leaves the room.

The skein of reflected light shimmering across the walls and ceiling of the flooded area is so dazzlingly fluid, so silent, that Melissa, on the dry catwalk, has the momentary illusion of being herself underwater, at the bottom of a sunstruck pool. It is a familiar illusion, and in the past she has encouraged it. Now, a banana quit that has become trapped in the room furthers the illusion by swooping frantically to and fro above her head like a fish. She reaches out to touch the railing, a small torrent of water rushes over her legs, and the illusion is dispelled. Peter, his mouth open slightly, is gazing up at her.

She lowers herself into the water.

"There you are, baby," she says. "There you are."

He draws himself slowly across the backs of her calves, curling his head close about her knees so as not to lose sight of her face, of her hands. She reaches down to stroke his belly. He says her name.

"You know, they told me all about your not eating and everything . . ."

He swims between her legs, the fronts of his flippers gently striking old bruises.

"How you just keep swimming around up here—in and out, in and out . . . I mean, look at you: you're so thin. I've never seen you so thin. Why are you?"

She kneels in the water. Peter says a word that sounds like "air." She runs a hand across the top of her own head, listening, and he says her name.

"Now, you see that? They even told me you'd stopped saying my name, but I . . ."

The sounds of water, so near at hand, have become as intimate to her as those of lovemaking. She begins to cry.

". . . but I didn't believe them."

Peter, floating on his side in front of her, watches her stand up again. She is shaking her head and crying. "Boy, is this fucked. I mean really, it is completely, completely out of hand."

Peter rights himself in the water and lifts his head above the surface. There is a sharp rush of air as he takes a breath, a snap as his blowhole closes upon it.

"Don't you think I understand what's going on? I mean, it's not gonna get better, you know. People go away. It's like that. You and I . . ."

Peter watches her.

"You and I . . . I don't know, we just . . . I just . . ." She is crying so hard she is afraid she will fall down. And it is as though to keep from falling down that she stumbles several slow steps backward in the water—away from Peter, but still facing him.

"Okay," she says. Tries to say.

Taking the waterproof bag from her shoulder, she reaches one hand in, fumbles around inside, and holds both arm and bag out at arm's length. Peter opens his jaw very wide. He says a word that sounds like "Nel-noon." *The light is so feeble in here,* Melissa thinks. But this is not true; she can see it is not true. She fires the first shot without removing the gun from the bag.

The sound of the first shot: in its echoes is contained the sound of all the shots to follow.

Peter is struck just behind the right eye; the impact of the bullet knocks him over on his side. For an instant, the corona of seawater his body throws into the air and the corona of blood the bullet throws from his body remain separate—a ring within a ring—then they fall together. And everything Melissa sees is red.

She discards the bag, steps forward, fires again. Peter swims sideways but makes no move to get away. Melissa becomes totally absorbed in the effort of counting the shots.

When she sees that the eye on the side where he has not yet been wounded is clear, she puts the gun barrel to the skin above it and fires. Then she fires and fires until there is nothing left to shoot. The dolphin rolls slowly over on his back in the opaque water.

From the observation deck, the waters of the cove, of the bay beyond, of the sea itself, appear perfectly calm. The fishing boats are still. It is the sort of day on which it is possible to imagine there is nothing laborious left to do in the world; it is the sort of world in which night seems a lifetime away. Beyond the boats and spits of land, in the farthest distance, sea and sky meet with a precision that no longer seems to Melissa arbitrary. She throws Diego's gun as far in that direction as she is able. Then, seeing that the water where she is standing is not yet tainted, she lies down in it for a moment to rinse herself before hurrying down the spiral stairs, walking back around the house, and entering it by the same door she had used less than half an hour earlier.

It does not alarm her that she hears the sound of the pump as the beating of a heart. The heart is hers.

Taking a towel from the larger of the two suitcases,

she strips, dries herself, and puts back on the clothes in which she arrived. Towel and leotard she bunches together into a ball which she tosses to the floor in the far corner. She looks at the two open suitcases. They are artifacts. From the smaller one she removes a sealed envelope with Ehrler's name on it.

As she is rummaging through her purse to be sure she has her airplane ticket, she pricks her finger on something. It is the sliver of mirror. Peering into it, she considers her eyes—first one, then the other. They are the eyes of someone who at one time was crying but now has stopped. She does not ask herself when it was she stopped but instead puts the mirror around her neck and, with one last glance at the suitcases open on the bed behind her, steps out into the light and heat.

Knolly is weeding the garden which Ehrler, to fulfill the terms of the local employment law, has had him begin. His forehead is shiny with sweat and he has removed both his shirt and tam. When he sees Melissa approaching, he stands up.

She holds out the envelope. "Would you give this to John when he gets back?"

Knolly looks from the envelope to the mirror fragment hanging from her neck. It is without color, harsh with light.

"I'm leaving, Knolly. I'm going into town now. There's a plane. I won't be coming back again."

She sees him staring at her toes and glances down to see what has attracted his attention. They are still. When she looks up again, he does too, and again there is intimacy in the exchange.

"Y'would like to use a lift," he asks almost tonelessly. He still has not taken the envelope.

"I'm going to walk," she says. "I'm leaving now."

He cocks his head and squints up at the house. She brushes a fly from the air between them.

"It's in the letter," she says. "You don't have to worry."

His eyes meet hers again for one last long moment, then he accepts the letter, lets the hand holding it drop lifelessly to his side and says, "Goodbye, white lady."

They turn away at the same moment.

WHERE WE LIVED
AND WHAT WE LIVED FOR

She walks a long distance without thinking about anything. The insects, which seldom trouble her, have formed a small cloud about her upper body, and in places they have drawn blood. The sun is low in the sky. The moon has yet to rise. She isn't tired.

And then, rounding a bend in the road, she is struck by a memory so vivid it is like something seen magnified before her. Like a movie, as they say. Except that it is not like a movie because it will play over and over for her—she is aware of it even now—forever:

Nona has just dropped her off at the train station. Melissa has just leaned out over the edge of the platform to see if the train is coming. When she looks back at the car, what Melissa sees is Nona: Nona twisting around in the driver's seat to look behind and, with one arm grasping the seat top beside her, backing out of the station at a speed that seems, then and at all other moments, incredible.

Acknowledgments

This book contains a few quotations and bits of paraphrase which go unacknowledged in the text:

page 61: The third and fourth lines of the song Knolly sings here have been taken from Bob Marley's song "Revolution" (Copyright © 1975, Cayman Music Inc./ ASCAP).

page 66: The italicized portion of the paragraph entitled "Sentimental Education" is directly quoted from Gustave Flaubert's novel of the same name (Part Three, Chapter VI). The translation is David Rieff's.

page 165: The paragraph beginning "Melissa began to explain . . ." involves a partial paraphrase of John C. Lilly's explanation of the same phenomenon in *Lilly on Dolphins* (Anchor Books, 1975), p. 97.

page 186: The synopsis of *Horror at 37,000 Feet* is a quotation of Leonard Maltin's description of that film in *TV Movies* (New American Library, 1975), p. 258.

page 188: "I hate traveling and explorers" is the opening sentence of Claude Lévi-Strauss's *Tristes Tropiques*, translated by John and Doreen Weightman (Atheneum, 1974).

pages 194–95: The paragraphs numbered 1 and 8 are quotations from Samuel Taylor Coleridge's "The Rime of the Ancient Mariner."

page 265: The song Melissa plays here is "Small Axe" (words by Bob Marley and Lee Perry, copyright © 1973, Cayman Music Inc./ASCAP).

During the writing of this book, I was awarded a stay at the MacDowell Colony, and received grants from both the Creative Artists Public Service Program and the Ingram Merrill Foundation. The assistance given me by friends and acquaintances is of a different order altogether and cannot be repaid here.

T.M.

About the Author

Ted Mooney was born in Dallas, Texas, grew up in Washington, D.C., and currently lives in New York City where he is an editor for *Art In America.* Ted Mooney's short stories have appeared in *Esquire* and *American Review.* EASY TRAVEL TO OTHER PLANETS is Mr. Mooney's first novel, and was nominated for The American Book Award for Best First Novel for 1981. It received The Sue Kaufman Award for The Best Work of Fiction for 1981 from The American Academy of Arts and Letters. Ted Mooney is currently at work on a new novel.

The
Best Modern Fiction
from
BALLANTINE